Coming Home

*Also by Dee Holmes
in Large Print:*

The Boy on the Porch

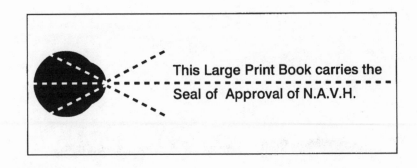

This Large Print Book carries the
Seal of Approval of N.A.V.H.

Coming Home

Dee Holmes

WHEELER
PUBLISHING

Published in 2004 by arrangement with The Berkley Publishing Group, a member of Penguin Group (USA) Inc.

Wheeler Large Print Softcover

The text of this Large Print edition is unabridged.
Other aspects of the book may vary from the original edition.

Set in 16 pt. Plantin by Elena Picard.

Printed in the United States on permanent paper.

ISBN 1-58724-655-4 (lg. print : sc : alk. paper)

Coming Home

As the Founder/CEO of NAVH, the only national health agency solely devoted to those who, although not totally blind, have an eye disease which could lead to serious visual impairment, I am pleased to recognize Thorndike Press* as one of the leading publishers in the large print field.

Founded in 1954 in San Francisco to prepare large print textbooks for partially seeing children, NAVH became the pioneer and standard setting agency in the preparation of large type.

Today, those publishers who meet our standards carry the prestigious "Seal of Approval" indicating high quality large print. We are delighted that Thorndike Press is one of the publishers whose titles meet these standards. We are also pleased to recognize the significant contribution Thorndike Press is making in this important and growing field.

Lorraine H. Marchi, L.H.D.
Founder/CEO
NAVH

* Thorndike Press encompasses the following imprints: Thorndike, Wheeler, Walker and Large Print Press.

Chapter One

"So are we going to set a wedding date for next spring?" Daniel asked, his tone somewhere between amusement and hope.

"Why do I have the sense you've been biding your time all day to ask me that?" Olivia Halsey, trying to sound merely curious, poked through a box of old china and glass she'd bought that morning at a Saturday yard sale.

"Let's see," he mused, "we made love, worked our way through those cartons and tables of junk —"

"You pulled that 1840s history book out of all that *junk*," she said while holding up a green glass plate to the sun. The facets catching the light were stunning, a signal it might be quite old, but she knew enough about vintage items to know that old didn't necessarily mean value. She wished Claire were here to look at it and tell her if it was genuine Depression glass.

"Pure luck," Daniel countered, stretching his legs out and crossing his ankles.

"Even luck has to start with something. You know what to look for in boxes of books, and today, voilà — a historical gem leaped right into your hands." Besides being a teacher of history, he had a diverse collection of leather history books, most of which he'd obtained in more sophisticated places than from someone with bad hair selling tired toys and too many generic florist vases.

Daniel had grumbled every Saturday about Olivia going to junky yard sales, a hobby she'd had since she and her mother made the weekend rounds back in her hometown of Bishop, Rhode Island.

Olivia's efforts to get Daniel interested had been met with rolling eyes until she gave him a World War II journal she'd found in a bundle of old table linen. It had been carefully wrapped in a yellowed napkin and appeared to have been tucked in the linens for safekeeping.

Finding the journal had convinced him, and since late March he'd been coming with her. He soon figured out that yard sales invariably treated books as musty tomes just a few steps from being shelved at the dump. He'd paid only fifty cents for the small volume he'd found today. "And speaking of history —"

"Oh, no, you don't," he said. "I'm not going to let you change the topic."

"I was afraid of that," she murmured, setting the green plate aside. Since she was getting together with Claire and Lexie next weekend, she'd take the piece with her. The three of them loved old things, and their combined expertise covered a wide variety of vintage items from linens to glass to silver.

"Just as a reminder of how much you want me . . ." He grinned, unfazed by her disinterest. "After the yard sales, we went for lunch, then came back here, where you lured me into bed again —"

"What a liar you are, Daniel Cafferty," she said with mock affront. "You were the one who had me half undressed before we got to the bedroom."

"You do have a way of making me forget the proprieties."

She grinned. "And here we are —"

"— with a question on our future," he finished, smoothly taking the subject back to marriage — where she definitely did not want to go.

Their future wasn't exactly the conversation Olivia envisioned on a lazy July afternoon; she'd prefer something light and noncontroversial like how to get a heavier blooming of her rosebushes, or even some comments on the new state-of-the-art auditorium the school committee was supporting.

Yet in all fairness to Daniel, he had been remarkably silent of late on the subject of marriage. And the more that silence con-

9

tinued, the better Olivia liked it.

They were sitting on her raised deck in cushioned wicker chairs that Olivia had brought from her late parents' home in Rhode Island. Funny how even though the house in Bishop was hers, and the rent money from the three-story monstrosity contributed to her income, Olivia's emotional attachment to the home where she'd grown up and cared for ailing parents ranged from ambivalence to disinterest.

Her parents had died four years ago, and almost three had passed since she'd put the excess furniture and boxes in storage and rented the house. She didn't dwell on her years there, and she hadn't probed closely as to why, or even why she was holding on to the property.

She'd almost convinced herself that not selling, so she could make a clean break toward the future, had nothing to do with keepsakes or family connections or small-town memories.

But it probably did.

Since simply leaving the house vacant wasn't prudent or wise, she'd opted to be a long-distance landlord, depending on a local realtor and a neighbor for day-by-day monitoring and to keep her updated on any problems. So far this had worked, allowing Olivia to have it both ways — not making a decision and not being involved.

Which, she decided, in that moment, was what she was doing wrong in her relationship with Daniel. She didn't want to make a decision, but she wanted to stay involved with him. That's why their relationship had hit an impasse, why he was urging her out of her too-obvious balancing act.

"Is your silence a sign of some serious thinking about us and where we're going?" He studied her from behind his sunglasses. Yet, she didn't need to see his eyes to know that he expected an answer.

While she was trying to conjure up a soft dodge, he asked again, "Are we going to plan a wedding?"

She wished he would demand or offer an ultimatum instead of being so graciously reasonable. Usually she avoided the topic of full-time commitment and forever-afters. Not thinking about them made them easier to dismiss.

Mostly Daniel hadn't pushed. But this was definitely a push, albeit a gentle one. He was sweet and wonderful, but he also detested fence-sitting and wishy-washy answers. Whatever stall time she'd gained by either finesse or silence had been played out.

She put the box of china aside and looked directly at him. "Oh, Daniel, this isn't easy. . . ." She paused, her voice catching. "But I don't have an answer for you."

"A non-answer sounds like a no."

11

She shrank from the disappointment she heard in his voice, or maybe what she *really* heard was that he wouldn't be asking again. That was what she wanted, wasn't it?

Obviously, or she wouldn't be searching for a way to avoid what she didn't want to say: *Stay with me, stay in love with me, be my lover, but don't ask me to make any long-range promises.*

And so she began with the truth. "I don't want to hurt you, and I don't want to stop you from seeking your own happiness . . . but then again, I don't want to lose you." She didn't know what else to say. No question she was being miserably selfish.

She cared about Daniel, and she enjoyed his company. She wanted their relationship to stay as it was. Warm and close and uncommitted.

He set his can of beer down and rose. Wearing old docksiders, jeans, and a soft denim shirt, he was handsome without trying. Hair a little too shaggy, and lines a tad too deep, contributed to an etched maturity that seasoned him without making him seem too cynical.

He was forty-five and six years divorced, with a daughter he adored and didn't see enough of, thanks to an ex-wife who rarely met Daniel halfway. That Caitlyn lived with her mother a hundred miles away didn't make it easy or simple, but to Daniel's credit, he saw her every week. He'd often told Olivia his truck could get from here to Greeley, Massachusetts, without him. Just fill it with gas and point it west on the Mass Pike.

"I love you, Olivia. I think you love me. Getting married isn't a trap. . . ." He paused as though searching for the words that would convince her.

"Daniel, we have everything a married couple has — probably more because we never fight."

"Surely you're not serious."

Her eyes widened. "I'm absolutely serious."

"Define *everything.*"

"What?"

"You said we have everything a married couple has. Like what?"

Why had she ever thought he wouldn't expect precise answers? In the past his straightforwardness had always gained her respect, but then it had never hit quite so close to the bone. "I don't know. . . . We like the same music, we both like to get up early in the morning, like to go to yard sales. . . . We always find lots to talk about, as in we're never bored with each other. . . . Uh, you're awful at directions, so I take the maps." Even to her this sounded like a recited and desperate list.

He raised his eyebrows.

"Don't look like that. It might sound silly, but general compatibility is very important."

"Yeah, I'm sure the biggest fights between adults are over who carries the maps."

Amused sarcasm — so much like Daniel. She sighed. "We have good sex," Olivia said. "And don't tell me couples with an *incompatibility* in that area don't have a problem."

"Correction," he said, looking down at her while sliding his hands into his pockets. "We have great sex, but I was under the impression that it was great because I loved you and you loved me."

"I do love you . . . at least I think I do. I don't know. You want me to be honest, don't you?"

"Honest? Sounds more like unsure to me." He walked to the deck railing, looking toward the gray shingled house beyond the row of lilac bushes.

She hurried to repair the breach. "One thing I do know for sure. I feel safe with you."

He dropped his head forward, shaking it slowly before turning, a resignation drawing the lines in his cheeks deeper. "Maybe what you really feel is comfortable. Like with an old friend or a favorite brother."

"And is that so awful?"

"I'd hoped we could do better than that, Olivia."

"Why are you doing this? Why are you pushing me when you know I hate it?"

"Because I'd like to believe our relationship is more than a collection of likes and dislikes.

14

Nothing stands still — it's either steps forward or steps back. When I first met you, before we really got to know each other, I admired that you weren't trying to wrestle a ring and a marriage license out of me."

Perhaps on some internal plane, this was exactly what had attracted her to Daniel. No expectations. She'd known that there had been women after his divorce, and she knew that he was considered a catch among the single women at school where she taught English. From what he'd told her, none of his past relationships were ever headed toward longtime serious.

"Someone you were involved with was pushing you?" *Like you're pushing me,* but she didn't say that.

He paused, taking off his sunglasses. His eyes looked weary, as if he knew he'd already lost her. "She was the mother of one of the football players." Besides teaching history, Daniel was the local high school football coach. "She was fresh from a divorce and thought she and I should hook up because her son was my starting quarterback and she loved to watch football."

"Something in common, it would appear."

"Football? Uh, no. I coach football, but I don't want to eat it and drink it twenty-four/seven. And why am I telling you about a woman who has nothing to do with us?" He shook his head more in self-derision than in wanting the question answered.

"Well, for one thing, that experience should make you understand the way I feel. You didn't like her pushing you —"

"I didn't like her period," he snapped. Then he held up his hand. "No more about her." Then, after about five beats of silence, he said, "Olivia, you intrigued me because you were so oblivious to men in general and me specifically. You didn't flirt, you didn't send out sex signals or lard up every conversation with a lot of trash talk."

"I was an utter failure with such machinations, so I quit trying a number of years ago."

"I loved that you were cautious and careful, but we're not strangers anymore. People who love each other commit to each other with more depth than sex and interesting conversations and" — he gestured to her box of china — "and picking through collections from yard sales."

Olivia scooped up the box and walked across the deck. Balancing the carton, she reached for the back door only to have Daniel pull it open for her. She went inside, setting the box on the counter.

When she turned around, he stood in the doorway. "It seems we've come to an impasse," she said.

"It would seem so," he murmured.

"Daniel, I really do care about you, and

16

maybe I even love you, but I don't want to get married, and because we don't agree on that . . ." *Okay,* she thought to herself, *just say it.* "It's probably best if we don't see each other anymore."

"Just like that."

Don't buckle now. "Yes."

There was a taut silence that caused her to want to take back her words before he agreed. But it was too late. He nodded and said softly, "All right, if that's what you want."

With a jolt she realized she'd just broken up with this wonderful friend and lover with the care usually reserved for a trip to the mailbox. Swallowing hard, she tried to keep her voice even.

"I think it best." But her heart was crying. He wasn't supposed to do this. He was supposed to kiss her and tell her there was plenty of time, that they could wait, that *he* would wait no matter what she said, that he wanted to be with her no matter what.

She was glad for the shadows in the kitchen so he couldn't see how the color had drained from her cheeks. *Be careful what you ask for . . . you might just regret getting it.*

But did she really? Deep, deep down, did she really? She would have something of value: a life with no worry about demands for marriage, no pushing her into areas where

17

she didn't want to go. Well, she'd just gotten what she wanted. She didn't feel all that good about it, but she knew this was also the fairest to Daniel.

"Then I guess this is good-bye," she said, shrinking from the moment that had left her with nothing but a melodramatic cliché.

He came forward, walking past her to her bedroom, where he emerged with the nylon jacket he'd brought with him that morning. He removed a small box from the pocket and placed it in her hand. A ring box.

She tried to give it back to him.

"Don't be ridiculous." He closed her fingers around it and then stepped back. "I bought it for you. It's yours. It's not complicated."

He started to walk away.

She didn't know what to do.

"Should I open it now?" What a totally idiotic question, she thought, realizing she would have asked him if the sun was blue if it would keep him from leaving.

"Do whatever."

She lifted the lid. Nestled in the scrap of velvet lay a gold ring with a filigree setting that held a pearl-size red ruby. It was delicate, vintage, and exquisite — similar to a piece she'd once seen at Brimfield and described to him in great detail. But that was months ago. Not only hadn't he forgotten, he'd managed to nearly duplicate it. "It's like

18

the ring I described to you."

"Yes."

"But I can't —"

"Don't tell me you can't accept it," he warned.

"Daniel, I just broke off with you —" Then realization flushed through her. "This was going to be an engagement ring, wasn't it?"

"Call it a farewell gift." He took it from the box and slipped it on her finger. Then it caught the light with the same intensity as he caught at her heart; in a smooth motion he slid his hands into her hair, his thumbs brushing her lobes. He drew her and she slipped forward, as though caught in a surreal web; her eyes fluttered closed and he kissed her. It wasn't a kind or sweet kiss, but it wasn't hurtful or angry, either. It was just sad.

"Take care of yourself," he said, his voice husky, his mouth still against hers. She blinked, trying to see through the haze of beguilement that he so easily generated in her. Then, before she'd regained her bearings, he released her, turned, and walked out of the house.

She stood there in the warm summer shadows, the places where he'd touched her suddenly cool and vacant. She tried to tell herself she'd done the right thing, the best thing, the only thing she could do. But when

19

she looked down at the ring, she wasn't sure if she should be sad because she'd disappointed him, or dismayed by the hold he still had on her heart.

She'd have to give it back to him, for she simply couldn't keep something that she knew absolutely was intended as an engagement ring. He could have just walked out without giving it to her, and yet he hadn't. Why?

To leave her with the symbol of what might have been? Or to rid himself of a ring he no longer cared about? The first made her wistful, the latter scratched at her like an unexpected claw.

Placing the ring back in the box, she returned to the bedroom where the sheets were still tangled, the ringer was off on her phone, and the scent of their lovemaking clung enticingly.

She put the box into a drawer and closed it, immediately understanding what she'd really done by not refusing the gift. She'd sent a mixed signal — she'd told him no to his proposal, yet had not insisted he take the ring back.

She scrubbed her hands down her face. *Oh, Daniel, why did you make this so hard?*

Chapter Two

For the most part the next two hours were a bust. The box of odd pieces of china that she'd been so eager to delve into held no interest. Flowers in her garden needed to be deadheaded, but she didn't feel like being outside. She sat down to correct some papers for an extracurricular summer English class that had concluded earlier in the week, but all the sentences in the essays blurred together. She tried calling her best friend Claire Fitzgerald in Lake Moses, Virginia, but got her voice mail. Then she tried her other best friend, Lexie James, in Chicago, but she wasn't home, either.

Olivia was disappointed — she wanted to whine and cry about what had just happened. Lexie would tell her that no guy was worth the angst and second thoughts; she should know and spoke from experience. Claire would be troubled. She relished making life work with what she had, and would be more ready to scold Olivia for pushing a good man away.

Olivia sighed deeply. Maybe she didn't really want to talk with either friend, at least until she'd sorted out her feelings about the decision she'd made.

Turning her phone's ringer back on, she checked her voice mail.

There were three messages. One for an overdue library book, one a return call from a summer student about her final essay paper grade, and one from Florence Kester.

"Olivia, it's Flo. Oh, my, I don't know how to tell you this, and I'm so sorry. It was my fault. I was away for a few days, and when I got home . . . Oh, dear, I can't just drop this in a message. Call me."

Olivia called immediately and Flo picked up on the second ring. As soon as Olivia spoke, Flo began.

"I've just been beside myself over the house."

Flo was a fretter and could get worked up over a pest invasion despite a dozen working mousetraps. "Now, calm down. What about the house?"

"Sometime while I was away — I was visiting my brother in Connecticut for a few days. . . . Edgar hasn't been himself since his daughter upped and moved to California with that free-spirited boyfriend who lives in his truck. Can you imagine? But that's another story. Edgar is lonely and worried, you know, well, of course you don't know, what with you not having those kinds of problems. Anyway, guess I should be thankful for that bus that he takes regular-like to Foxwoods every week. He does have a good time with the slot machines. Won five hundred dollars last time on the quarter slots, then he went and lost most of it."

"Flo—"

"Now, me, when I win, I take it home with me. Bought me a new stove with my last winnings. Always good to have something to show for your money — that's what I say. But Edgar, he always thinks he's on some streak. . . ."

When she paused for a breath, Olivia jumped in. "Lucky streaks do happen. Now, about the house . . ."

Finally, Olivia thought.

"Vandals — they, they just made a terrible mess. Probably those boys from down around Brace Road. Never did understand why the police don't arrest the lot of them. Just a nest of scalawags always up to no good thing." She rambled on about wild kids and careless parents and police who should be doing their job.

Olivia sighed. She liked the chatty Flo, but keeping her on one subject long enough to get details was frustrating.

"I checked the house before I went away and everything was as it should be. Someone or a lot of someones broke in and put spray paint on the walls, broke that old mirror in the upstairs hall, gouged up the wallpaper — you know I never did like that wallpaper, but never mind — with dirty words, and well, it's just disgusting. I called the police and they sent that Trent McGraw. Been awhile since I'd seen him. You remember him, don't you?"

She certainly did; she also remembered that he'd grown up on Brace Road. She hoped Flo didn't. Before she could redirect Flo's rambling back to the house, she said, "Sure you do. You and those two friends of yours were always giggling about him."

"We were in high school — giggling about boys was the reason we went to school."

"Just the same, I remember your mother and I would roll our eyes and wonder what nice girls saw in him." Then she muttered, "I still wonder."

The tasty lure of rebellion, Olivia remembered, before she recalled that Trent mostly ignored her. Funny how that glimmer of teenage angst could roll into her mind with such clarity after so many years. The last time she'd seen him was at their tenth reunion, and he had barely recalled her name. "Guys are like that," Lexie, the guy expert, had told her. "Most don't even know which one they sacked and which they blew off. They just move on to the next."

"He's divorced now, you know," Flo said,

bringing Olivia's attention back to the present.

She didn't know. He and his wife had looked happy enough at the reunion; she'd been awed by Tanya with her smart black dress, flawless makeup, and perfect figure. Beside her, Olivia felt like a small colorless nobody. Their entire exchange of polite smiles and greetings left her more than a bit queasy — it had hammered home why Trent barely remembered her name. Olivia in a word, was ordinary.

"Tanya getting caught in that townhouse with an old rival of Trent's — leastways, that's what I heard — well, once it all got public and made Trent look like a fool, he dumped her. Course there's more — no angel, that Trent McGraw, just too cocky for his own good if you ask me, but I have to say he looked very precise in his uniform, like a real professional."

"I'm sure he did," she muttered, wondering for a vague moment what had caused Tanya to cheat. She shook away the question. Who cared about the trials and misfortunes in Bishop, she thought firmly. She had enough of her own messes.

"The realtor should be here in a few minutes," Flo said, pausing, and Olivia could picture her glancing down tree-lined Steeple Street as though expecting Peter to arrive in that moment. "I know he's going to say the

Marlowes won't want to rent the way it is. Oh, this is all my fault. If I'd only stayed here . . ." Then she started to cry.

Olivia reassured her that she wasn't angry and that when she'd volunteered to watch the house, Olivia never expected her to be a full-time guard.

"Things happen sometimes despite our best efforts. I want you go and make yourself a glass of iced tea and relax. I'll drive down this afternoon."

"Oh, I think that's a very good idea. Do you want me to get a handyman — I could call Rosa Lauder. Her boy fixes things. I could ask her to send him over."

Rosa Lauder was a friend of Flo's and even more talkative, plus she asked endless questions. And Olivia was already talked out. "No, let me take a look first." She glanced at the clock. "I'll see you in a little while."

She tossed some items into a duffel, closed and locked the windows, then realizing she was low on cash stopped at the ATM, where she ran into a colleague who was handing out flyers in support of the new school auditorium. Energetic and with the grace of a jackhammer when she embraced a cause, Karen Clancey rambled on, finally asking Olivia to put the papers on car and truck windshields at the mall the next day.

"I was going to drop them by tonight," she said, as if it was a foregone conclusion that

Olivia would be doing it.

"Sorry, I can't. I'm on my way down to Bishop." She wasn't really sorry — spending her Sunday cluttering up windshields and the mall parking lot with discarded flyers didn't interest her. Going to Bishop was suddenly an adventure. Karen was tough to duck, and Olivia had no doubt the woman would have rung the "you care about the school, don't you?" bell until Olivia caved.

"Oh." Her disappointment was obvious. Then, "What's in Bishop?"

"The house I grew up in."

"That's all? I thought it was an emergency."

"Actually, it is," she muttered, saying good-bye and hurrying to her car.

As she drove out of town, she realized that this diversion was a good thing — it would help to filter out her loss of Daniel. And it definitely got her out of doing flyer placements. Besides, now that she was on her way, she was kinda looking forward to seeing the old Steeple Street house again.

Bishop was referred to by coastal Rhode Island residents as a seaside potty stop for folks either on their way to Newport in the east, or Westerly and Connecticut to the west. Undaunted by what some observers claimed was an insult, Bishop basked in its small-town quaintness. Their tourist traffic was minimal, their "mall" consisted of four stores linked by a roof, but their shoreline was one of the state's best kept secrets. Gull Beach had two miles of sand meeting water nestled into a cove of rocks that offered spectacular views of breaking surf while providing small inlets for clam diggers and waders.

Her teenage summers were spent at Gull Beach, where she and Lexie and Claire wiled away their days lounging on blankets, wearing skimpy bikinis, slathered with lotion and drinking frozen Del's Lemonade when they weren't carrying sand umbrellas and chairs down to the sand for the summer locals. The girls took delight in beating the boys out of all the great tips.

It was a time of dreams and promises and eagerly planned futures. Olivia had wanted to open an antiques store, Claire, to marry her boyfriend and have lots of kids, and Lexie, well, she wanted to be a star. Not just any kind of star. A big-time, big-money, big-talent star who was recognized everywhere.

Olivia smiled now at the rush of memories. Lexie, who was always filled with ripe confidence, refused not to believe in herself. Her energy was contagious, and Olivia knew that a lot of her own one-time confidence in herself had come from Lexie's "be what you want to be" attitude.

But circumstances at home had altered her antiques-store dreams, and they ebbed away like the tide. As time brought other more pressing responsibilities, that dream became even more remote until she simply gave it up as if it had been a smoky mirage.

Now, driving down Beach Street with the shoreline on her right and the stacks of houses and local stores on her left, she felt as if she'd only been away for a few days. Little had changed. The post office, all brick and corners from so many revamps over the years, had its window box filled with impatiens because, as she recalled, they were the only annual the postmistress couldn't kill. Murphy's Park and Shop, a kind of general store, still had as many items on the sidewalk as there were inside. Near Ned's, the barbershop, a leashed shepherd sat beside Wes Gunther, the only Yankee fan in town, or at least the only one to admit it. He was Lexie's uncle, and Olivia had fond memories of the yearly spring rivalry between Wes and her father on the Red Sox versus the Yankees. She waved, and to her surprise, he waved back, tipping that Yankee ballcap that, her father had once told her, Wes planned to be buried in.

Wes "The Yank" Gunther wasn't thinking about dying and getting buried — he was still watching the red Camry with the Mass plates making its way down Beach Street. He pushed his cap back, told Roger to stay, and ambled inside Murphy's. Cold beer dispensed by the soda machine kept the regulars happy during the dog days of summer. But for the three men by the counter, and Fritzie, the owner, the "real" customers were busy with their shopping, not tuning in to the local chatter.

"Not gonna believe who I just saw." Wes announced this as if the answer might be the current *Playboy* centerfold.

"Mickey Mantle?" Fritzie asked, then laughed, drawing the others in, too. Wes sometimes liked to think that the old Mick was settin' up the Yankee plays a way up yonder. Wes liked to think the departed were doing useful things, not just flying around testing out their wings.

"Nope. The Halsey girl. Haven't seen her around these parts in years."

"Heard some punks messed up the Halsey house. Been a bunch of vandalism lately. Just goes to show what happens when you let these little punks get a foothold."

"What foothold? They sprayed some paint, broke some stuff, and did some wall art. Compared to the stuff we used to do . . ."

And for a few moments they all reminisced about what they did, when mischief-makers were called delinquents, not vandals.

"She even waved to me. Imagine that; didn't think she'd remember me."

"She remembered you cuz you're a Red Sox traitor."

"Ya think?" But it wasn't worry in his voice, it was pride. Being called a traitor to his country, well, he'd be pissed at that. But only gluttons for pain would be loyal to the Sox. "Heard from Lexie that she's got a boyfriend. 'Bout time."

Fritzie said, "Sure do remember when Lexie and Olivia and that other one —"

"Claire."

"Yeah. Her. Anyway, our boy Trent was after one of them — don't remember which."

"Trent was after every female in town," Wes said, scowling. He was no prude, but Trent McGraw had always been too much of a bragger when it came to women. In Wes's day, guys didn't talk.

"So has McGraw got the guys who messed up Olivia's place?"

"Heard something about the Klayton kid, but if you ask me, they oughta be lookin' at those rich kids who come humpin' down here every summer." Then he said, "Maybe me and Roger will wander over and see if we can help her out with the cleanup. Neighborly like, you know, for old times."

"Like when you were bonkin' her ma?"

Wes gave the men a hard stare. "I did some cleanup of trash she wanted to get rid of after old Stan got laid up and couldn't do it — never got no closer to the lady than a handshake."

"Yeah? We heard different."

"What you heard ain't worth a pail of warm spit."

While the men in Murphy's debated rumor versus fact, Olivia drove past Ike's Ice Cream, the usual cadre of kids crowded around the take-out window. A patrol car sat in the parking lot, and Olivia wondered fleetingly if it was Trent. Admittedly her curiosity about him had been piqued, but then she was also curious if Ike's Ice Cream tasted the same. The red-and-white sign — HOMEMADE ON THE PREMISES still hung in the same place. Before she left town, she most definitely planned to sample.

Funny, she thought as she made the turn that would take her to Steeple Street, how coming back had her musing on why she'd moved away. Oh, she knew the big reason — too many years trapped in one place. Caring for her parents had been an obligation that hadn't felt suffocating at the time, but rather necessary and supportive. But once they'd passed, she couldn't get out of town fast enough. And the house that she'd once loved, well, she'd abandoned it right along with Bishop. Nothing would ever make her come back . . . nothing.

Get a grip, she chided herself, shaking off the nostalgia. Bishop is a small coastal town that hasn't changed in thirty years and probably never will, plus all the best and the

32

brightest moved away. She would have done it sooner than she had but for her parents. There was nothing here for her after their deaths, and there was even less here now.

She planned to leave as soon as she'd seen and assessed the damage. Whatever needed to be done could be handled via the phone. After all, how complicated would it be to hire a few painters and repair people?

When she turned into the brick drive, the weeping willow in the front lawn brought back thoughts of happier days — memories of shaded afternoons under the drape of the long, feathery branches. The tree fit the house — both oversized and old. The brick and clapboard monstrosity with its ivy-laced playhouse were where Olivia had spent the carefree summers of her childhood. Then when she was twelve her mother had turned it into a garden shed.

You're too old for a playhouse. Time to grow up and quit pretending.

Olivia had never quite forgiven her.

The house itself was a triple story with an eyebrow window just below the central peak at the center front and tiered rooflines that sagged a bit at the corners. While one of the largest houses on Steeple Street, it was also one of the most expensive to maintain — high ceilings, big rooms, drafty windows, and an acre of open land to its north that pushed the howling winds of fiercely cold winters through the drafty structure.

The house looked weary and lonely, making her feel as if she'd somehow contributed to its exhaustion. The lawn, parched and brown in places, gave evidence of the dry summer they'd had. Her mother's flower gardens gave barely a hint of their one-time lushness, now reduced to only scraggly perennials. Looking at the tattered, shabby surroundings suddenly made her feel sad. Her father's mantra about most things was that "neglect harvested waste," and she supposed that applied here. While nothing excused vandalism, an empty house was an inviting target.

Flo hurried across the yard wearing a pink flowered, precisely ironed cotton dress, her graying hair a mass of short curled springs that only emphasized her bouncy pace. At sixty-seven her skin was leathery from years in the sun without a hat. But her face was kind and Olivia recalled many a day when Flo and her friend Rosa Lauder had come and stayed with her parents to give Olivia a break.

"I'm just so upset about this!" Flo wailed.

Across the street Rosa and Edna-Mae Wetchner, who lived four houses away, peeked out of Rosa's front picture window that was dressed with gauzy curtains stamped with painted daisies. A few doors away the phone rang in Evelyn Gunther's Cape

Codder. Rosa was calling with the news that Olivia had arrived. Evelyn's shades were drawn due to the fact that she'd lost three rosebushes to aphids this season, and in a self-sacrificing gesture, she had promptly re-signed as president of the Bishop Garden Club. Always one to deliver the grand, if overdone, gesture, she intended to repeat all the scintillating details on a planned vacation to see friends in northern New York. But right now her attention leaped from rosebush-mourning to the arrival of Olivia.

Olivia hugged and reassured Flo. "It will be fine. I'm just as glad you weren't here, be-cause I know you would have come over and you could have been hurt."

"I would've had my gun."

Olivia shuddered, not even wanting to think about that scenario. "I deserve some blame, too," she said as they walked up the brick drive to the back door. "I shouldn't have expected you to watch the house."

"You know I wanted to. Your parents were always so kind to me. It was the least I could do."

"Well, we'll get things fixed up for the renters." She used the key and opened the back door. "Let's take a look."

"Wait, before you go in, there's something I haven't told you."

Olivia frowned. "About the vandalism?"

"No, the renters. The Marlowes called last

week and said they were going to be in Boston this weekend and wanted to drive down and measure for drapes. I said it was okay, but that was before —"

"This weekend?" Today was Saturday. "When are they coming?"

"In about three hours."

Olivia closed her eyes and drew a deep breath. "Terrific."

Then stepping inside, the familiar smells of ancient wood, the ever-present lavender cologne that her mother practically bathed in, the lingering memory of old illnesses and ordinary stale air swirled around her in such a thick wave, Olivia had to suck in her breath at the breathtakingly clear flashback:

But your life, Olivia, you had so many plans and we're a burden.

There's plenty of time.

Then, on another day, there would be the terror of abandonment that she'd see in their faces, like the time she went away for a weekend with Lexie and Claire.

You're coming back, aren't you? Promise us, you'll come home again.

Her parents had health insurance, but the bills that weren't covered always loomed. Her mother's diabetes plus her father's prostate cancer had been debilitating both physically and emotionally. They weren't old enough to qualify for Medicare, so despite a lot of juggling and trimming, money became tight.

Olivia, looking for any source of cash, gently suggested selling some of the many items her parents had collected and no longer used; they'd both whitened in horror. *Sell our beloved antiques? How can you even suggest it?*

The idea was abandoned before it found footing, and Olivia continued to cut corners while using her salary from teaching to pick up the slack. She could have argued, she could have secretly sold things, but she did neither.

Instead, they lived hand-to-mouth in a house full of furniture and bric-a-brac, some of it quite pricey. To Olivia, it was the ultimate irony. Going without while surrounded by wealth, their ill health finally taking its final toll four years ago.

Funny, that afterward, when all the antiques were hers to sell, burn, or give away, she'd taken none of those options. What she hadn't stored, she'd taken with her. At that point all she'd felt was the pull away from the tight strangle of Bishop to someplace else — anywhere else. She'd ended up in Parkboro, Massachusetts.

Moving away, living away, staying away provided more much-needed distance than just the hundred miles between here and there. As her friend Lexie had observed at the time, "Who cares where you live? When you don't know where you belong, anyplace will do." Olivia, who usually made decisions only when she had a zillion facts, found a kind of weird comfort in Lexie's "just do it" advice; she promptly picked Parkboro when she learned they'd been looking to hire teachers.

"Well," Olivia now said to Flo. "We'll just have to manage. . . ." Her words died as she caught sight of the kitchen's scribbled walls, the gouged counters, and the spray paint of red, black, and orange that looked more gross than damaging. "Not very imaginative art," she muttered, stepping to the sink and turning off a dripping faucet.

"Art!" Flo folded her arms and sniffed. "Your mother certainly would not have called this stuff art, I can tell you that."

Her neighbor followed behind her as if to catch her in case she fainted or got sick at the sights before her. They made their way through to the dining room and into the living room, where the expensive floral "New York wallpaper," as her mother had called it, hung in jagged tears, exposing naked walls beneath.

Flo caught her breath as though seeing it for the first time. "Oh, my, Alva would just roll over if she saw this. I wonder if it could be repaired," she commented, drawing in for a closer look.

I hope not, Olivia thought, having never cared for the overly busy print. While Flo examined the ripped paper, Olivia returned to the back area of the house, this time entering a one-time summer kitchen that her father had converted into a small study. It was here where Stanley Halsey had written what later became an insightful guide to hunting and finding antique treasures. She recalled the hours he'd spent organizing pictures and illustrations, making notes, retracing over and over again the research paths he'd taken to show readers the steps necessary to authenticate each find.

Olivia particularly remembered a piece of yellow pottery reportedly used by Mary Lincoln before her husband became president. When it became known that the piece had been seen in the northeast, it became a "race to locate" for many collectors. But no one was more diligent than her father. And when his efforts paid off, Stanley Halsey traveled to northern Maine in the midst of a blizzard, found the elderly woman who'd been using the piece for a cat dish, and paid her a handsome sum for the yellow pottery. How proud he'd been and how envied by dealers that he'd gotten it for such a reasonable price. A woman in an old wooden shack with a valuable Mary Lincoln pottery piece seemed an odd mix, but one of the fascinating delights of antiquing was where these unique finds turned up.

Then just a month after the purchase of the Halsey find, as it became known within the industry, an expert on Lincoln memorabilia met with her father and after much discussion and examination concluded the piece was fake. Other experts later concurred.

Her father never fully recovered either professionally or personally. The Halsey find became the Halsey fraud. And from that came a lesson she learned well. Be absolutely sure before you stake your name and reputation.

Perhaps, she realized now with the distance of objectivity, her parents' reluctance to sell their antiques had been more about fearing the discovery of another fake than slavish devotion to their collections. In retrospect, her own delay in selling could have sprung from the same underlying unease.

How sad, she realized, that a lifetime of work could come under question because of one mistake.

She kneeled down and ran her fingers over the indentations in the floor where her father had rolled back and forth in the wooden chair with rusty castors. The window above the desk framed the driveway and beyond to the side yard, where the seasons changed with a comforting ritual. Her father had often called her in to show her the artistic drifts of January snow or the embryonic leaves of April. "Mind keepers," he called those moments, when nature showed her power and beauty.

"Hello?" A woman's voice called from the

kitchen. Rosa Lauder, Olivia guessed.

"Anybody here?" came the second female voice, this one a bit higher pitched. Had to be Edna-Mae Wetchner. Unless things in Bishop had changed drastically, Rosa and Edna-Mae were still the cousins who lived and acted as if they were joined shoulder to hip.

Flo appeared. "Now, you know we're here, seeing as you two have been watching since Olivia came home."

Edna-Mae Wetchner held tighter to the bowl she was carrying. "You don't have to be rude, Floie." She looked around. "However will that poor child get things fixed in time?"

"Olivia is quite efficient," Flo said defensively, although she'd been thinking the same thing until now. Agreeing with the flighty Edna-Mae or the know-it-all Rosa, well, she just never did that.

"Looks mighty messy to me," Rosa said, approaching the torn wallpaper and looking more closely. "This will be a job to get off. Remember when I stripped paper with one of them steamers?" She shuddered. "Thought I'd never get done."

"Alva loved this paper, and Olivia is going to have it repaired," Flo said, crossing her arms and glaring at Rosa.

Rosa shook her head, making a sweeping gesture of the room's walls. "Waste of time. It needs to come off, then maybe some paint.

41

Besides, wallpaper in public rooms is a mistake."

"And just when did you become such an expert?"

"I read it in a magazine."

"I bet I could find one that says different," Flo retorted. "And besides, who asked you anyway. I'm taking care of things, so you can run along." She eyed Edna-Mae. "Both of you."

"Edna-Mae, we've just been insulted," Rosa said with a sniff.

"And told to leave." Edna-Mae's flyaway hair fanned out as she bobbed her head at her own words.

In the small study Olivia preferred to wait until the ladies left. Flo and her friends were known for these verbal tussles, as her mother would call them, and getting into a "taking sides" position was a bad idea.

Hearing only silence, she peeked out.

Flo stood like a sentry surveying her options. On the one hand, they were her best friends, but they were always butting in before she was ready for them. She wanted Olivia to herself so they could talk and discuss what needed to be done. Since Flo had been watching the house, she certainly had first dibs on first advice. Rosa and Edna-Mae were always full of opinions about what Flo should or shouldn't do. The fact that sometimes they were right . . . well, lots of times they were wrong, too.

Since it seemed to be a standoff, Olivia came out of the study, in time to greet yet another neighbor who'd just come in the back door. "Why, Olivia, it's wonderful to see you. Let me look at you." Marion Gunther, Wes's sister, seemed awed as she came forward, grasping Olivia's hands and spreading her arms wide, much as Marion had done when Olivia was a little girl. The only thing she didn't do was ask Olivia to twirl around. Smiling and looking her over, Marion said, "My dear, you look lovely. Last time I talked to Lexie, she said you were quite happy with a new man in your life. And a very handsome one, too, or so I hear," she added, the interest unmistakable. "You know what they say about being in love."

Olivia smiled in spite of herself. Marion was such a romantic and so open about her opinions on love that it was hard to ever get in a huff about her being nosy. "No, what do they say about being in love?"

"Why, it makes a woman glow," she said, peering closely to see if that was indeed true. She brightened when Olivia nodded. "I believe Lexie said his name was Daniel. Always did like that name. Is this forever-serious? I certainly hope so. Weddings are so lovely and you're due one. Time is passing, my dear. Children won't wait forever."

"No, they certainly do not." Olivia made a

mental note to choke Lexie for filling her aunt's head with too many rose-blossom scenarios. "Seeing you reminds me I have to call Lexie and Claire and cancel our plans. What with the mess here at the house, I'm going to be tied up here for a while."

It was then that the other two women appeared with Flo at their heels. Rosa Lauder and Edna-Mae Wetchner were first cousins on their mothers' side, if she remembered correctly. It was one of the many quirks or charms of Bishop, depending on one's view; touting that you're part of the town's family branches, almost everyone was related somehow.

Olivia had notably not kept up with the Bishop news; when she lived here the women were both widows and Edna-Mae had a daughter somewhere that no one ever mentioned. "Troubled" was all that was ever said.

"Flo has told us to leave," Rosa said, her cheeks bright pink discs, and just the slightest flare to her nostrils.

Rather than getting into that battle, Olivia said, "The renters are going to be here shortly, and Flo and I were trying to decide just what to do. The condition of the house certainly won't be inspiring."

"I offered my son Jimmie to help you out, but Flo —"

"Told me what a wonderful worker he is," Olivia interjected with a smile and put her arm around Rosa. "He's a handyman, isn't he?"

"Why, yes he is." She peered at Flo suspiciously. "She said he was a wonderful worker? I didn't hear her say that."

"It was before you came over. And a handyman is what is needed here, that's for sure." Then she added quickly, "Flo and I are going to need some help. Do you think Jimmie would be willing to come and take a look?" Olivia hadn't even seen the rest of the house, but stalling about the work that needed to be done was silly. If she expected to keep the Marlowes from looking elsewhere, she'd better at least appear prepared when they showed up — she glanced at her watch — in less than an hour.

"I brought a bowl of pasta," Edna-Mae chimed in, interrupting Olivia's thoughts. The small woman gripped the bowl tighter.

"Why, thank you, but really you shouldn't have fussed."

"Oh, this was leftover from a picnic. It's too much for me to eat alone."

"Well, I appreciate you sharing it." Olivia took the bowl to the kitchen and put it on the counter. The refrigerator door was open to prevent odors, since it wasn't plugged in, plus the vandals had filled it with empty, sticky cans lying in puddles of spilled beer. Just as she was debating on what to do, Flo appeared.

"It's not cooked."

"Excuse me?"

"The pasta isn't cooked."

Sure enough, when Olivia removed the foil from the top of the bowl, inside were a box of macaroni, a tomato, a small onion, a green pepper, and a small jar of mayonnaise. Edna-Mae had even included a few packets of salt and pepper that from their packaging came from a local fast-food place.

Flo said, "Edna-Mae hasn't turned on a stove since her husband passed. It was food poisoning that killed him."

"I didn't know that. How awful for her."

"Oh, it wasn't her cooking, it was him eating stuff that should have been thrown away. Milton never would throw food away and it finally did him in. As for Edna-Mae, she hates to cook, always did. Whenever there's a 'going-on,' she doesn't like to 'not bring a dish,' as she calls it. We're all kinda used to her raw surprises."

Olivia glanced once again at the bowl of ingredients and then she laughed. Really laughed for the first time since she'd arrived in Bishop.

Chapter Three

"Daniel, you can't say no. Please. It will only take an hour, maybe less. I promised I'd have these flyers distributed today."

"Karen, look, I'd like to help, but I can't. Why don't you get some of the kids to do it?"

Daniel was in line at the local Wal-Mart with an arm full of items when Karen Clancey zeroed in on him from four aisles away. He hated to shop for stuff, whether it was grooming or clothes or food. Even prowling through one of Olivia's junky yard sales appealed to him more than a winding trip through kids, noise, and cart-jammed aisles.

Now here he was not only behind a woman with seven-hundred craft items that would take forever to price-scan, but his wait had just been made even more agonizing by the enthusiastic arrival of the school's roving volunteer.

Karen was bubbly and known to be adventurous in her social life, and Daniel liked her — but in small doses. He was all for enthusiasm, but Karen tended to make everything she volunteered to do into some high religious calling complete with pleas for help and a merciless application of pressure if one didn't see things her way.

And today he was in no mood to be pressured or cajoled. In fact, he was cranky and sullen and nursing rejection wounds; he didn't want to talk or smile or feel compelled to alter his glum mood.

Why hadn't he kept his sunglasses on? He'd been avoiding her for days and now he was stuck.

"You're very difficult to get ahold of."

Apparently not tough enough since you found me. He toyed with the ramifications of verbalizing his annoyance. The line moved a fraction of an inch, and Daniel took a step, hoping Karen would get the message and retreat. No such luck.

"You're the athletic director," she said, her voice rising in chirpy energy as if stating the obvious was supposed to sway him.

"So I am." Daniel watched an eight-year-old push a cart filled with bags for his mother. Maybe he'd just put all these items down and walk out.

Karen continued in his ear like a buzzing gnat. "You of all people should be leading the parade of volunteers." She drew closer to him. "I think you could give me a better reason than you can't."

He looked at her. Now he really glared at her, hoping she'd get the message and slink away. No deal. "What difference does the reason make if I'm not going to do it?"

"So there isn't a reason. You're just being stubborn, not being a team player."

Shoppers were beginning to look and the noise that just moments ago bellowed around him had dropped about ten octaves.

"Look, I don't want to do it. That's about as clear as it gets."

"But why?"

The urge to come back with something thoroughly outrageous teased around the parameters of his mind. A few people were looking at him as if waiting for him to say something. You're a chicken, Cafferty. The woman deserves to be embarrassed. "Goodbye, Karen."

Instead of going away like most people would do, she whined, "How can you do this to me? You promised me in June, and now you're backing out."

"I never promised you anything," he fired back, realizing instantly he should have kept his mouth shut. Her top-volume complaints had been overheard, and Daniel didn't need to look around to see the disapproval from those in the vicinity. One woman with a straw hat tied to her head by a frayed green ribbon remarked, "You don't look like a man who would break a promise. This poor lady looks like she's about to cry. Why are you being so mean?"

"Ma'am —"

"Some men have all the nerve," muttered her companion. "Kind of move my ex would make."

As a few others chimed in, Daniel was sure he'd been sucked into some kind of fun house. Then just when he thought it couldn't get any worse, the school principal, Frank Fisler, strolled by with his wife pushing a cart full of items including a gigantic new coffeemaker.

"Daniel, good to see you." He extended his hand, and Daniel juggled his items, dropping a package of razors, shampoo, and a bag of caramels.

"Frank." He shook his hand, then picked up the items, with Frank getting the caramels.

"Used to eat these, but they wreck your fillings." He handed them to Daniel. "You should have gotten a basket."

"I should have gone to the drugstore," Daniel muttered.

Fisler laughed, although for the life of him, Daniel found nothing funny. "Why, Karen, hello," he said, as if she'd been sent in to make this a party. "I almost didn't see you. How are you? I hear you're working hard on the fund-raising for the new auditorium."

"Yes, I am. Daniel and I were trying to work out some details."

"Ah, then, you two are together?"

"No," Daniel said firmly. Karen simply smiled, saying nothing. Fisler looked from one to the other and then frowned. He leaned close. "You and Olivia have an argument?"

"No. Olivia and I are fine." Stupid lie, Cafferty. It's sure to be out by midweek that the two of them were no longer a couple.

"Glad to hear it. Olivia is a lovely lady. Well, guess we'd better get finished up," he said when his wife nudged him. "Coffeemaker died this morning, so here we are. Can't imagine reading the morning paper without coffee." Daniel managed a smile while Karen rambled on about brands and why the one the Fislers had wasn't the best. Daniel tuned it all out. Finally good-byes were said, and he was left — once again — with Karen.

"Too bad she won't be able to make the silent auction tonight," Karen said, keeping parallel to him in line.

"Mrs. Fisler?"

"No, silly. Olivia."

"Oh." There was no way he was going to ask how she knew. Besides, he knew and that's what mattered; she wasn't going for the same reason he wasn't. They'd planned to go together, but now . . . "There's always another auction," he said, breezing the words out and then moving quickly to put his items down when the craft buyer's items finally moved along the counter. Then the woman checking out launched into what she was going to make with five grapevine wreaths for the curious checker.

Daniel's back teeth began to ache. This was absolutely his last trip to Wal-Mart on a Saturday.

"That's an odd thing to say given she was called out of town on an emergency."

This got all of Daniel's attention. "What emergency?"

"You didn't know? Oh, perhaps I shouldn't have said anything."

"Knock it off. If she told you, it's not a secret."

"But she didn't tell you?" Karen asked, totally missing his dig that she was a full-time blabber.

"How could she? I've been in this line for most of the day."

She waved her hand. "You men are so impatient."

"Mostly we're just tired. What emergency?" he gritted out.

She shrugged. "Oh, I don't really know, you know, like exactly what it was."

"Just answer the question, Karen."

"Something in Bishop," she said quickly. "I saw her at an ATM a little while ago, and she said she was going to Bishop." Then she added, "You really didn't know, did you? I thought she told you everything."

Finally his items were checked out and being bagged. He turned his back on Karen to pay for them. Olivia and the word *emergency* had him feeling suddenly inadequate and worried.

He didn't turn around again. Pocketing his change, he took his bag and exited the store before he ran into anyone else he knew. Emergency in Bishop. But what? Her parents were dead. She had no ties there but the house. And what kind of emergency would that be unless there was a fire? He tried her cell phone, but as usual, it wasn't on.

He drove home, then changed his mind and drove to her house. One look at the closed windows, and he knew she was definitely gone. He used his key, went inside, and checked Olivia's phone number list. He quickly called the Kester woman, but it rang and rang until he finally hung up.

He tried Olivia's cell one more time, but nothing.

Well, there was only one thing to do.

He returned home, changed his clothes, and headed south to Rhode Island.

"Oh, Claire, the place is a mess. The Marlowes came to measure for drapes and, of course, saw nothing but the gouged woodwork, torn wallpaper, and broken windows. They stayed only long enough for Mrs. Marlowe to get hysterical about where they were going to live. He was marginally less upset, but clearly, this threw them. Moving is hassle enough, but making a presumably pleasant trip only to learn that the house you were excited about looks like a war zone isn't anyone's idea of fun. I wasn't sure if I felt worse for them or for myself."

"Livie, what are you going to do?"

"Try to get the place fixed for them. I did tell them I wouldn't hold them to their lease, but if they do back out, then I'm going to have to get someone else. It sounds greedy, but I need the income from the rent."

"Not greedy. Prudent. Leaving the house empty will only encourage more vandals."

Olivia was curled into the corner of an old leather couch in Flo's TV room. The one-time extra bedroom had been converted after her last child got married. The decor was a combination country and thrift shop. Beside the leather couch, the other item of note was Flo's grandmother's huge antique school clock that hung on one wall over a pine desk. The room had changed little since Olivia had lived in Bishop, and it was as invitingly cluttery as she'd remembered.

"This is lousy, but I'm going to have to cancel our get-together," Olivia said. She hated doing that, for their reunions didn't happen often enough and the three of them had been looking forward to this one since May.

"No, let's just move the date."

"By the time I'm done here, I'll have to be back for the new school season. Anyway, Lexie probably has her vacation time already set." Disappointment filled her. "Believe me, I hate doing this. . . ." She sipped a glass of lemonade Flo had fixed for her. "I'll call Lexie — I know she's going to be annoyed and ask me for the umpteenth time why I don't sell the place."

"No, let me call her. I needed to anyway. I'm worried about her."

Alarmed, Olivia asked, "Why? She hasn't hooked back up with that last jerk she divorced, has she?" Lexie had a habit of believing that she could control any relationship, and often waited too long to get out of the bad ones. With two divorces, and a fairly recent new boyfriend, Olivia and Claire feared she'd take the plunge again.

"I don't think so — that Eric who she's been dating — seemed to be going okay. Nevertheless, she sounded distracted when we talked last week. I felt like I was carrying the conversation. You know Lexie, she never wants to admit it when things are going badly."

Oh, she knew Lexie, all right. She hated admitting any kind of failure, and Claire would, as she'd done for Olivia, offer more of a sympathetic ear than a lecture.

Listening to Claire express concern for Lexie caused Olivia to realize all over again how truly blessed she was to have two such good friends. Despite the distance, Claire in Virginia and Lexie in Chicago, they talked a few times a month, did e-mail more than a few times a week, and made a point of getting together as often as all of them could swing it. What with jobs and family obligations, they still managed to see each other at least three times a year. Now, with Claire's concern, Olivia felt twice as bad about canceling. "Do you suppose it's her job that's upsetting her?"

"I hadn't thought about that. It's always been the one thing that goes right in her life."

Lexie was an investigative reporter for a Chicago television station and had filled in as anchor on the weekends — proof, Lexie had told Olivia, that her next promotion would be to an anchor desk.

"Don't worry, I'll find out," Claire said, her determination evident. "That girl needs to understand we're her friends and we want to be there for her instead of her trying to cope all alone." Olivia could hear Claire's grit and resolve. Always the nurturer, Claire made it a point to make sure neither Olivia nor Lexie had trouble or problems that couldn't be solved with conversation laced with straightforward advice and a few sage solutions. "In the meantime, I'm going to come up to help you."

"Oh, Claire, that would be wonderful — no, getting to see you would be wonderful even if you lounge in the yard and bark orders."

"I might do that, too. You do have that lovely willow tree. All right, it's settled — extending our visit, well nothing could make me happier. Jeff's off on another can't-cancel business trip, Lara is visiting cousins in Richmond, and Tony . . ." Olivia heard her catch her breath at the mention of her self-indulgent eighteen-year-old son. She didn't ask. She didn't need to. Tony had managed to wrap up every parental disappointment into one nasty package. Claire ached for him, and Olivia and Lexie ached for Claire. "He called and wanted money and I sent it," she blurted out, and Olivia groaned. "I know what you're thinking, but I can't help it. He's my son, Livie, and I can't just turn my back on him."

But he's turned his back on you except when he needs something. "You're a soft touch, Claire, and Tony knows it," she said gently. She refused to say she understood, because she didn't. She'd never had kids and hadn't a clue how she might act in the same circumstances.

"But what am I going to do? Hang up on him? Lecture him?" But without waiting for Olivia to offer an answer — and thankfully she didn't, because Olivia had none — Claire added, "Jeff will be furious with me, but I don't care. If the man stayed home once in a while, he'd know how I feel about these rules he lays down and then leaves me to enforce."

Olivia sighed. "What can I say? I'm no expert on kids or on having a husband." Or men in general, she thought, noted by the swift way she'd just dropped Daniel. Come to think of it, just what was she an expert on? Suddenly she felt at loose ends and rather silly to be wasting energy worrying about something as trivial as a house when Claire's "Tony" problem was much more significant. Vandalism hardly ranked up there with a wayward son so desperately in need of . . . of something. "Hey, if you can come, I'd love it, but if you can't . . ." She glanced up as Flo came in the room.

"The police are here," she whispered. "They want to talk to you."

She nodded. "Gotta go, Claire. And let me know about Lexie, okay? I worry about her."

She turned the phone off, rose, and followed Flo down the small hall, through the country-style kitchen and out to the back porch, where Olivia came to a halt when she saw the officer standing, sunglasses on, next to a patrol car with a teenage boy slumped down in the backseat. Another officer sat in the front seat writing on a clipboard.

When he removed his sunglasses, she knew immediately. Tall, dark-haired, and still with that undefined ability to make women look just a smidgen too long. "Trent McGraw, how nice to see you." She started to extend her hand, then wondered if you were supposed to do that with a cop. Suddenly she felt ill at ease. When he didn't say anything, she wondered if her greeting sounded too personal with a man who didn't even know her name the last time she'd spoken with him.

Then he came forward and smiled. "Olivia? Wouldn't have thought you'd remember me. We haven't seen you around these parts in years."

"Actually, Flo told me you had been to the house —"

"So you assumed I'd be the officer following up." He smiled, his eyes warm, and for that moment, when he seemed to focus on her, her emotional recall became immediate. All those teenage tummy flips from a long-ago summer when she had a major crush on him and he hadn't a clue who she was.

"Yes, I guess I did."

"Well, too bad we're meeting under these circumstances." It sounded logical, it even sounded true with a heavy dollop of regret,

59

but his expression belied his words. If she'd simply run into him in town, a chance meeting, without a connection to the house, he would have been totally blank.

Then again, what did it matter? "Flo said you wanted to talk to me."

"Yeah. We picked up some kids for knocking down mailboxes about a block or so away just a little while after your house was trashed. Right now it appears these kids might be the culprits."

Olivia kept looking in the backseat at the boy scrunched into a near fetal position. His blond hair, the most visible and striking thing about him, was spiked in Irish green.

"Is he one of them?" Olivia whispered.

"Him? Just taking him home." But she noted he didn't specifically say he wasn't. "Since I was passing this way, I wanted to update you that we've made some arrests."

She thought it odd that the police gave rides home, but since no other information was offered, she didn't ask. "I appreciate you stopping to tell me. What happens now?"

"If they're charged and plead guilty, they'll probably get fined, required to make restitution, perhaps be ordered to do some community service. Most of our judges don't look kindly on this kind of mischief."

"How reassuring," she said, remembering a few cases where slaps on the wrists and "be a good boy" were the gist of the punishment.

The boy in the backseat turned, and something clicked in Olivia's mind. "Isn't he Kitty Klayton's son?"

Trent raised his eyebrows. "Yeah, it is. How do you know him?"

"His mother once worked for my parents."

Trent scowled. "Kitty? Had to be a while ago."

She walked closer to the patrol car. The boy didn't look up even though the window was down. "Raymond, hello. I'm Olivia Halsey. You probably don't remember me —"

Then he turned and looked at her. She saw a long scratch on his cheek as well as dirt smudges. But it was his eyes that made her heart break. Pain, defiance, hardness — they were all wrapped up in one of the most direct looks Olivia had ever had from anyone.

"I knew your mother — she was a big help to me in the months before my parents died."

For an instant the boy's expression carried an edge of softness, but it was gone just as quickly.

"How is she?"

He shrugged.

"Well, please say hello for me."

Again, he shrugged.

She straightened, her teacher-instinct that something at home was terribly wrong. She turned to Trent, keeping her voice low.

"Is Kitty all right? I mean, is she still in

61

Bishop, still living at home?"

"She's still on Brace Street," he said with a deftness in the art of avoiding answering. "We gotta go. I'll get back to you in the next few days." Then he glanced in the direction of her house. "Looks like you got company."

Olivia looked across the street just in time to see Daniel climb out of his black truck.

Chapter Four

Lexie James tried never to dwell in the past. Life was too full of attractive angles and ripe opportunities to muddle around in the dreck of mistakes or disappointments. At least *this* approach had been her philosophy until two months ago.

Once, someone told her that distance was a better evaluator of circumstances than a magnifying glass. But Lexie needed neither to see the ripples a couple of major changes could bring.

Take this morning. As the bright July sun threw dazzling streaks and sparkles across Lake Michigan, Lexie was fifteen minutes into her morning run and trying not to think about the night before. Running cleared her head, and man, oh, man, today it needed clearing. She liked the early morning — less traffic, less noise, and a better possibility that she wouldn't meet anyone she knew.

Or at least better than any other time of day. There were runners and joggers and walkers, but none that she knew. Her friends into afternoon runs or they'd escaped to ocal gym or fitness center where they ould sweat in air-conditioned comfort.

Lexie had gone with them until she began to beg off with a fleet of excuses. It had been a bit disconcerting that her patently transparent reasons were all so readily accepted. But hey, what could she expect? No one she knew in Chicago was into deep analysis unless it was about themselves.

Truthfully, she'd always preferred running alone and doing it outdoors; she liked the fresh air, she liked hearing the birds, and the sweat she raised was for real. And unlike the fitness fashion crowd, she liked her paint-splattered shorts, the Chicago Bears tee that was as least as old as her last divorce, and sneaks that should have been replaced a summer ago.

Replaced, she thought drearily. Her life had too many of yesterday's hopes that in today's reality had about as much chance of happening as a snow burst. She needed to get on with it, but with what? And therein lay her dilemma. Where was her life going? Hardly the question for the lead reporter from *"Live at Five"* with Lexie James reporting. Yeah, well, whatever.

A blue truck rumbled toward her; the driver waved and she waved back. She didn't know him except that he drove this route every Saturday. There was something comforting about consistency.

She rounded a corner, crossed the road, and continued picking up her pace and increasing her heart rate.

Three miles later she began to slow down, allowing her body to cool and her breathing to even out.

At the entrance to her building, her neighbors were just waking up. The smell of coffee wafted from open windows along with the ambrosia of Mark Allison's weekend bacon and waffles.

Her tummy growled and she decided that she'd treat herself, starting with Bessie's homemade pastries. She'd shower, and then while her coffee was dripping, she'd run to Bessie's.

Inside, she took the stairs two at a time and disappeared into her four-room apartment that until two months ago was so affordable, she barely minded paying for it. Now the rent was chewing away at her savings with more vigor than a starving wolf.

She'd chosen the contemporary style of clean lines and black and white accessories because they were refreshingly different from the staid, stuffed, and patterned clutter that she'd grown up with back in Bishop.

She'd liked this minimalist feel, but like so many things of late, even for her furnishings, the word *replace* had drifted too frequently to mind. Suddenly that old dinged and scratched rocking chair of her grandmother's that she'd left with her aunt in Bishop had more appeal than the tubular and leather chair she'd once thought she couldn't live without.

She eyed it now and could count on one hand the number of times she'd actually sat in it.

She pulled off the sweaty headband, her blond hair damp and stuck to her head. She ran her fingers through it, clearly unconcerned about its disorganization. Then she saw him.

"You should have waited for me," he said. Fully dressed and obviously showered, he looked out of place and too satisfied.

"I run alone."

"Always?"

She shrugged, going to the kitchen, and taking a bottle of cold water from the refrigerator, she guzzled it down.

He came up behind her, nuzzling her neck. She was sweaty and she stank, but that didn't deter him. "You were good last night," he whispered.

"I know."

"I like a woman who knows what she's got."

"I like men who know when to go home."

But instead of being offended, he merely chuckled as if they were exchanging clever barbs. "So when are we on again?"

"I'll let you know."

He didn't chuckle this time, deciding she wasn't teasing, but very serious.

Good, she didn't play games, and the sooner he figured that out, the sooner she'd be alone.

Then he turned her around as if he might be talking to someone other than the lonely Lexie James. "Let me know? What is this? Playing hard to get?"

"I am hard to get."

"Not last night you weren't." She allowed him to cup her breast, mostly because men liked that morning-after indulgence, and that's all he was going to get.

"Guess you got lucky," she said, not caring if he was offended or not.

"So did you."

She rolled her eyes. Was there anything worse than a performance ego?

Lexie looked at him fully and wondered what she had been thinking. Attractive in that instant handsome way that came from expensive clothes and attentive grooming, but take those away and she doubted if he'd stand out in a group of male mannequins.

Then again, last night had been a haze of margaritas and smoky music.

By the time they'd arrived at her apartment and were out of their clothes, Lexie, suffering a bout of lonely self-pity, wasn't looking for a precursor to a new relationship, but for a quick intimacy, the sweet lies, and that silly rush of an unexpected encounter. She certainly wasn't thinking about the morning after or conversation and questions. And absolutely she hadn't even considered if he was worthy enough to meet her lover standard, never mind engage in seductive quips.

And that was the rub. Last night she'd been feeling desperate and sorry for herself, and since men mostly knew the score, that trinity of reasoning justified letting Bob or was it Rob? — into her bed. In her usually well-arranged world, she was distressingly picky about men. In fact she was picky to the point of prudishness.

She did sorta know this guy, so it wasn't as if he were just some club crawler looking to score.

Lexie hadn't totally screwed up. She never went to bed with strangers or boyfriends of friends and especially not with ex-husbands, as was the habit of her cousin Shelley. Shelley figured sex was easier, safer, and never complicated when it was an ex-husband.

Lexie could top that since she had two ex's, but sex with them turned her off faster than smelling sweaty feet.

"I'm serious about seeing you again, Lex."

"Please don't call me that."

"Lex? I kinda like it."

"I don't." Well, for her best friends it was okay.

"Hey, whatever you say."

He walked over to her coffeemaker and poured himself some, filling her Bishop mug that Olivia had found to replace the one Lexie'd had since she was a kid. The original had been broken when she moved from Bishop to Chicago. The mugs had been made in the seventies and were nearly impossible to find. Olivia had located one in a little shop in Vermont and gave it to Lexie last Christmas. She'd had her morning coffee out of it every day since. Watching this guy drink from it made her feel as if she'd been invaded.

He said, "I was about to go out to Bessie's for some pastry when you came in."

She scowled. "I don't eat pastry." *And what gave you the right to make coffee anyway?* She wanted him gone. She'd planned on him leaving while she was running. Her apartment felt crowded and hot and smothering. When she blew off the wake-up cuddle-sex, she figured he'd take the hint.

She finished her water, debating whether to be polite or just tell him to go away. "Bob, look —"

"It's Rob."

"Okay, Rob. You're probably a nice guy, but I'm not looking to get tied into anything." She refilled the bottle from the tap and guzzled down another six ounces.

"Hey, me neither. We had fun last night and . . ." He paused, dropping his voice and moving closer to her. "You were so hot for me, babe. It was the best sex I've had in years."

Lexie turned away, a sour thump rolling through her stomach. She went to adjust the window to let in more air. What had she done with him? She remembered the cab ride home, the heat, and the impatience, but honestly when they got to her bedroom, it became a blur.

Not good, kiddo. Blurs and sex are a dangerous combo.

"Look, I have an appointment, so if you could just finish your coffee and leave, I'd appreciate it."

Suddenly his easygoing nonchalance crumbled, and he looked stunned, as if he realized she really meant it. "You're throwing me out?"

She crossed her arms. "That's a fair guess."

"What kind of a woman are you?"

"A bored one."

Now he just looked sucker-punched; Lexie didn't blink. Not nice, not very ladylike, but then she was no lady last night, so why should she expect herself to be one in the morning?

He dropped her Bishop mug into the sink, black coffee splashing up onto the clean dishes in the drainer. She heard it break and with a fury most reserved for priceless porcelain, she shouted, "You stupid jerk! You broke it!"

He looked at her with a kind of goofy startle that made it clear he had no clue what she meant.

She fled to the sink where she retrieved the pieces one by one and laid them on the counter.

"That mug? You're calling me a jerk over a cheap mug?"

She whirled around, fury gathering with tornado speed. "Get out."

"You're whacked, lady. Totally whacked." He stalked out of the kitchen. She followed him as he gathered up the rest of his things.

"You broke my mug," she said again, fists clenched and heart pumping faster than after a hundred-yard run up hill. He could have just put it down he didn't have to *drop* it in the sink.

"You're some kind of headcase." He threw a five-dollar bill on the messy bed and said curtly, "Buy a new one."

She grabbed the bill and ripped it up and flung it at him. His eyes widened as if he'd met a true loony, and she stomped toward him, trying to look her looniest. The jerk fled the apartment like a wiped-out bully.

In the living room she pulled the curtains back and hoped he'd look up so she could sneer at him. He did try a cautious over-the-shoulder glimpse that she returned by making a wretched face. He hurried down the street and around the corner.

71

She let the curtains go and returned to the kitchen. Maybe she *was* a headcase. Whacked out. Paranoid even. Nevertheless she folded her fingers around the broken mug pieces as if they represented all that was broken in her life. . . . And there was a lot broken.

Yet still, screwed-up life or not, at that moment she felt better than she had in weeks. Nothing like a good rant of invectives at an idiot to clear her head of the webby strands of failure.

By the time she climbed into the shower, she was humming and thinking about Bessie's fresh pastry.

"I don't know how you do it, Claire," praised Tricia Culpepper, the president of the Homemakers Club. "Every time I'm here it all looks so perfect. Doesn't anything ever get mussed or dusty or out of arrangement?"

"I love my home and I love puttering, so things don't get ahead of me."

"Well, this certainly has been a pleasure, hasn't it, ladies?" The six other women all smiled. "I wish more had been able to come. Perhaps we could do a tour again in the fall, Claire?"

"It would be wonderful to have you all come back."

"I for one ate one too many of your delicious scones. But as I always tell my exercise class, giving myself permission to have something exceptionally decadent makes it a treat not a cheat."

Claire wouldn't have called her scones decadent, but she didn't argue. The others all agreed with Tricia, and those burdened with a few extra pounds all seemed to make mental notes. If skinny Tricia could indulge without guilt, so could they.

Claire, too, admired Tricia's success. Not because she wanted to be on the same diet, but because of the changes she'd effected in her life as a result of her diet. The change in Tricia's looks and confidence had been dramatic. Tall and flat and slender, she barely resembled the chunky, somewhat busty woman of a year ago. Of all the questions and interest Claire had ever heard expressed by those in the group, the ones about Tricia's diet had been by far the most common.

"Well, I'm glad they were such a hit, and I'm so pleased that you all could come."

What they had come for was an outing for the Homemakers Club of Lake Moses, Virginia. For years — long before Claire and Jeff and their two children had moved to Lake Moses — the women had gathered to make baby quilts for newborns at the local hospital. The lovingly made quilts were then given to the babies' mothers to take home and keep. The very first quilt, done eighteen years ago, was still treasured by its owner who was now on her way to college. Tricia called this creating history to be passed to future generations.

The quilts were pieced and sewn at weekly meetings followed by lunch. Then twice a year the women gathered to tour homes in the area. They weren't necessarily historical homes, although more than a few had been designed and built well over a hundred and fifty years ago.

Claire Fitzgerald's home had been suggested after Tricia and her husband had been there for a Christmas party, and Tricia had raved about how Claire's house looked like something out of a Christmas showcase.

Because the waiting list of homes was extensive, the actual tour of her house by the Homemakers Club came three years later.

Honored and thrilled to have her home even suggested, Claire had eagerly agreed. She loved showing off her flair for color and the impeccable taste she'd inherited from her late mother, a hostess of some repute back home in Bishop.

The Virginia house was a large two-story brick with the Federal style influence; Claire and Jeff had wanted it the moment they saw it. At the rear was a large patio–porch where, after the tour, Claire had served iced tea and her grandmother's scones with her own homemade strawberry jam.

Tricia said, "Before everyone leaves, I did want to announce that our next house tour will be at Piedmont House. It's recently been turned into a bed-and-breakfast, and the new owners have done a great deal of refurbishing."

Then she said to Claire, "Can we count on you next weekend for the quilting?"

"Regretfully, I'm going to be away."

"A getaway. How lovely. Just you and Jeff?"

Just her and Jeff . . . how lovely and exceptional that would be . . . and how utterly improbable. She couldn't recall when she and Jeff had gone away alone for even an overnight. His job with International Systems Data, a computer company, had him traveling so much, Claire felt more like a widow than a wife. "Actually, it's a few days with two friends I grew up with."

"Well, we will miss you." Tricia glanced around. "We should be going. Again, thanks so much, Claire, this was most generous of you. I'm sorry we missed seeing Jeff."

"I'm sure he'll be disappointed, too," she said. Not really. Oh — if he were home — he'd stick around long enough to say hello and then escape to the golf course even if he didn't have a game. "He's away on a business trip."

Even as she said it, the reason sounded clichéd. Then again, Jeff was away all the time.

Claire accompanied the women as they walked down a flagstone path bordered with impatiens. The driveway of inlaid brick, its uniqueness one of the main reasons she and Jeff wanted the house, was one of only three that she knew of in Lake Moses.

Believing this was the conclusion of conversation, the women all exchanged good-byes and some quick hugs before departing for their respective cars. But Tricia stayed behind and Claire braced herself.

More questions, she knew. Tricia wasn't especially nosy, but Claire knew that she herself aroused a certain amount of curiosity because she wasn't a talker or one to share every facet of her life with anyone who was around. Small-town living, as she knew from her years in Bishop, didn't allow one to just meld into the population. One had to partake and contribute. She wasn't standoffish, but she didn't pry others with questions and would have preferred to be treated the same way. This was a trait that came directly from watching her mother.

Her late mother, Elaine Murray, practiced and taught Claire that family problems should stay in the family. Airing the dirty linen, as she'd called it, only created unseemly opportunities for others to judge, criticize, and advise. Admittedly, Claire's natural instincts were toward prudence, but she also wanted people to think the best of her. Approval, she knew, but also to counter a long-held childhood fear of not quite measuring up.

Certainly her son's recent activities fell into that category; just contemplating the idea of telling everyone and having them feel sorry for her was anathema.

Claire was aware that she was in the minority in an era where the most intimate of issues was confessed and wept over on television and in the magazines.

Not that Claire didn't have more than a few things worth her tears and frustration. She did. And when she needed comforting ears to hear her, she went to Livie and Lexie; they were best friends, best since high school. And while she liked Tricia and the others, the tenor in Lake Moses was one of perfect families, perfect kids, and perfect lives. And Claire wanted everything to be perfect; it was a standard worth striving for and one she'd embraced because it was the way her own mother had lived.

What's wrong with wanting everything to be perfect? she would ask Jeff when he rolled his eyes and muttered something about her perfection obsession.

She objected to obsession, it was more a matter of order and not settling for second best. At her most logical she knew absolute perfection was impossible, but that didn't change her deeply ingrained habit of expecting the best of herself . . . and of her children. So when conversations and questions began to veer into areas where she didn't have ready-made answers, Claire got nervous.

Like now.

She glanced over to the neighboring yard, where Dennis Roche, a charming man in the midst of a divorce, was playing basketball with a couple of teenage boys.

Last spring Dennis had literally saved Claire's daughter from an ex-boyfriend who tried to force her into his car. Since then he and Claire had become friends as well as neighbors. Often they shared a glass of wine in the afternoon, and recently when he found her weeping about Jeff going on yet another trip, Dennis had taken her in his arms and held her. Claire had thought a lot about those few moments, not about missing Jeff but how good it felt to not cry alone.

In fact, she was lonely and Dennis was good company. She seriously doubted Jeff was just sitting in hotel rooms with room service and HBO for *his* companions.

Tricia, sunglasses in place, glanced in Dennis's direction. "Too bad about what his wife did. Weren't they married more than twenty years when she left him?" His wife had filed for divorce the previous winter and moved in with a used-car salesman from a nearby town.

"Something like that," Claire murmured.

"A real tragedy. And here I'd always believed it was the men who got itchy. How's he doing?"

"I guess all right. He doesn't say a lot." Unsaid was that Claire didn't probe, either. Dennis seemed reluctant to talk and she respected that. "He keeps to himself."

"You don't ever talk to him?"

"Well, of course, we're neighbors, but we don't talk about his divorce or about Jenny."

Claire thought that Tricia was ready to leave when she said, "Oh, I know what I wanted to ask. About Lara. Some of the teenagers are getting together to do a park cleanup. Would Tony and Lara be interested in joining them?"

"She's visiting relatives in Richmond. She and her two first cousins are quite close. Last summer they came here and this year was her turn."

"How nice. What about Tony?"

"He's — uh — he's not here either . . . he's traveling through the Midwest."

"My, that does leave you all alone, doesn't it?"

"I have lots to do, believe me." She hoped she didn't sound defensive or, worse, snooty.

Tricia didn't seem to notice and instead crinkled her forehead. "You know, speaking of Tony traveling, it must be the new thing for teenage boys. My Josh has been begging us all summer to let him go with some friends to New England. George and I have been very reluctant, but as the time grows close, I'm afraid he's wearing us down. I'd

79

like to talk to you a bit more about it. Perhaps you could tell me some of Tony's experiences and if he's had any problems."

Claire felt as if she were on the verge of a panic attack. She didn't believe that Tricia was digging or being coy, but Claire was getting a headache trying to answer questions she didn't want to answer. "I really don't know a lot. You know boys. They never say anything that might worry you."

"Do you worry?" At Claire's odd expression, she added, "I didn't mean obsess — some mothers do that over every little thing. But surely you must be concerned. Lake Moses is a small, close community and probably more than a little insulated from the bad stuff in the world."

Not as insulated as you think. "He's my son, and, of course, I'm always concerned about his well-being."

"What is he doing for money if you don't mind my asking. Is he picking up jobs along the way or are you and Jeff financing him?"

Claire didn't know what to say. She already was hip deep in a lie, but there was no way that she was about to blurt out that Tony had stolen money from them, walked out after graduation, and she and Jeff hadn't seen him since.

She shuddered even now just recalling Jeff's reaction and implicit instructions that if Tony was so determined to be on his own, then he was welcome to it. The whole problem was complicated and stressful, but there was no way that the perfect Claire Fitzgerald was going to admit to the one woman in town with impeccable credentials when it came to child-raising that she was an utter and total failure.

Finally she managed a vague answer of "I guess you could say it was a little of both."

"Well, I'm sure he's having an adventure and learning a lot about how people live in other parts of the country."

"Adventures and boys do go hand and hand." She cringed at her vagueness. She was getting pretty good at labeling Tony's continued absence as "his adventure" and had used it often when asked.

That Tony was doing drugs, probably having unprotected sex, and didn't care that his family knew about both so disturbed Claire that she simply couldn't talk about it. Instead, she'd created this myth of a young vagabond traveler off to see his country and learn from all its diversity.

Finally Tricia said, "Perhaps I am being too worrisome."

"I think you should trust your instincts, Tricia. You know your son and you know his friends." She paused, hearing her own words and realizing what message she was giving Tricia. One that Tony was trustworthy and was on this "adventure" with her and Jeff's blessing. "I'll be honest, Jeff and I weren't happy about Tony roaming around without any particular reason or a place to go. But he is eighteen and we couldn't stop him. I do worry and every day I pray he stays safe."

It wasn't the whole truth, but it was certainly a partial.

"Oh, Claire, I had no idea. How unsettling it must be to not know and wondering. . . ." And with that Tricia gave her a warm hug. "Sometimes letting go is the hardest part."

Claire nodded, feeling the heavy emotion grip her chest. Tricia could have been talking about Claire as well as Tony.

"Have a good time with your friends," Tricia said warmly. "And if you need a friend here in Lake Moses, I would be honored."

"How very kind of you," Claire said, realizing that opening herself up just a bit had the unexpected benefit of finding a potential friend.

Later when Olivia called, Claire realized just how much she needed to see her best friends. She had lots to tell them, but even more she was eager to be with them.

And even later, when Dennis brought over an Italian wine he'd brought from a recent trip to Florence, Claire allowed him to kiss her and made no attempt to stop him.

It wasn't betraying Jeff that loomed in her thoughts, it was only that she wanted Dennis to be Jeff and to care enough to be with her, to talk to her, to bring a bottle of wine.

It was her husband she wanted, but it was the neighbor who was making her feel wanted and cherished.

Chapter Five

"What a mess."

"But most is fixable. A little time and some intensive labor," Olivia said, determined not to act swamped even though she felt it.

Daniel had been through the downstairs, disgusted by the damage and clearly annoyed by all the work that had been created. Now he stared at her as if she was crazy. "You're sounding like you're going to tackle this yourself."

"Why not? I can do most of it. What I can't, I'll hire out. Besides, many of the rooms needed to be updated, so this is an opportunity to do it."

"Olivia, this isn't just buying a few gallons of cleaning stuff and painting some walls," he said, squatting down to examine a spattering of dark stains of unknown origin on the living-room carpet. Then he walked over and ran his hand over the rips in her mother's torn New York wallpaper. "This is a major overhaul."

"I'll manage."

"Manage with what? You need ladders and rug-cleaning equipment and a steamer to get the paper off, never mind buckets and brushes and a good variety of repair tools."

"Claire and Lexie will be here in a few days."

"And they're bringing all the things I mentioned with them? Whew, now I'm relieved."

She glared at him. "Did I ask you to come here? Did I ask your opinion? Did I ask you anything?"

"No, but I wish you would," he said, obviously frustrated. "Why couldn't you be just a little like most women — tears, hysteria, and desperation?"

"Ah, and is that the way most of the women you know react?"

"It was a joke. Lighten up."

But she barely heard him. "I take it that those hand-wringing women then give you the opportunity to be a hero and run to the rescue?"

Even as the words tumbled forth, she knew she wasn't describing Daniel. Suddenly she was feeling undone and out of control. The house, the damage, coming home, a flock of good-intentioned neighbors, Trent who barely remembered her, and Daniel, who knew her too well just appearing as if he'd been to the drugstore for toothpaste.

Yet with all but Daniel she'd been patient, kind, and soft-spoken. She sighed. Maybe she just needed to send him on his way. She didn't want to alienate him, and yet . . .

He held up his hands in a I'm-backing-off gesture. "My point is that I'd like to help you. So how do I do that? Ask permission or wait until you ask me? The latter probably will occur when condos are common on Mars. Since I've been lacking in heroic deeds or skills during my rather uneventful life, when I saw this mess, I had a momentary relapse into those days when doing something for someone else wasn't an insult."

She didn't know what to say; she felt small and snippy and most of all ungrateful. He was a good man who'd gone out of his way to come and offer assistance, and she acted as if his arrival was an act of war.

"Okay," he said with a sigh, when her silence continued, "I get the message." He started to walk away when she touched his arm. It was the first time she had since he'd arrived.

"I owe you an apology," she said, thoroughly annoyed by her own behavior. "And I am sorry. You drove down here to be supportive and offer to help, and I'm not acting very grateful."

But instead of taking her hand or using the advantage of her gesture to draw her close, he stepped away. "Perhaps there's some residual tension because of earlier?"

"I guess," she said, thinking that was too

easy an excuse for her being so bitchy.

He jammed his hands into his pockets and leaned against the staircase, looking at her but without guile or amusement. When they were together she used to call it "the look," to which he always seemed puzzled, claiming to have no idea what she meant.

It wasn't an empty stare, but more one of inner knowledge. Like he knew the answer before she thought of the question. It was a side of Daniel that had always intrigued her.

"Your sudden arrival just threw me. I wasn't expecting you."

"And you don't like surprises."

She realized how very transparent she was, realizing, too, how well he knew her.

"I tried to call a number of times," he added, as if reading her mind.

"It's just that you, well —"

"What?"

"Well, sometimes you sound a lot like the proverbial bossy boyfriend."

"Ahh, and I'm not your boyfriend any-more."

"No, you're not."

"Noted," he said, straightening. "I'll make sure I don't forget." But she saw his mouth twitch as though he were working to prevent a smile. "Look at it this way. By my coming you actually saved me."

"Huh?"

"Karen and her flyers." He told her about

the meeting in Wal-Mart and Karen's flyer fervor. "I have a feeling she'd've been ringing my doorbell, and then I couldn't have avoided her."

"Maybe she has the hots for you." Yet, even though she'd said it with an airy lightness, something disturbing ruffled up within her along with a fleeting visual of the nubile Karen climbing all over a willing Daniel.

"Yeah, there's that," he said, as if considering the possibility was worth some thought. "Now that I'm available."

Not about to show that his comment pricked, she added, "Just don't come crying back to me when she makes you crazy."

"Back to you? Now, that sounds promising."

"Well, one never knows, does one," she said, deciding that obviously he'd gotten over their breakup and was simply teasing her to get a reaction. "Come on, let's take a look upstairs."

Olivia led the way as they climbed the staircase to the second floor. She hadn't yet done a close inspection of the upstairs beyond a glance before the Marlowes arrived. She didn't need to see and deal with the destruction any sooner than necessary.

Because of the broken glass from the mirror, Olivia had hoped the Marlowes wouldn't want to see the second floor; she'd been right. The downstairs was horrific enough.

And now as she approached the shattered glass, she knew what had been the source of her reluctance. She'd not wanted to see the destruction of her father's beloved mirror.

The old glass with its two-inch bevel had resided in a heavily detailed gold frame. Her father had found the mirror in an abandoned barn about to be torn down. He'd been there to salvage the discarded barn lumber that eventually became the floor for Olivia's playhouse. He'd found the mirror in one of the cow stalls. The wrecking crew knew nothing about it, and her father, assuming it had been stored and forgotten, hauled it out, put it in his truck along with the barn wood, and brought it home.

The mirror had hung in the upstairs hall as long as Olivia could remember. When she'd decided to rent the house, she'd considered taking it to her new home in Massachusetts. In fact, she'd even had it off the wall and ready to be carried out by the movers. But the empty space where it had resided for so many years looked so barren, she'd had the movers rehang it.

The empty frame remained hung now, albeit crooked and damaged, the reflective guts jagged and broken at her feet.

"Destructive jerks," Daniel muttered in disgust. His hands were low on his hips as he looked at all the broken glass. "You said earlier the cops arrested some kids — sure hope the judge doesn't give them a walk."

Olivia turned away, tears threatening. How strange and unsettling that the tears would come now with Daniel here. Flo's comfort would have been a dry hankie and glass of cold lemonade. Daniel would be kind and careful and too easy to lean on.

Truthfully, she'd had no intention of crying; she'd actually been considering selling and ridding herself of the responsibility of the house. Yet here, now, among the splintered chards, Olivia felt as if that once clear option had been broken as soundly as the mirror.

She felt his hands close over her shoulders. "This could have been avoided" — she took a small gulp — "if I'd taken the mirror with me."

"No self-blame, sweetheart. You couldn't have known."

"But I should have. What idiot rents a house with an irreplaceable mirror full of old memories? What was I thinking?"

"Probably that getting away and starting your life had more value than glass and nostalgia."

"I can remember my father telling the story of how he found the mirror every time a visitor commented on it. It was one of his special treasures."

"Olivia . . ."

"Look how I treated it!" She pushed away

from him, sweeping her hands wide. "I might as well have put it on the curb and walked away."

"But you didn't do that. It's a thing, sweetheart. Valuable, sure, but just a thing."

She backed away, suddenly chilled. "How dare you say that. It's more than just a thing."

Their eyes held for a count of more than ten seconds.

"Whatever you say," he murmured, not about to get into another go-around disagreement.

When she didn't move, he did, drawing away as though his eyes might see things she didn't want to hear about. "Tell you what. I'll get the busted stuff out of here. Take it to the dump. You need to get rid of this glass before you or someone else gets cut." He picked his way through the glass and walked down the hall.

Olivia didn't move, still bristling at his easy dismissal of what she saw now as a lost family heirloom.

Finally he said, "Are you staying here tonight?"

The question was simple, guileless, and might have been asked by a passing bystander. "Of course I am."

He stood now in the doorway to the master bedroom, which was untouched — the vandals had either ignored it or gotten spooked before they could think up any mischief. The original bed for the room, her parents' four-poster, was in another bedroom. A king-sized frame with a fairly new mattress and box spring was angled from the alcove.

"At least you have a bed."

"Yes." She walked to the window to open it wider. Despite the ceiling fan above her, the room was close and she was hot and sticky.

"Don't look so nervous."

She turned. "About what?"

"That because there's a bed between us that I'm going to fling you down, kiss you, and see where that goes, and thereby blow away our nonrelationship."

His eyes met hers directly, and she forced herself not to look away. "You wouldn't do that unless I wanted you to."

"And here I expected stony silence or a brusque dismissal. Most interesting."

She walked back around the bed and out of the room without him trying to stop her, flinging behind her as she went, "I'm going to be far too busy for lovemaking."

There, she'd said it. He wasn't the only one who could toss out a line and see what got reeled in.

She expected a snappy retort, but he merely chuckled. Truthfully, she was grateful that he didn't push her or zing her with some clever comeback, but what she was most pleased about was that he hadn't tried to kiss her. For then she feared she would have been lost.

How easy it would be to lean on Daniel, and she was tempted, oh, was she ever tempted. But mostly she was annoyed with herself for having such a needy reaction. It was just that she knew Daniel and cared about him and just plain trusted him. And it would be so easy just to let him hold her and . . . allow herself to give in to the obvious — tears, hysteria, and desperation.

While she had limited use for women who used such machinations to get what they wanted, the truth was she felt like doing all three. Maybe she needed a hero after all.

"Will you and the girls be too efficient and organized to accept some extra help?"

He'd always referred to Claire and Lexie as "the girls." Lexie always bristled and Claire said it made her feel fifteen. Olivia dismissed it, knowing he only did it to tease them. "Let me guess. You're the extra help?"

"I can't be here all the time, but I can drive down long enough to make sure you three haven't partied yourselves into jail."

"Very funny."

"I was thinking I could help with some of the heavy work. Bring my ladder, do the rugs."

"You'd do all that? I would think you'd be looking for the quickest way out."

"After a few days of being bossed by you three, maybe I will." He glanced at his watch. "But right now I have to split. Caitlyn is expecting me and I promised her I'd be there tonight."

"Tell her hello for me."

"I will."

He started to leave the room, passing her without touching her. She waited until he was at the staircase before she said, "Thanks for coming."

"Thanks for not telling me to get lost."

"I wouldn't say that to you."

"Ah, then maybe there's hope."

"No, not hope. Just a lot of work."

"Maybe there's not a lot of difference." He winked at her. "I'll get some boxes and get rid of the glass."

"Thanks," she called, adding, "I'll be seeing you."

Over the next few days Olivia organized, assessed the damage and what repairs she could reasonably do herself and what would have to be hired out.

Wes Gunther came, with his dog Roger, and offered to make some dump runs. She thanked him, saying Daniel had taken it all, but she'd be in touch if she needed him later. She called Rosa's son, Jimmie the carpenter, and had him lined up to come so they could discuss what needed to be done.

One door needed some repair where it had been kicked from its hinges. There was a fist-sized hole in the kitchen wall, and some wooden shelves in her father's study would have to be repaired. The shelves hadn't been vandalized, but Olivia recalled her father always talking about having the shelves fixed. Funny how she'd not given those shelves more than a cursory thought when she'd lived here. Now they'd made it to her priority list.

Sheets and bedding were added to the list that she purchased on Monday at Priscilla's Linens, a specialty shop that smelled of lavender and verbena and had the most sumptuous fabrics. She paid a horrendous sum, but she loved nice bed linens, and just because this was a temporary stay didn't mean she had to have scratchy sheets and cheap foam pillows.

She bought for the four-poster rather than the king-on-a-frame, which for reasons that made no sense struck her as insulting to fine linens to put such elegance on a mattress that resided on such plain generic support. The four-poster had family history and patina scratches, plus it was high and cozy. Her parents had gone to the king and frame for ease of getting in and out of bed. The four-poster had been on its way to the attic when Olivia intercepted it for her room, where it remained, thankfully untouched by the vandals.

But an unexpected occurrence happened just a couple of hours after Daniel had left on Saturday evening.

She'd been wandering through the house, making a list of supplies for cleaning and repairs. She borrowed bedding and some towels from Flo until she could get to Priscilla's on Monday. Since she needed some personal necessities, she decided to drive to Bishop Drugs.

Business was light, due no doubt to it being Saturday night. She wandered the aisles, adding things to her basket, thinking how much more interesting a local drugstore complete with a fountain was than the chain where she'd shopped back in Parkboro.

She bought the necessities, plus a jar of peanuts she didn't need, a bag of caramels she shouldn't eat, a new romance release she wouldn't have time to read, and a flea market guide that featured a nearby flea that had expanded and added about fifty more dealers since the last time she'd been there. If Lexie and Claire came, she decided, they could make a day of it. If they didn't, well, she'd drive over by herself.

As she rounded the corner and spotted the popular fountain with its spinning stools and black marble counter, she couldn't resist. She sat down on a stool at the fountain, setting her basket and handbag on the floor beside her. The menu, up on the same blackboard that had been there when she lived in Bishop, listed all the old favorites she remembered and loved. Including chourico and pepper sandwiches; the spicy Portuguese sausage was considered a basic necessity to a Rhode Islander's diet.

The teenage girl who waited on her had the name Jessica pinned on her shirt. She looked vaguely familiar, but Olivia decided it was because she resembled most teenage girls — lovely skin, latest hairstyle, and a wispy-slim figure. She smiled, her eyes darting from Olivia to behind where she was seated.

"Do you know what you want?" she asked.

"Yes, a chourico sandwich with peppers and a cherry Coke."

"Fries?"

Why not. "Sure. With vinegar, please?"

The girl wrote it all down, hung it up on the order belt and sent it down to the cook. Then she laid down a place mat depicting a map of Bishop, added silverware and a bottle of vinegar. Her gaze darted once again over Olivia's shoulder, while she made the cherry Coke and then set it down with a straw.

Had to be a boyfriend, Olivia thought, but when she turned around, Trent McGraw, in boots, jeans, and a yellow jersey shirt, stood at the magazine rack.

"Hello again," Olivia said. "You checking up on shoplifters? Or are girls going for older men these days?"

For a split second he looked bewildered, a kind of "who are you" look, and Olivia wished she'd just smiled and sipped her Coke. "Olivia Halsey, remember? My house on Steeple Street was vandalized?"

"Olivia, yes. Guess my mind was elsewhere."

An awkward pause followed, and when Jessica once again glanced over at him he seemed to take no notice of her and said, "Mind if I join you?"

What could she say? "No, be my guest."

More silence.

He laid a small bag on the counter, glanced around the fountain area, and then asked, "You planning on staying in town until the house is fixed up?"

"Probably. I'm a teacher, so I have a few weeks before school starts."

"Well, if you need help, give a holler. I do part-time handyman stuff. Extra income, you know, when I'm not on duty. Lots of unexpected bills lately."

She digested this, wanting to ask, but of course she didn't. Flo had said his wife walked out on him, so perhaps divorce bills were what he meant. "What kind of work do you do?"

"Paint, a little carpentry, some electrical — you know, basic stuff. I do runs to the dump and regularly mow a few lawns every week. It's amazing how many people want little

98

things done, and when they call one of the pros they get a shock at the estimate. That's when they start looking around, and well, I get called. Been doing this for a couple of years, and word of mouth has spread. If you need some references, I can give you some names."

Olivia was thinking of a retired army sergeant in Parkboro who she often called for minor repairs. He was honest, fast, and reasonably priced. "I'll keep you in mind."

"Sure would appreciate it."

Jessica came and put down the sandwich and fries. Then just as Olivia's tummy growled in appreciation, Jessica, in a low voice, said to Trent, "Did my mother send you over to spy on me, cuz if she did —"

"She's worried about you. I told her I'd make sure you weren't being bothered."

"By who? All those imaginary men she thinks want to pick me up? How am I ever going to have a steady boyfriend if she's got the cops following me around? I have my rights, you know."

Trent held up his hands. "You do, indeed. And just for the record, I wasn't following you."

"Then what are you doing here?" she snapped, her voice as accusing as her words. No question she looked angry, trapped, and scared.

He opened the bag and held up a bottle of

aspirin and a sports magazine. "Do these pass the quiz?"

Jessica huffed her disbelief at what she clearly considered a ploy, swung around, and went to wait on another customer. Olivia, who knew a little about the frustration of feeling surrounded, put down her sandwich. She'd barely had more than a first bite. Trent, who didn't seem the least bothered by Jessica, simply raised his eyebrows when she scowled.

"What?"

"That was smooth."

Now he merely looked perplexed.

"Your excuse to come in here."

"What excuse? I have a headache and I like sports magazines."

"And it had nothing to do with Jessica?"

"Nope."

She wasn't sure she believed him. Jessica could have ordinary teenage "no one understands me" angst or Trent could be splitting hairs. He didn't come to check on her, but as long as he was buying something . . .

"So then why are you still here?" She was amazed at her own annoyance over something that she knew nothing about. When he didn't have a quick response, she countered with her own. "And please don't say it was because you saw me. You didn't even remember me."

"Uh-oh. Do I detect some exasperation?"

"Actually, yes, given that we just spoke a few hours ago at Flo's."

"You're absolutely right, and I apologize," he said, looking suitably contrite. "It's been a hellish day, and I was trying to wind down and unfocus."

"It's not just about me. Jessica looked at you a number of times. You had to notice that if I did. You're a cop. Aren't you supposed to be observant? I don't like being used to draw her out."

"Use you? If I'm not mistaken, you were the one who spoke to me."

He had her there, but nevertheless, she still felt used, which meant she flat-out didn't believe that he didn't recognize her.

She sighed at the tangle she'd created simply by some silly old, and quickly growing vaguer, interest in a guy who never knew she existed. And what was she doing getting into a conversation that had nothing to do with her? Or acting huffy because she didn't leap to the forefront of his memory?

She didn't know Jessica — perhaps her mother had reason to be worried. For that matter, she didn't even know Trent. And it was abundantly clear that she'd made zippo impression on him if she had to keep reminding him who she was. Was this self-immolation or what?

Suddenly the sandwich and fries had lost their appeal. She picked up her bag to pull money out for the check when he touched her arm. "Come on, don't go. Better yet, why don't you let me buy you a drink. Ricky's is just down the street."

She knew Ricky's, oh, she knew it well. She and Claire and Lexie had gone there for their first legal drink and more than a few afterward.

"I think not." She put money on the counter, plus a generous tip, and gathered her things.

"Come on, Olivia. One drink plus I'd like to find out why you seem to know me so much better than I know you."

It's quite simple. I had a major thing for you once upon a time, and you didn't know I was alive. "I'm really not in town to do social things."

Then, as if she'd accepted, he took her arm, leading her away from the fountain, "What are you doing?"

"Ah, come on. Lighten up. It's Saturday night, it's early, and going back to that big house to be all alone — how fun is that?" Then somehow his arm got around her shoulders long enough to draw her close and murmur, "Please?"

He was a charmer. The grin, the eyes that seemed to look at her as if she were the only woman in his world. The light touch that was confident yet not pushy. She could feel herself weakening. And while she was wavering, they'd walked nearly to the exit door when she realized she hadn't paid for her purchases.

"Good idea," he said, steering her to the counter. "I'll wait here."

She paid for the items and started to exit when he fell into step beside her. "You're persistent, aren't you?"

"I prefer the word *patient*. One drink . . . I promise." He held up his hand as if swearing an oath. A gesture, she concluded, that had no doubt disarmed many a woman in the past.

Was there really any harm in one drink in a public place? "All right. One drink."

A few minutes later they walked into Ricky's. This was one place that had changed. Updated to an art deco style, plus the clientele seemed a bit more sophisticated than the blowsy, loud crowd that she re-called. Trent led her to a table.

"What's it gonna be?" he asked once she was seated and trying to adjust her eyes to the dimness.

"Merlot is fine."

He returned a few moments later with her wine and a bottle of beer for himself. He raised his bottle to toast, and she raised her glass. "To refreshing my memory about you," he said with a grin.

"Might be pretty boring."

"I'll take my chances." He winked and

lifted the bottle to his mouth. She sipped her wine, thinking this had to be the most unexpected moment in a day filled with them. Breaking off with Daniel, the vandalism, the trip here, seeing Trent, and now having a drink with him. All in the space of less than twelve hours. Truly remarkable.

"So how come I haven't remembered you?" It wasn't a question as much as a verbal musing and a hope she might provide the answer. He leaned forward as if to look at her more closely. "I must have been blind as well as dumb, but then my mother always told me I let all the nice girls get away."

Nice. A suitable synonym for *boring.* Which undoubtedly she had been to guys like Trent. Ergo no memory of her. "We weren't in the same crowd."

"That's no surprise. You're a classy type from the careful part of town. I hung out in those dark places with centerfolds on the walls."

"I know where you hung out."

This seemed to amaze and horrify him at the same time. "Uh, oh, did I hit on you and forget?"

She laughed. "No, but if you had —" Just in time she stopped herself. What was she doing? Teetering on the verge of telling him she once had a raging crush? That if he'd hit on her back then, she would have led the way to the nearest bed?

"Don't stop now," he urged. "If I had you'd've what?"

"Probably been terrified and fascinated at the same time." Then before he could get any mileage out of that, she added, "I was sixteen, about Jessica's age, and a little bit awed by the Brace Road boys." More like endlessly curious and loving a kind of flirt with the forbidden.

He leaned back, studying her, and instead of picking apart her confession, he let it lay and asked, "So who did you hang with?"

She reeled off some names, ending with Claire and Lexie.

"Now, those two, I do remember."

"Oh?" Now she felt really left out.

"Everyone knew Lexie, or knew who she was," he said carefully, as though not wanting to say anything disparaging. Lexie would find that amusing, given that one of her favorite self-descriptions was that she "liked to slut around," although her talk was more outrageous than her actions. Lexie had been popular, plus had a sexy figure that she showed off without apology — then there was her trait of always being the one who broke off with a boyfriend. That intrigued guys. They all wanted to think they would be the one she wouldn't ditch. And because Lexie had always been so forthcoming about who she dated, Olivia was pretty sure Trent hadn't been among them.

105

Anyway, Lexie knew of Olivia's crush and for friendship loyalty alone she would have kept her distance.

"Lexie was indeed popular. And Claire? You remember her, too?"

"Claire was no Lexie."

"Much more reserved and proper?"

"More like perfect. Guys were sure she wasn't real." Then, as if old knowledge was returning, he added, "She was different."

Olivia began to relax.

Then he said, "We hooked up for a while when she broke off with that guy from Boston U. she'd been dating."

The Merlot that Olivia just sipped turned sour in her mouth. "You and Claire dated?" The idea of Claire and Trent was so out-there, Olivia barely held her gasp.

"She never told you?" That either surprised or amazed him, she wasn't sure which.

"Oh, she probably did, must have slipped my mind," she said quickly, hoping she sounded dismissive.

"Yeah, well, as I said, it was just a short while — maybe a month. She ended up getting back with the guy —"

"She married him," Olivia said flatly. She did indeed recall the short period that Claire and Jeff broke up. Olivia and Lexie had been supportive pals, listening and sympathizing while Claire sobbed about Jeff ignoring her and taking her for granted. Lexie had told her she was too high maintenance a girlfriend for a guy like Jeff, who viewed getting his career started as a first focus. If she wanted to keep him, she needed to get a grip. Olivia agreed, but because she always ended up a little uncomfortable with the "too truthful" opinions of Lexie, she'd said little. Now, listening to Trent, she had a whole barrel full of questions that needed answers — starting with why Claire had never once mentioned or even hinted that there'd been a relationship with Trent.

Which meant sex. Trent McGraw wouldn't have "hooked" with some girl who just wanted to be friends.

Suddenly she wanted to leave, and she wondered what had possessed her to resurrect this part of her past. Maybe she'd hoped that some trigger in Trent's memory would recall her, but instead she'd learned stuff she really didn't want to know.

"Hey, you okay? You got pretty quiet. Wine all right? I can get you a fresh glass."

She looked at her watch, simply to give her a moment to add a smile and frame an excuse.

"Actually, I remembered I'm expecting a phone call." She rose to her feet. "Thanks for the wine, Trent. See you around, I'm sure." And before he could stop her, she waded through the clustered tables and out to the street.

By the time she got home, she'd decided that she didn't need to lighten up and she didn't need to get involved in the people and places of Bishop. That was one of the reasons she'd left, wasn't it?

Chapter Six

They arrived on Wednesday while Olivia was trying to get it across to Jimmie, who turned out to be a know-it-all, dismal excuse of a carpenter, that the shelves in her father's study only needed to be repaired, not replaced.

"I want wood, Jimmie, not particle board."

"Repairin' them be costly," he said darkly, causing Olivia to envision some astronomical figure. "Why throw good money at old beat-up shelves." It seemed to be a pronouncement, not a question. "Particle is cheaper and the stuff they make today, you can't tell the difference."

"I *know* the difference, but that isn't really the reason. The shelves have family history and I want to preserve it." She glanced around the cozy study; its history of the time that her father had spent here was important to her — a necessity to hold on to.

"Seems to me you should've thought of that when you was leavin' the place empty. But that ain't my business."

"You're right." He wasn't saying anything she hadn't already thought of.

"I am?"

"Yes, but that was then and this is now. The original shelves stay, and I'd like some wood corbels for under support."

"Corbels?"

"Yes, you know nicely turned, curved? About three inches wide. Not just L-shaped. The ones along the roofline will give you an idea."

"She wants corbels," he muttered, clearly taken aback at what he'd gotten himself into.

She should have anticipated his viewpoint when he asked why she hadn't replaced high-maintenance outside painted clapboards with no-maintenance vinyl. Jimmie was not only disinterested in the integrity of keeping the past, but definitely a guy who thought that being hired meant an expectation to follow his advice, no matter how ill-conceived it was.

What she needed, she realized, was a craftsman, not a garden-variety carpenter. She recalled Trent mentioning checking references, and it occurred to her that they not only vouched for honesty and workmanship, but the *kind* of workmanship.

"This is what I want." She handed him a piece of paper from her pocket where she'd sketched the style she wanted as well as some general measurements.

Jimmie took it, looked at it, and then scratched his head. "You want I should make wood braces? What's wrong with metal?"

Somehow wood braces didn't sound like corbels to Olivia. And she seriously doubted the finished product would resemble them. "No metal."

"You know how to make corbels?" Lexie James asked, causing Jimmie to swing around to face the doorway as if he'd been spooked.

There stood Lexie in high-top work-style boots, a denim playsuit, her blond hair a tangled mop twisted onto her head that on anyone else would look like an allergy to a mirror. On Lexie it was stylish, sexy, and deliberate.

Beside her was Claire — in a pretty lemon-and-lime sundress with a sweater casually over her arm. Shimmery rose pink toenails peeked out of white strappy sandals. Her darker hair was soft and brushed and, well, like all of Claire, perfect.

Olivia grinned, thrilled to see them. "When did you two get here? I didn't hear you!" she exclaimed, hugging both of them.

"Just in time it would seem," Lexie said sternly, while Claire winked at Olivia. Then indicating Claire, she added, "The domestic-bliss queen, here, started a list before we got through the kitchen."

Olivia giggled. Claire and her lists were legend.

Lexie walked closer to the shelves in question, looking at them as if shelf brackets were her specialty. "Nope, Jimmie, metal braces just won't do."

He tried to look miffed that his suggestion was being challenged, but there was no question that the sudden appearance of the curvy blond had brought on a slack-jawed stare. Then, self-consciously, he straightened, closed his mouth, and wound it up into a miff again. "I can make corbels," he asserted.

Lexie patted his cheek. "I knew you could."

Jimmie preened.

Olivia grinned. "Think of it as a job opportunity to show off your skills."

"Huh?"

Claire said, "She means that Ms. Halsey wants wood."

"Wood corbels," Lexie added, lowering her voice so that it sounded more like a sexual caress than carpentry instructions. Jimmie practically dissolved into a puddle.

"Wooden corbels, yes, ma'am." He pulled out his measuring tape and approached the shelves.

"Geez, Lex," Olivia whispered as they left the study. "If you'd kissed him, I'd've had him making them for free."

"If I'd kissed him, he'd be unable to work for a week."

Claire and Olivia nodded and said in sync, "How true, how true."

Olivia put an arm around each as they walked through the dining room, around the corner, and into the kitchen. "Am I ever glad to see you guys."

"I told you we'd come to help," Claire said warmly. "Lexie got an early-morning flight and mine was in about the same time, so we met at Green, rented a car, and here we are."

"Good thing, sweetie, or you'd have metal brackets, and God knows what else — probably metal bookcases in the living room." Lexie poked in the refrigerator, pulling out a can of orange soda. "This all you've got? No beer?"

"I didn't know for sure if you were coming."

"Any decent fridge has beer," she muttered.

"Tomorrow, we'll buy beer."

"Lexie almost didn't come," Claire offered.

"Didn't come?" Olivia studied her. She did appear more restless than usual. "Why?"

"Thanks a lot, friend." Lexie glowered at Claire, then fiddled with the soda can. "Things have been busy."

Olivia said, "You're always too busy."

"Yeah, I know. Claire harassed me for two days about it. See what happens when she's left alone? She makes phone calls."

"She's not telling you what she planned," Claire said, unfazed by the accusation.

"Uh-oh."

"She was going to blow off our weekend, too."

"Lexie, you weren't."

"Like I said, I've been real busy." She swilled down soda. "It's all been a royal pain, and since I've had so much on my mind — never mind. Who wants to talk about all that crappy stuff anyway? Not me."

Olivia and Claire exchanged looks. Lexie working long hours was hardly a news bulletin, but that had never stopped her from attending their previous get-togethers. Their weekends were sacrosanct unless there was a dire emergency. And while Olivia had planned to postpone their weekend because of the house, a total canceling? No way.

The comradely silence put Lexie on the defensive. "Stop peering at each other as if I'm involved in some plot to shake up the WCG news department."

"I think you did that already."

She grinned. "Yeah, we did, didn't we?"

"Last year. We want to know about now."

Olivia crossed her arms and tipped her head to the side, waiting. Claire sighed heavily, waiting, too.

"What?"

"That's what we're asking you. What have you been so busy doing?"

"Jeez, I've been here ten seconds and already you're on me."

"Lex, just tell us?"

"We're the easiest to tell, remember?"

"You're both nags."

"Friendship rule number fourteen. Real friends nag."

Lexie muttered a couple of colorful words, then reluctantly said, "Okay, okay. Only because you two will poke and prod until you make me crazy. And if I tell you, I don't want any should've, would've, could've lectures about this."

"Us lecture?" Claire's eyes widened and Olivia managed to match the look. "What's the chance of that?" The giggles were barely concealed.

Lexie put the soda can down, crossed her arms, and scowled. "I don't like making myself look like a total jerk."

"Lexie, we love you," Olivia said, wanting to reassure her.

"Even at your most stubborn and at your jerkiest," Claire added.

Lexie nodded, fiddling with turning the can this way and that. "I picked up a guy in a bar, got drunk, had sex with him when I would have had more fun if I'd done a strip on Lake Shore Drive. I threw him out the next morning after he broke my Bishop mug, and now he's telling people I'm a whack job."

Both Olivia and Claire looked at her in confusion.

Finally Claire said, "For this you were

going to cancel us? Why? Surely you didn't think we'd be shocked."

She shrugged. "It was just stupid and I don't like myself when I do stupid things. And, having some clueless jerk call me a whack job because I was upset about the mug . . . it just pissed me off."

"Okay, we know you getting pissed can be dangerous. What did you do?"

"Tried to forget it happened."

Then Olivia knew. "Word got back to Eric, right?"

Lexie paled. "I don't want to talk about him."

Claire filled in. "You two had a fight and you told him to go to hell, he walked out, and now you won't talk to him." Claire sighed. "Lex, you should have just explained and apologized."

"Eric's a loser," she muttered, "and that's all I'm saying." Her chin lifted, her eyes hardened, and Olivia knew that was the end of the discussion, at least for now.

She walked over to Lexie and squeezed her hand. "I'd've been pissed about the mug, too. We'll just have to go on a hunt for another one."

"Absolutely," Claire said.

Lexie looked only marginally mollified.

Then Olivia said, "Come on and take a look around. You can give me your opinions, which I desperately need. The cleanup is mostly done, but the fix-up is going to be long."

They did a quick tour of the house, with Claire taking the king-sized bed and Lexie choosing the room with a daybed. Both were aghast at the vandalism, and both had some ideas on doing the repairs.

"Daniel doesn't think we can do it alone," Olivia said. "He volunteered to come and help."

"I hope you said yes."

"I —"

"Livie, you didn't say no."

"We broke up and I think he'll get the wrong idea if I let him get involved."

"You mean, like you might *need* help?" Lexie asked dryly.

"I don't want to talk about him," Olivia said, wishing she'd kept her mouth shut.

"But you will," Claire said. "Just like Lexie will talk about Eric." She linked arms with Lexie and Olivia. "We've got days and nights and we'll all get caught up."

Then it was back to the kitchen, where Claire opened the refrigerator and took out a bag she'd put there on her way in. Lexie presented a bottle of wine. "To go with the sandwiches."

"Wine for lunch. Uh-oh, so much for getting much done today."

"You look like you could use a day off," Claire noted.

"I'm with Claire, Livie. You look beat. But no more. We're all pitching in and this place will be rental-ready in no time."

She looked at each fondly, saying for the umpteenth time, "I'm so glad you guys are here."

"Yeah, we are, too," Lexie said.

Claire opened the bag and pulled out thick sandwich wedges that had been cut from a long loaf of fresh crusty bread and piled with a buffet of fillings. In addition there was a bag of chips and a jar of pickles and three pieces of the inevitable cherry cheesecake.

"That makes it all official," Olivia said, eyeing the dessert.

"Hey, what would life in Bishop be without Sorenson's cheesecake?" Claire said. "I stopped to just get that and then realized I didn't know what you had. So we splurged at the deli. And then while I was waiting for Lexie, who was getting the wine, I overheard someone say that there's been a spate of vandalism and that your house wasn't the worst."

"Oughta lock the five little monsters up," Lexie said, producing a cork remover from a bag that was large enough to hold a midsized stereo system.

"How'd you know there were five? I hadn't heard an exact number."

"Livie, you got to keep up. Walt —" At their questioning looks, she said, "Walt at Walt's Liquors."

"Didn't he die?" Claire asked.

"This is the son."

"Figures. If there's sons, Lexie will find them."

Lexie huffed. "He's married with twins and he drives one of those freaky vans." She shuddered and Claire and Olivia laughed. Lexie hated vans. "You wanna hear this or not?"

"Go."

"Walt said the kids were all released to their parents, and a couple of the fathers were getting their boys lawyered up. One father was already beating his breast about being divorced and not having custody and his kid going through a tough time, rebellion, not his son's fault and blah, blah, blah. Gist of it was that no one confessed and that you shouldn't hope for a resolution or restitution any time soon."

"Sounds like I should have talked to Walt instead of the police," Olivia groused. "Trent sure didn't give me those details." She took some paper plates and cups from a cupboard, and led the way out to a small porch that faced the south yard. Olivia had dragged her mother's old wooden lawn furniture from out of the playhouse the day before. She'd scrubbed them down after brushing away the spiderwebs and a few years' worth of dust. The cushions that thankfully had been covered in old bedsheets were faded but still fat and cushy.

Claire pulled one of the chairs around so it was away from the direct sun. "Trent, hmmm. Now, there's a name from the past. Trent McGraw, right? I had read in one of the class newsletters that he was a police officer," Claire said fondly, reminding Olivia of what Trent had said about "hooking" up.

Lexie wasn't so generous. "Trent 'kill all the cops' McGraw?" Lexie hooted with laughter. "He did more running and hiding from the cops than anyone on Brace Road. Geez, hadn't thought about him in years. Didn't he marry that prissy Tanya Fatter something or other?"

"Fatterstone."

"All I remember is the Fatter. No wonder she got married. Yikes, what a name."

"They're divorced." When both glanced over at her, Claire said, "Unlike you two, I read the monthly digest from Bishop."

"You do have time on your hands," Lexie said, pouring the wine and settling back in one of the chairs. "Police Department must have been desperate to make old Trent a cop."

"Don't be so hard on him, Lex. Trent just grew up and matured like the rest of us." Claire's pronouncement had Olivia wondering if this was a general assumption or she knew it firsthand.

To Olivia, she asked, "So what did he say to you about the vandalism?"

Not as much as he said about you. The instant thought sprang like a bumped sore. "Very little. They arrested some kids and they were being questioned and they — the police — would be back in touch."

"A stall if I ever heard one," Lexie muttered.

Claire handed out full plates. "You should go and talk to the police, Lexie. You're a reporter. You could probably gets lots of info."

"Hmmm."

"I don't even know if I care that much," Olivia added.

Olivia settled into her chair, a friend on either side, and decided she was indeed doubly blessed.

It truly was a lovely day, relaxing and lazy. Birds fluttered around a nearby birdbath when they weren't ducking from Marco, an exploring orange tabby who belonged to Rosa across the street. He was a good mouser and had found a lucrative spot near the playhouse, which he stealthily stalked in the early morning while Olivia watched, relaxing with her coffee and *The Bishop Daily News*.

Lexie, lazy in her chair, raised her cup of wine. "To our very special friendship."

"Here, here."

Well, of course, it had been a whole bag of excuses — not exactly big lies, but just the same, she'd deliberately used that disastrous

Saturday to not have to say what was really going on.

In fact, on her flight, she'd glommed on to it as the perfect answer for not telling the real truth. Pretty handy. She actually should thank the hapless Bob or Rob, or whatever his name was, for providing such a ready-made reason.

You gotta love them. Lexie thought fondly of Olivia and Claire as she began her morning run the following day. Confessing to pickup sex and being totally wasted caused barely a yawn.

They were her best friends and they knew of her past sexual exploits, that she liked dirty movies, that marriage was a disaster for her, and that she had had no compunctions about telling them just about anything. Most stuff was meaningless — easy to confess, or whine about, and always knowing she'd get advice when she wanted it and silence when she didn't.

But her real problem, no, two problems were too humiliating — her pride, her sense of self-worth had been decimated. She had a hard time even thinking about them for very long; she couldn't bring herself to tell them. To see and hear the pity; Claire and Olivia rallying and ready to defend as they'd done when Lexie went through her two divorces.

These two lost wars, though, were far different.

Of course, one of them at least was no secret in Chicago. It was, as they say in the news business, a non-event to the world in general, but to Lexie it had been major and devastating.

The other — she still felt the sting of humiliation about the other. If anything she'd learned that being alone was far preferable to involvement. And being alone was where she intended to be for a long, long time.

In town she slowed down her pace, taking in the familiar sights and waving to Walt as he opened the liquor store for the day. She'd called her aunt last night and promised to come over this afternoon, but right now her curiosity was drawn to the Attic on the Corner, a combination antique and junk store that had sat on the corner of Ocean View and Wave Avenue since Lexie had been a little girl.

She crossed the street, stopping to peer into the dusty windows when she saw that the door was locked. She cupped her hands and leaned close to the glass, but the darkness inside prevented her from seeing much except that it looked like she'd always remembered. Cluttered, disorganized, and wonderfully intriguing.

A small sign on the door corner said the store was open 9–4. She'd come back later, and as she turned away she realized how long it had been since she'd been in a store

where the owner was as familiar and as interesting as Helene Duprey. She wasn't much
older than forty in years, but because she'd
come from Paris, she'd always seemed far
more mature to Lexie. She wondered now if
she'd ever made the trip back to her beloved
France, a dream Helene had often shared
with the star-in-waiting Lexie James.

That star junk was long past waiting, she
thought now as she turned from the window
and resumed her run. In a weird kind of way,
she was almost glad.

Chapter Seven

"We're going to Bishop? Really, Dad, really?"

Daniel raised an eyebrow at his daughter's overwhelming enthusiasm. She'd been staying with him for a few days longer than usual since her mother wanted more time with her boyfriend. Daniel didn't mind; his choice would be for Caitlyn to live with him permanently.

While there'd been nothing much different on this visit than on others, he had found her a bit more preoccupied than usual. Marsha had said she'd discovered boys, not something Daniel wanted to think about, but realistically he knew those days of Caitlyn pronouncing all boys as gross toads were on the wane. Still, such an excited reaction about going to Bishop was baffling; the town was seventy-five miles from where she lived with her mother.

"We're going to Bishop," he confirmed, wondering if he sounded like a Pied Piper leading the way to the nearest Gap. "I told Olivia I'd help her out. Her parents' house was trashed by some vandals."

"That's sucky." The dreamy look on her face didn't quite fit her words.

"Yeah, it is." He filled in some more details, watching Caitlyn try to hold on to each word with rapt attention.

Caitlyn was fourteen, rushing full tilt with the energy and curiosity of an official teenager. All those physical parts that just a few years ago had been awkward and seemingly scaled wrong had, with startling speed, shaped themselves into a lovely young women. Her teeth fit her mouth, her leanness had rounded into young curves, and her face that once seemed too big for her wide smile and small nose had shaped itself into a near perfect fit. To Daniel's relief, so far there'd been no unexpected surprises like a tattoo or a nose ring.

This morning he'd just finished his second cup of coffee, casually mentioning Bishop, when Caitlyn erupted as if he'd announced he had scarce tickets to some hip-hop concert.

"This is just so cool." She bounced around, hugging herself. "When are we leaving? Oh, wait, I can't wear this." *This* was biking shorts and flip-flops, and one of those tops that very clearly announced she had breasts and a midsection. He tried to not be a stuffy old father about what she wore; he saw enough at the high school to know

Caitlyn looked modest compared to some.

Whirling, she pulled the top off and ran back to her bedroom. When she reappeared, her hair was loose and flying, her shorts were shorter and her top had the word "Hottie" emblazoned in a run of glittery neon colors.

"Hottie?"

"Huh?"

"The shirt."

"Cool, huh?" She took a yogurt from the fridge and a spoon from the drawer and sat down at the table. "So when are we leaving?"

Daniel took a slow breath. Hottie. The *early slut look* leaped to mind. It was a term he'd heard another teacher use when referring to the current crop of skimpy sexual styles worn by girls — some so young they could have been barely out of diapers. He'd found the comment more than a little bit truthful, but when it came to his own daughter, there was no equivocation. The truth barreled in like a punch in the gut.

"Caitlyn, don't you think the shirt's a bit provocative?"

"The shirt?" She looked bewildered, then grinned, licking the yogurt spoon. "Oh. You don't like it? I do. It's sexy, and besides, all the girls wear them."

"Does your mother know you're buying clothes like this?" Daniel knew Caitlyn often went shopping with a credit card without her mother. He also knew she was very adept at playing their differing opinions about rules and behavior to her own advantage. His awareness of this plot convinced him to always be wary of entangling arguments.

"She bought it for me." She had that "I got the last word" look.

Terrific. How the hell did he counter that?

"Well, you're not wearing it."

"What?" She looked up, genuinely stunned. "You're telling me how to dress — like — like I was some goofy dork?"

"Humor me. Okay?"

"I'm fifteen going on sixteen."

"Sweetheart, you won't be fifteen until November, and even if you were —"

"I'm not a baby!" she shouted, coming to her feet and kicking the chair back. She planted her hands on her hips and "Hottie" worked up and down with each quick breath.

All this for some slutty shirt? Maybe. *Lately, she gets very huffy over the silliest things.* Marsha's comment had been whispered to him after Caitlyn was in the truck.

"You're certainly no baby," he said casually. "In fact, you're a beautiful young woman who doesn't need to advertise her sex appeal."

"It doesn't mean anything. It's just a shirt."

He set his coffee mug in the sink, then put the cream in the fridge, and fished around in his pocket for his truck keys. He rounded the island, passing her where she still stood by the table, and headed to the back door. He knew her eyes were following him, waiting for him to realize how "out of it" he was. She was so delightfully innocent and so wonderfully young, and Daniel wanted to give her anything she asked for.

At the back door he glanced at his watch. "Time's passing and I'd like to get to Bishop by midmorning. Better go change so we can get going."

"Change? I don't want to change."

"I know you don't, but this isn't negotiable."

She folded her arms and tipped her chin up. "What if I say no?"

He dropped the keys back into his pocket. "Fine. Then we don't go."

"But what about helping Olivia?"

"Another time."

"Dad!"

He shrugged.

She muttered something, then swung around and flounced out of the kitchen, down the short hall, and Daniel winced when she slammed the bedroom door.

He didn't like these dustups, but he felt a huge obligation as a father, and even more so because he and Marsha were divorced. Watching his daughter display herself like some sex kitten — it pained him and it worried him, and as long as she was with him, it wasn't going to happen.

And what was the matter with Marsha? He knew she was all caught up with some boy-friend, but buying some "do me" shirt for their daughter . . . Then he realized that "do me" clothes were what Marsha wore when they were dating. Not as in your face as a "Hottie" shirt, but low tops with nipples showing; he remembered one shirt with a zipper. Yeah, he remembered, all right.

He'd married her because she'd been preg-nant, and while blaming provocative clothes was a bit simplistic, there was no question sexy outfits were a real turn-on. And yeah, he could've been careful, he could've been smarter, he could have kept his own zipper up. But he didn't and she didn't and there they were.

Daniel went out to his truck and loaded up his ladder and went into the garage for his toolbox. He put that in, plus the steamer he'd rented to take off wallpaper. He was on his way back into the house when Caitlyn appeared in a pink T-shirt, arms crossed, pout in place.

He knew better than to comment. She'd done as he asked. Case closed. "So what's the big attraction in Bishop?"

"My boyfriend." She glared, as if expecting an argument.

Ah, that not only explained the shirt, it scared the hell out of him. "You have a boy-friend in Bishop?" he asked blandly, hoping he hadn't made Bishop sound like a rave sex club. "Seems a long way from home."

"Actually, he lives in Acton and I go to school with him. His parents have a summer house in Bishop and a boat, and they told me I could come anytime I wanted."

Daniel was relieved. "That was nice of them. How come you never mentioned him before?"

"Because you treat me like a baby and Mom said you'd get all upset if you knew so I've never told you."

Thanks, Marsha, just what I need. You conspiring to keep secrets with our daughter.

"So how long have you had this boy-friend?"

"Since way last Christmas," she said, making it sound like six years instead of six months. "And he's cool and popular and someday —"

"You're going to marry him?"

She blinked, and he could almost see her mind trying to process what didn't fit her idea of how he would react. "I didn't expect you to ask that."

"Sometimes I do manage to surprise you."

She lowered her head, the grin coming slowly. Daniel wanted to hug her, pleased that she wasn't going to just dismiss his questions.

"Do I get to meet him?" he asked. "When we get to Bishop, I mean."

This time she frowned, but he could see her defenses scrambling back into position. "Is this some sort of trick?"

"Nope. Just thought it would be, you know, polite and appropriate."

She didn't look quite convinced. "You're not going to ask him a lot of dumb questions, are you?"

Like are you having sex with my daughter? "I'll watch myself."

Then she smiled. And he dropped an arm around her, kissing the top of her head, the confrontation over the shirt controversy slipping away. Now all he had to do was wonder about this boyfriend and whether his fourteen-year-old daughter was still a virgin.

"Why, Claire, is that really you?"

Olivia, high on the ladder she'd rented from the rental center, scraper in hand, glanced across the living room and saw Trent McGraw walking toward Claire, who'd been washing graffiti off the baseboards.

She dropped the sponge into the bucket of sudsy water, wiped her hands on a towel, and rose to her feet.

"Hello."

"Hi, yourself," he said with a smile. "Let me look at you." He took her hands, swinging them out and whistling low. "You're more gorgeous than I remembered."

Claire blushed, looking all flustered and a

132

bit uneasy. "In these old shorts and T-shirt? I think you need glasses."

"No, ma'am."

"Well, thank you. I'm very flattered."

Then, with a straightforward steadiness that seemed more Lexie-like than Claire-like, she said, "Now that I've lapped up all those nice compliments, I really must tell you that I don't know who you are."

Trent looked dumbfounded, and Olivia couldn't help the spurt of *gotcha* that warmed her ego. Now he knew what it was like to be forgotten. Or was Claire just acting clueless because Olivia was watching? Which was totally silly and Olivia was ashamed of herself for thinking such. Claire was married and anything between her and Trent — if there had indeed been anything — most likely had been embellished and revised by Trent.

"You don't recognize me?" he asked, clearly affronted. And then before she could say no, he added, "Trent McGraw."

"Trent! Of course," she said, nodding and smiling. Olivia couldn't tell if she was surprised or relieved. "Actually, I kind of thought it was you, but it has been a few years."

He looked slightly mollified, but clearly Claire's late recognition excuse hadn't set well.

Claire glanced up at Olivia with just a hint of panic in her eyes. Olivia relaxed. Whatever that conversation with Trent about him and Claire, it was clear that her friend's reaction revealed she'd never been as stuck on him as he'd indicated.

"Trent," Olivia said, drawing his attention. "What brings you over here?"

Claire casually slipped her hands out of his and threw Olivia a grateful look.

Instead of answering her, he said, "Saw Lexie in town. Boy, she's sure changed."

Olivia hadn't thought she looked all that different. "Oh? In what way?"

But before he could answer, Claire moved into his line of vision and said, "I understand you're a police officer."

"Ah, you must have been talking to Olivia," he said, as if Olivia had disappeared into another room. "Yeah, for about four years. Worked some private security before that, but the company went belly up, so I decided to get into something that wouldn't. I got this thing about having job security."

Olivia recalled that Trent's father had been unemployed most of the time that she'd lived in Bishop. Part for lack of jobs, but Amos McGraw was also slothful and lazy. If it didn't come to him, he couldn't be bothered.

". . . so the way I figure it," Trent continued, "most jobs get boring, but being a cop, there's always something going on. A few more bucks would help, but hey, this isn't Providence, where there's lots of overtime. Besides my ex lives in Providence, and she's dating a cop. My luck we'd end up partners. How are things going with you?"

Olivia listened, realizing he'd given a résumé of answers about himself all in response to one observation by Claire. By contrast, Olivia learned virtually nothing at Rickey's. Perhaps she needed better skills.

"Oh, I'm fine," Claire said. "Busy with lots of projects in Lake Moses." At his puzzled look she added, "It's a small town in central Virginia. Right now my family is away, so I came up to help Olivia."

Olivia noted she didn't say Lexie had come, too.

Trent glanced up at Olivia. "Been meaning to stop over and see if I could help. You got home all right the other night? No problems."

"I got home fine."

Claire tipped her head, eyebrows raised with a "you didn't tell us you were out with him" quizzical look.

She hadn't deliberately kept her drink with Trent a secret; she'd just found the meet-and-greets with Trent a bit depressing. Plus they'd both given her grief about her breakup with Daniel, so getting into any talk of Trent would have sent Lexie into rebound-teasing that Olivia didn't want to hear. Now, thanks to Trent, she was positive she'd get grilled by Claire and probably Lexie, too.

Diverting attention, Olivia asked, "You have anything more on the vandals?" She ran her scraper forcefully beneath a big strip of loosened paper, then pulled it down and dropped it on the floor.

"Not much. They got lawyers and outrage that they've been accused, but no one has flipped or confessed. Steamer would make that go quicker."

"The rental place didn't have one."

He walked over to where Olivia was perched on the third step of the ladder, chatting as he approached. "By the way, you forgot to call me." He said it as if she'd missed a date. "So, I decided to just drop over and see where I can offer my services." He went on to name some of the odd jobs he'd done, which to Olivia's ears sounded more impressive than they had in Ricky's. She also decided this rendition was to impress Claire, who Olivia noted had knelt back down to retrieve her sponge.

"I didn't forget, Trent, I just hadn't gotten around to it."

He shoved his hands in his pockets, looking contrite. "Look, I shouldn't have just charged in here. I probably sound like some pushy salesman. It's just that I hated to see you trying to do so much in so short a time."

"I appreciate your concern," she said, tossing a few more scraped sheets onto the floor. What she didn't tell him was that the realtor had called and said the Marlowes feared the house wouldn't be ready, and what with wanting to get settled in time for school to start, they'd found a place in Westerly.

That removed the time pressure, but Olivia wasn't as disappointed by the Marlowes' decision as she thought she'd be. Being in the house had filled her with a zest for homey nostalgia that surprised her. Or perhaps it was the reality of the vandalism that had left her with a personal sense of invasion. Seeing the deliberate destruction in the home where she'd grown up had filled her with remorse layered with knots of disloyalty and had suddenly made her protective of the one big tangible she had from her past.

As with the broken mirror, she had a sense that her years of disinterest in those things her parents had held dear brought this on. She'd walked out, locked the door, and left its care either in the hands of strangers or in no hands at all.

"I have an idea," Claire said. "We were talking this morning about the lawn and that it needed to be cut and trimmed. What do you think, Livie?"

"Okay with me. Do you have equipment, Trent, because I don't."

"Got it all."

"All right."

And with that settled, he walked over to

137

Claire, hunkered down beside her and leaned close, whispering something Olivia couldn't hear. Claire nodded, again dropped the sponge in the bucket, and rose to her feet. Trent turned and nodded to Olivia. "See you later."

Once he'd gone from the room, Claire hurried over. "I'll be right back."

"What's going on? I thought he was doing the lawn."

"I don't know. He said he wanted to talk with me privately." Then she whispered, "I'll fill you in later."

"Wait a minute. Why did you interrupt when he mentioned Lexie? Is something wrong? I didn't think she'd changed all that much. A little thinner, but that's all."

She sighed. "I don't know what it is, but she's distant, and her not wanting to come here . . . that's just so unlike her."

"But she explained that."

"I know she did. . . ." Claire went to the dining-room window and peeked out to where Trent was moving a lawn tractor off the back of his truck. "Take today, for example. She's not here helping us, and I know it isn't because she's avoiding the work."

"She was going back to the Attic to see Helene."

"She could have done that this afternoon. No, I think she's afraid."

"Lexie? Afraid? Of us? Come on, Claire.

138

That's ridiculous. Compared to her, we're the wimps in this trio."

"I'm telling you what I think."

"Hey, Claire, did I lose you?" shouted Trent from the kitchen.

"We can talk later."

Olivia watched her hurry off to join Trent and moments later saw them in the backyard, walking toward the playhouse.

She climbed down from the ladder, and because she was preoccupied with Trent and Claire and now Lexie, she wasn't watching where she was stepping and one foot ended up in the pan of hot water she'd been using to soak the wallpaper. Startled, then furious, she hopped out, slipping on the slick, wet old-glued paper and frantically grabbed for the ladder.

Too late. Her feet were already sliding, and in the next second she was on her rear.

Getting to her feet and looking at the mess, she gave in to her frustration and kicked the pan of water, sending it flying into the wall. Water poured down the wallpaper.

"Shit," she muttered.

"Nothing like a well-placed cussword, as my uncle Chester used to say."

She swung around, glaring at Daniel, who was carrying what looked like a brand-new wallpaper steamer. "This seems to be my day for men sneaking up on me," she muttered.

He plucked a piece of shredded gooey

139

paper off her rear end and said, "I told you —"

"Daniel Cafferty, if you say I told you so, I'll throw that other bucket of water at you," she warned, marching over to the one Claire had been using.

"Back it down, babe. I was going to say, I told you when I was here on Saturday I'd get a steamer. And if you'd leave your cell phone on, I could have let you know that I was on the way with it." Daniel took the bucket and set it a safe distance away.

"You know I hate cell phones. And you're a chicken."

"And one who prefers dry feathers to wet ones. Cluck, cluck."

"Don't make me giggle."

"Never."

But she did anyway. She couldn't help it. None of her catastrophes or screwups ever rattled Daniel. Always practical and always able to turn down her temper and over-the-top outrage. Sometimes she thought he didn't take her seriously enough, sometimes he was entirely too logical and yes, even a bit too overbearing. But to his credit he didn't get testy over minor stuff, took most of what she threw at him in stride. Well, most things.

What other man would not only bring equipment, but supply himself to help out his ex-girlfriend? Not any that she knew.

"Besides, I'd never say 'I told you so' to

you." He hauled the steamer over to an electrical outlet.

She sagged against the wall, suddenly tired and feeling as grubby as she looked. "I'm sorry for being bitchy. I'm glad you're here."

"Really?" He brightened and she laughed.

"Don't look so surprised. You're always a big help, and you always seem to have what I need before I need it."

"Ah, now that was worth the trip." He grinned and she was reminded of everything she loved about Daniel. His wit and his concern and his sense of knowing what to do when she seemed to be flying in a dozen different directions.

"I didn't know you were coming today."

"I'm getting the team roster set up for the fall game schedule, and next week we start drills. Rounding them all up has been about as easy as, well, catching you with your cell on."

"I'll try to do better."

"No, you won't."

She shrugged.

"Anyway, I had today free. Oh, and I brought Caitlyn with me." He explained about the extra days he had with her before launching into the news that she had a boyfriend in Bishop. "His name is Brian Torgan. Ever heard the name?"

"No, but there's a ton of new families here since I moved away."

"These are summer people. I dropped her off at their house, a place down near the water. Met the parents — the father was only marginally interested in meeting me or Caitlyn. I think he would've rather been sailing his boat. The mother looked at Caitlyn, said all the polite, welcoming things, but I definitely had the impression she was irritated with Brian for not warning her. Caitlyn, of course, had only told Brian she'd be seeing him this summer. Nothing specific. Then, as I was leaving, I heard his mother mutter something about another new girlfriend. Brian and his girl-to-do list is obviously extensive."

"How old is Brian?"

"Sixteen. And that I only learned from a very defensive daughter."

"It sounds as if you and Mrs. Torgan have the same goals. She thinks her son is too girl crazy and you don't want Caitlyn with a guy who might hurt her. All very normal." Olivia folded her arms, amused by the usually unflappable Daniel. "So what was Brian like?"

"Nothing was pierced, thank God. Polite, called me sir — you know, the usual stuff when you want to make an impression."

"It could be good manners."

"I suppose." But he didn't sound convinced.

"What you really want to know is if they're having sex."

"What I really want is to lock Caitlyn up until she's about twenty-five."

"A tad impractical."

"Yeah, I know." He paused as though debating on continuing. "Never mind. New subject. Saw your neighbor and two of her friends outside. They're going to bring lunch over and put it in the refrigerator. I got the impression they don't want to be a bother or get in the way."

"That would be Flo and Rosa and Edna-Mae. They're very sweet and they want to help, but I said no to climbing ladders and getting down on their hands and knees. Truthfully, they aren't as agile as they used to be. We compromised on them making lunch."

"Sounds like a good plan. Also, I saw Claire. Who's the dude trying to pick her up?"

"Pick her up?" Olivia laughed. "He's a local guy that Claire has known for years."

"Tell her to be careful. Can I use that bucket to fill the steamer? It will take a few minutes to heat up."

"Sure. Just rinse it out good." Olivia watched him take the bucket, go to the kitchen, and then return to pour water into the steamer. Then he plugged it in.

"I'll bring in my ladder."

"Daniel?"

"What?"

"Why did you say Claire should be careful?"

"Because the guy is moving on her big time."

"Don't be silly. Claire's married and adores Jeff. She has no interest in Trent. She's just being nice."

"No argument there, but Claire's also naïve."

"Come on. She's forty. Naïve is for Caitlyn's age. Not Claire's."

"I disagree. If it were Lexie, I wouldn't have mentioned it." The steamer began to whoosh and gurgle.

"Daniel?"

He made a few adjustments until the noise lowered to a steady hum. He rose to his feet and looked at her. "That should do it."

"What if he tried to make a move on me?" It was a totally self-centered question, but she was deeply curious as to how he perceived her.

"That would be different."

"How?"

"I'd have to kill him."

And with that he went out to get the ladder, leaving Olivia feeling warm and cherished and wondering why Daniel knocking off Trent seemed the most rational thought she'd had all day.

Chapter Eight

By late that afternoon Olivia was amazed at all they'd accomplished. Lunch from Flo and the girls had been delicious and appreciated, Trent had done the lawn, trimming and manicuring, including some cleanup in the long-neglected flower bed. The perennial garden looked perkier, albeit a bit straggly and in need of some fresh additions. A trip to the garden shop would be a nice diversion after wrestling all day with wet shreds of wallpaper.

She and Claire and Daniel had worked tirelessly to get the paper off the wall in the living room — a dirty, tedious job that Olivia vowed she'd never do again. Actually Daniel had been the tireless one. She and Claire would have quit hours ago if he hadn't been so dogged.

"You want to get this done or look at it again tomorrow?" he asked from high on the ladder, working at the edges near the ceiling.

"Whose bright idea was it to do all this anyway?" Olivia snipped, picking bits of the paper off her arms.

"Yours," Claire said, guzzling from a bottle of water.

"Next time tell me to hire someone."

"Next time I'll bring a crew, not just a ladder and a steamer," Daniel said.

By five o'clock they were almost finished when Lexie came in; actually she kind of danced in as if she'd spent the day shopping in Paris with an unlimited letter of credit. Wearing leather sandals, white pants, and a frilly lemon tube top that emphasized her throat, breasts and her tan, she stashed her packages, then gave a wide-eyed, head-bobbing scan of the room.

"You guys have done a great job. How could I have missed out on all of this fun?" She looked around, swinging so that her blond hair flew like waving wheat.

Olivia, who felt as if she'd been clawing her way through a wallpaper wasteland, caught the eye of an equally exhausted and cranky Claire. Olivia asked, "Do we kill her now or make her cook for the rest of the week?"

Claire crossed her arms and set her mouth in a thin line. In a voice dripping with vengeance she said, "Killing her is too easy. Let's make her cook."

"That might kill *us*."

Lexie, whose cooking non-skills were legendary, played along like the third leg in a tag team. "You two can't survive without me.

No one else knows where to get the best porn videos."

"Oh, brother," Olivia said, rolling her eyes.

Daniel chuckled.

"Lexie James, that's a lie," Claire said, a pink blotchiness climbing from her neck to her cheeks. "We never sent you out for dirty movies."

Lexie laughed, neither defending or taking back her exaggeration. She swaggered over to Daniel, sliding her arms around him, unconcerned about the remains of sticky wallpaper getting on her clothes. "Hi, stranger. How'd they wrangle you into this girly-girl scene?"

Daniel played along. "Someone had to make up for you flitting around the local bars."

"Damn, you had to tell them."

"I cannot tell a lie."

She laughed, letting him go.

Neither Claire or Olivia even smiled.

Daniel said, "Uh, I think you're in trouble, Lex, for totally blowing off paper-stripping duty."

She turned to look at Olivia and Claire, who were staring back at her, more bemused than angry, but trying very hard to look serious. "I'm here now. What can I do?"

"Where were you all day?"

"I was laying the groundwork for having fun."

"Like in a field trip?"

"Hmmm. I found a couple of junk places

to explore, plus — drumroll, please."

Olivia did a drumroll impression.

"I was talking to Helene and you'll never guess what she told me." She looked at everyone, noting they were all waiting and listening, and she wanted to savor her news a little bit longer. Turning toward the kitchen, she said, "I'm starved. You guys leave anything to eat? Any beer left?"

"Wait a minute."

"Lex, tell us. What?"

She grinned, excitement filling her voice. "Helene is going to sell the Attic and have a big closeout sale, and she said we could come before she publicly announces it and get first dibs on her stock."

Claire beamed. "Now, that works for me."

"What fun. Like having our own private antique store," Olivia said, thinking about the pleasure of poking through all of Helene's inventory. "Why is she selling?"

Lexie went to the kitchen, Olivia and Claire trailing after her. Lexie rummaged in the fridge, plucking a stem of grapes from Rosa's fruit salad. Taking the pitcher of Flo's lemonade, she poured a full glass.

"Business has been struggling, plus she said she wants to go back to France, where she still has some family."

"Too bad I live in Lake Moses. It would be fun to have an antique store."

"So when do we get to sweep up the

goodies?" Olivia asked.

"In a few days," Lexie said vaguely, pouring more lemonade and popping a few grapes in her mouth.

"What does she have?" Claire asked. "I remember old linens and pretty dishes."

"Lots of those." Lexie named off other items such as old metal, framed pictures, and silver flatware that she'd seen in her visit to the small store, commenting that a better presentation would have made the story easier to browse through. "Things are just stacked in piles rather than arranged into vintage eye candy that make customers *want* to buy."

"Frankly, that surprises me," Claire said. "Helene was always conscious of pretty displays."

"Maybe she's lost interest and just can't be bothered."

While Lexie and Claire discussed French china and Italian linen, Daniel took Olivia aside.

Brushing the pieces of wallpaper off his clothes and looking at his watch, he said, "Hate to do this, but I'm going to have to split. I have to pick up Caitlyn in about fifteen minutes."

"It's okay, the worst is done. Thanks for coming and being such a big help."

He studied her and she wondered what he was thinking. Not about leaving to get

Caitlyn, she decided. Feeling ridiculously uneasy and as tongue-tied as a teenager on her first date, Olivia's skin prickled. The warm summer air suddenly felt as thick as her thoughts.

Tension danced between them, and though no personal or private words had been exchanged in the past few hours while they'd worked together, now Olivia could sense the edges of intimacy wrapping around her.

"We love each other," he said bluntly and without any pretense or apology.

"Oh, Daniel."

"It's what you're thinking, it's what I'm thinking."

"But it makes being with you very awkward."

"Better awkward than bored. Relax. I haven't made any moves on you, nor have I been reminding you every five minutes of what we once had. I just think we should be honest about what's still between us."

"I don't know what you want me to say."

He cupped her chin, lifting it, but not bending to kiss her as she expected. Or was it hope? Certainly not dread.

"You haven't denied what I've said. You haven't denied the reality of what we had, what we still have. That's enough for now." He paused and she held her breath, afraid to swallow or breathe for fear she would betray her feelings. "I have to get Caitlyn." He ran his thumb along her jaw and then her lower lip. "I'll be in touch."

She wanted to call him back, she wanted him to kiss her, she wanted him to stay. But he was already out of the living room; she heard him say good-bye to Claire and Lexie. She walked into her father's study in time to watch him climb into the black truck, back out of the drive, and disappear down the street.

She drew in a deep breath. What did it all mean? She honestly didn't know.

Claire, as she had done every morning since Tony and Lara were in the primary grades, awakened at five-thirty. The birds were chirping with snappy chatter, the sun promising a warm day. Claire had always been a morning person — the time of day when her energy was at its highest. She took great pride that when most of the world was just waking up, she had her house straightened, kids out the door to school, Jeff off to work, her appointments for the day mapped out, the newspaper read, and was happily on her third cup of coffee.

But Bishop wasn't Lake Moses, and even if it had been, Claire had very few family reasons in recent years to get out of bed so early at home — no longer were there kids to care for and Jeff traveled so much for his work, he barely needed her when he was home. She'd missed those pleasant and fulfilling duties despite a plethora of activities that usually filled her days.

Maybe that wasn't very independent or progressive, but Claire had drifted away from her feminist leanings in college. The truth was she'd loved being a wife and mother, caring for her family and putting their needs ahead of her own. She'd never felt deprived of an outside career nor did she feel guilty for not using her spare time for some cause. Her family was her cause, and she solidly believed that getting her kids raised into responsible adults was a full-time responsibility.

The disappointment, however, was that despite her dedication and her loyalty, she had an absent husband and an unemployed vagabond son. Lara, thank God, had turned out fine; a warm, sweet daughter that any mother would take pride in.

She wished Lara were here. Her daughter so enjoyed Olivia and Lexie, and Claire would have taken great pride in showing her off. She was a testimony to her mothering skills, and Claire clung to that as if Lara were the only thing she'd done right.

Now she arose, showered, dressed, and left a note for the still-sleeping Olivia. Lexie had already gone on a morning run.

But instead of making coffee and enjoying it outside in the morning sunshine, Claire, wearing beige slacks and a sage green blouse with a lightweight sweater casually knotted around her neck, drove into town.

That this was the third morning she'd wound up in Muriel's, the local coffee shop, was not a coincidence, but she'd convinced herself she'd done so simply because it was where the locals congregated. Why have coffee alone at Olivia's when she could have some here and catch up on the local color and the newsy chatter?

Muriel's was charming and clean and where Trent McGraw had coffee every morning.

Claire ignored that gremlin hidden deep within her that whispered she was coming here because Trent, rather than Muriel's, was what charmed her.

Trent was an old friend and there was nothing wrong with enjoying the company of someone she'd practically grown up with. Trent himself had pointed this out when they'd gone outside to chat a few days ago. She'd been fascinated by the police work he'd done and especially his work with a drug rehabilitation program for teenagers.

Claire found herself talking about Tony and what she'd come to suspect was his serious cocaine problem. Trent listened — really listened — while Jeff seemed only to get angry. Vividly she recalled their heated discussion about their son.

"He's got a problem and he needs to deal with

it. *Sending him money doesn't work.*"

"*So your solution is to let him starve.*"

"*Get serious. That cash is going up his nose, not to buy burgers for his belly.*"

"*You want to turn your back on him. I can't do that.*"

"*So you enable him. How's that working for him?*"

That had been the last go-around she'd had with Jeff, ending with his orders of sending no money when Tony called and asked for it.

Of course, she'd ignored Jeff, and didn't give a hoot that he would be furious about it.

She'd told Trent a little of her and Jeff's division over Tony, and Trent had listened, understanding that for her there was more than just tough love. This was her firstborn, her son, and she could not, would not abandon him no matter what he did or didn't do. Trent had understood that Claire believed in redemption and second chances; she firmly embraced the cliché that the best was yet to come. Deep down she was adamant that her son was a good kid who would get straightened out if only she remained supportive emotionally and yes, financially. Now, as she walked into Muriel's, she saw him and liked that he was there and glancing up and motioning her to come and join him. With one long breath of reality, she knew she

154

wasn't here for coffee or chatter, but to see him.

That he grinned at her as if he just realized that the sun had come up . . . well, nothing in recent days had given her such a full and overflowing sense of well-being.

"Good morning," she said.

"Good morning. I thought you weren't coming today."

You would have missed me? "And start the day without Muriel's coffee? Not on your life." She slid onto one of the stools.

The coffee shop was doing a brisk business; patrons on their way to work, take-out with a decent-sized line of customers, and a few families at the tables. WBIS, a local radio station, gave traffic and weather as well as up-to-date reports on a warehouse fire in the early-morning hours.

The smells of frying bacon and hot coffee and warm cinnamon rolls along with the Bishop radio station reminded Claire how little life in Bishop had changed.

A cheerful Muriel put a cup and saucer on the counter and filled it. No prepackaged half-and-half, but a china pitcher with real cream was placed in front of her. "Fresh raspberry scones this morning."

"Sounds yummy."

"Trent, how about you?"

"Sure. I was waiting to see if Claire came in."

"You were?" For the silliest reason this made her heart jump. How long had it been since anyone waited for her?

He shrugged. "Sure. Food always tastes better when enjoyed with a pretty woman."

Oh, boy, it was so schmaltzy and probably a lie, yet so utterly wonderful to hear. "You are the flatterer."

"So what are you and the girls up to today?"

She grinned. "That's what Daniel calls us — the girls."

"Daniel being?"

"Oh, a friend of Olivia's."

"So what's up today? More wallpaper stripping?"

"No, that's done. Olivia has a painter coming in. Today we're going to go through Olivia's parents' things that she put in storage when she rented the house. Are you on duty today?"

"Actually, I was last night. I'm on my way home to sleep."

Claire found her mind running to areas that were too rattling as well as just plain unacceptable. What she needed to do was excuse herself and leave. "You worked all night?"

"Yep."

"That has to be hard. Sleeping during the day, I mean."

"At first, but then your body clock adjusts.

156

What is tough is dating."

Dating? She wasn't sure she wanted to go down this path. "I imagine you do have a lot of girlfriends."

"None at the moment."

So much for her resistance. "That's hard to believe."

"Just can't seem to hook up with the right one. None around like you, Claire."

Her eyes widened at his easy segue from general dating to her. She quickly sipped her coffee, trying to catch a side glance. *See what you've gotten into by coming here to meet him?* She quickly changed the subject. "So if you worked all night, you must be exhausted. Why are you here when you could be home sleeping?"

And without a beat or a pause or a breath, he said, "I wanted to see you."

Claire swallowed, her heart responding as if it were a thirsty garden, while realizing that she'd stepped into some very deep weeds.

"I'm sorry," Trent said. "I've embarrassed you."

"No, no. I — I'm just not used to — never mind. It's not important."

He was hunched forward, arms resting on the counter, head tilted toward her. Overnight stubble darkened his cheeks and his eyes — a compelling smoky green. Funny, she hadn't recalled that they were so deep and so enticing.

She looked away, watching a couple at a table trying to restrain an active toddler. She didn't know what to say and realized how out of touch she was with this kind of flirty banter. For indeed, that's all this was — friendly attention from an old friend she'd known years ago.

Get a grip here, she scolded herself. He said he wanted to see you. You wanted to see him, too, or else you would have stayed in Olivia's backyard and had your coffee. You're here, he's here. It's public and nothing is going on.

Muriel put two plates down with the scones and refilled their cups. "Anything else I can get you folks?"

Claire said, "Could I get two of the scones to take back to my friends? I know they'd love them."

"Sure." She wrote them down on her order pad, and moments later she returned with a sack that she placed on the counter in front of Claire.

"Thank you."

She nodded, tearing off the check and leaving it between them. "You want any more coffee, give a holler."

Ignoring the check, Trent broke his scone in half, dunking it in his coffee.

Claire laughed. "You remind me of my son. Tony is a dunker."

"Dunking's the best."

"So he says." She carefully broke hers and took a small bite.

"Go ahead."

"What?"

"Dunk."

"I don't think so. It's too messy."

He grinned as if seeing her messy would be an intriguing sight. "I dare you."

"You dare me? To dunk a scone?"

"Live dangerously. You know you want to."

"I don't, Trent. Really."

"Yeah, you do, Clary, yeah, you do."

Clary? She hadn't been called Clary in years, not since — "How did you ever remember Clary?"

"There's lots of things about you I haven't forgotten. Besides, Clary would definitely be a dunker. Clary would relish living dangerously," he added, flashing a sun-bright grin.

Whether it was the challenge or the fact that she hadn't done anything even remotely dangerous in years, she dunked the scone. The pieces crumbled in the hot coffee, dropping off, hitting the hot liquid, splashing up and splattering her top. She took the handful of napkins from Trent, but they were of no use on her splotched blouse. She cleaned her hands and dabbed at her mouth.

"Sorry."

"I should have taken my own advice."

"Want me to have Muriel get something to clean your top?"

She shook her head. "That's okay."

How silly she'd been. Dunking scones. What did she expect? What she needed to do was leave; right now she should gather her things and get out into the fresh air to clear her head.

"I have to get back to Olivia's."

"Yeah, I need to roll, too." He slipped off the stool, standing, and then reached for the check. She did, too, and their fingers bumped. Claire wouldn't have said sparks crackled, but it was no ordinary hands colliding. And rather than jumping back as though she'd noticed, she glanced up at him. "Let me get the check."

"On one condition." He paused, watching her, those smoky green eyes too intriguing to allow her to look away.

"What's the condition?" she asked, her mind racing into absurd possibilities.

With the check still a question, neither had moved their hands. She was more tempted by his attention than she wanted to admit.

"My treat tomorrow morning." His voice was almost a caress.

"Oh." Idiot, she thought, just what did she expect? Something obvious and bluntly sexy? And what was she doing here anyway? Coffee in a public place seemed innocent enough, but suddenly her enjoyment of his company . . . She pulled her hand away. "Uh, well, I don't know if I can make it tomorrow."

"The following morning, then."

Now thoroughly flustered, Claire felt trapped, forcing a measure of good sense to return. "I have some plans with Olivia and Lexie —"

"Look, I'll pay to have your top cleaned."

"Don't be silly. I made the mess."

He stared at her a long time as if he wasn't sure he believed her. "Whatever you say," he said, dismissing her from his attention. Taking one last gulp of coffee, he nodded to her. "See you around."

"Sure." And she watched him leave with a sinking disappointment wrapped in a dose of mortification. What had she expected? Those innocent sparring and flirting chats of years ago? She'd come here because the last two times had been fun and lighthearted and she had believed that Trent truly enjoyed her company. And she liked his attention. Why was that wrong? It wasn't. At least to her it wasn't.

Now he walked out of the coffee shop and never looked back. She fumbled in her purse, pulling out some bills and leaving them on the counter. Muriel appeared to clear the dishes and clean off the counter as Claire was adjusting her sweater.

"He's a heart-wrecker, that one."

"Oh, we're just friends from a long time ago."

"Friends? With Trent? Is that what he told you?"

"Well, not exactly." *He didn't tell me anything but good-bye.* "I just meant, well, that I've known him for a long time."

"Yeah, well, that can be said of a lot of women in Bishop. Most of 'em, he just ignores. Trent is fussy about who he hooks with. In fact, haven't seen him in here with a girlfriend since last winter."

Girlfriend? Is that the impression a cup of coffee with an old friend gives? "None of that has anything to do with me."

Muriel lined up the napkin holder, salt and pepper, and sugar jar. Giving the counter a final wipe, she said, "Weird. I figured he'd taken a real shine to you, you know, what with you coming in here to meet up with him. You got some spots on your top."

"Yes, I know. And I wasn't coming here to meet him —"

"Just a coincidence, huh? Like yesterday? Like the morning before?" Muriel grinned. "Hey, it's okay. Your secret is safe with me."

"There's no secret," Claire snapped and then regretted it. Nothing like acting as guilty as she felt.

Muriel leaned across the counter and whispered, "Honey, he's a great guy. That slut Tanya wasn't worth his time or the grief he got from her. Trent's a real charmer, but like I said, he's a heart-wrecker. Just so you know a lot of women have left their panties in his bed, but ain't none of them been able to get

162

a ring on their finger."

Claire digested this piece of unnecessary intimate information and changed the subject. "I know my friends will like the scones." And with frigid finality, Claire turned and walked out of the coffee shop.

Chapter Nine

At a little before seven o'clock, Lexie stopped
to cool down about a block from Olivia's.
Bent over, hands clamped on her knees, she
took slow, measured breaths. Sweat glistened
on her skin, and even her shorts and sports
bra felt too restrictive. Too bad Olivia didn't
have a pool. That new condo development
she'd looked at yesterday had a nice one.
Lexie had been walking near the pool when a
grimy maintenance guy sidled over and told
her she could come and swim anytime she
wanted. The invite, of course, had nothing to
do with his leer at her legs that was supposed to flatter her.

Then there was the beach. She hadn't been
to Gull Beach since she'd arrived in Bishop.
Maybe that's what she'd do. Get into her suit
and wander down for a dip in the surf.

Her sweaty body notwithstanding, one
glance at the broiling sun and she knew
today was going to be a scorcher. Too hot
for any kind of hard work, so she intended to
suggest they sort through the boxes they'd

brought from the storage unit. But right now even that usually enjoyable chore didn't appeal.

Now contemplating a cool shower, she was just three houses from the driveway when she saw Claire zoom in, rock the car to a stop, then burst out, slamming the door. She carried a sweater — a sweater? What was she doing with a sweater? It was hot as Hades. Also in her hand was a small bag.

Lexie broke into a jog, calling her name before Claire could get in the house.

But either she didn't hear her, or she ignored her, because she yanked open the door, disappeared inside, and the door rattled closed.

Seconds later Lexie walked into the kitchen in time to see a puzzled and barefooted Olivia, in shorts and a tee, eating a bowl of granola and peaches, her attention on the fast-moving Claire.

"Claire? What's the matter?" Olivia called, setting her bowl down and starting after her.

Lexie asked, "What's going on?"

"Don't know, but she looked furious." Olivia pointed to the bag on the counter and then peeked inside. "She tossed this as she sailed by. Scones."

"Probably from Muriel's. Wonder if her fury has to do with charm-boy Trent."

Still looking in the direction Claire had gone, Olivia turned her attention to Lexie, who was running water in the sink and dousing it on her face and arms.

"Trent? What about him."

Lexie took a long drink from the faucet, then wiped her hand across her mouth. "She was having coffee with him at Muriel's. Amazing what you see when you run early in the morning."

Olivia felt totally out of the loop. How would Claire even know Trent was at Muriel's unless they'd planned to meet? Ridiculous. "Why would she be doing that?"

"Why not?"

Olivia didn't like the direction her mind was taking. "She's married for starters." Truthfully, Claire sneaking off to meet Trent didn't annoy her at all compared to what she knew her reaction would have been a week ago. Lost in some old nostalgia about a guy who could barely remember your name — well, she might have had a few moments of silliness, but now she had her head clear and steady. No question that her friendship with Claire meant ten times more than trying to get attention from Trent. And then there was the whole question of Daniel. . . .

"So she's married. So what? They were friends a long time ago and they're friends today. Why does someone have to give up a male friend just because she had the misfortune to marry a jerk?"

"Um, are we talking about Claire or you?"

Olivia asked gently. Lexie had gotten a boatload of criticism from her second husband about her close friendship with a guy she ran with in the morning — a friendship that had preceded her marriage and continued after her divorce and into a new relationship. Lexie had always maintained she would have never gotten involved with Eric if her ex hadn't been such a possessive jerk.

"I'm talking about men who defend their friendship with women, but get testy and nasty if their wives enjoy men as friends."

"A double standard. What else is new."

"It sucks."

Olivia sighed.

"As for Jeff, do you see him around? Has he called her once? Has he ever given five seconds of thought about what she does or where she is?"

Olivia noted that Lexie, too, hadn't heard from Eric — at least not that she knew of — so perhaps she was just generally ticked about men who didn't make regular phone calls. To Olivia calling could also be checking up. "Jeff is somewhere in the Far East for that computer conglomerate. Besides, why would he call? He trusts Claire."

Lexie pulled a bottle of water from the fridge. "Gee, let me think," she said, her tone leveled with sarcasm. She drank thirstily. "I've got it. He might want to talk to his

167

wife, as in I miss you, I love you."

"Okay, you're right. Hey, cut me some slack. I've never been married."

Lexie pointed the bottle at her. "You're the smartest of the three of us. Remember this conversation when Daniel comes calling with a ring and a date."

He already did. But instead of blurting that out, she simply nodded.

"Come on, we need to go see if she's okay."

Lexie, followed by Olivia, climbed the stairs and approached Claire's room. "Claire?"

"I'm okay." The pause was clearly filled with a few fading sobs. "I-I'll be down later."

"Claire, we're coming in."

"No!"

But it was too late, Olivia had the door open and they both walked into the sunny yellow bedroom. A bay of windows faced the east, and the early-morning sun streamed in across the hardwood floor to a yellow damask slipper chair and onto a heap of clothes at Claire's feet. Tossed clothes were very un-Claire-like.

She stood in a lacy blue bra with matching panties, the kind of stuff Olivia would have worn on an anticipated date with Daniel. But this was Claire, who always dressed perfectly right down to silk underwear. Her hair was messed and her face was streaked with tears that she now tried to hide. She looked crushed and humiliated — so much for

168

morning coffee with an old friend being a day-brightener.

"Claire? What in the world happened?"

"Nothing. It's stupid and I'm an idiot and —"

Olivia walked over and put her arm around her. "You are never an idiot." Olivia glanced over at Lexie, who'd made herself comfortable, waiting for whatever details there were to play out.

"You waiting to pounce?" Claire glared at Lexie.

Startled, Lexie scowled. "Thanks a lot. That's how I treat my best friends. Pounce and claw when they're bawling and beating themselves up."

"Oh, I'm sorry. This has not been a good morning."

"Yeah, we noticed. So, girl, fess-up time." Claire eased away from Olivia's comforting arm.

"You're probably going to hate me —"

"Never happen."

"Well, you're definitely going to be pissed at me."

"Sounds more like you're pissed at yourself," Lexie observed.

"Royally," Claire muttered.

"Why do I feel like I'm the only one who is in the dark here?" Olivia asked.

"Because you are," Lexie said, with a soft bluntness. "Claire's been meeting Trent for

169

coffee the past few mornings while you were still asleep. And no, she didn't tell me, either. She passed me that first morning on her way to Muriel's. Never even saw me, did you, Claire? And me being the snoopy sort, I went into town and — hey, it's a small town and there isn't much open at six in the morning. And there they were at the counter in Muriel's."

Claire scowled at Lexie. "Thank you for that newsy bulletin. If I ever need a personal spy, I know who to call."

Lexie shrugged. "At your service. I could give lessons on guys like Trent."

"You don't know him."

"I know his type. Anyway, Livie does, and even she'd agree that he's a jerk."

"He's lousy at remembering names, that's for sure," Olivia muttered.

"Well, I happen to like him," Claire said, crossing her arms as though hers was the final word.

"A few moments ago he had you in tears and calling yourself names. Now you're defending him."

"So what if I am. You —"

Olivia interrupted. "Hold it. Hold it. This isn't getting us anywhere. Obviously, we all have different opinions of Trent. Okay, Claire, fill me in. Why are you meeting him and why has it upset you?"

"It was just coffee and some conversation."

She was almost pleading to be believed. "When he came to do the lawn — that day we went outside, we got to talking and he told me about some work he was doing with messed-up kids — naturally, I thought of Tony. Lexie James, don't you dare roll your eyes."

"I'm listening, I'm listening."

"Anyway, he said he'd love to talk to me about Tony, even said he had some tips and advice. How could I just say no to that?"

"You couldn't. Of course you couldn't," Olivia soothed.

Claire spared a glance at Lexie. "I know what you're thinking."

I'm thinking you're headed for trouble, my friend. But Lexie remained silent, just shrugging instead.

"Anyway, he offered to meet me for coffee. I mean how sinister is that? It's not as if he was inviting me to his apartment."

"And would you have gone if he had?"

"I — well, I — no, of course not."

"Lexie, leave her alone. Go on, Claire."

"So I met him and the first morning we talked about Tony. And yesterday, too. Then, when I was leaving, he asked me to come back, saying we could just have coffee. Nothing heavy or serious or complicated. So I went back today."

Olivia and Claire exchanged glances.

"So what happened?" Olivia asked.

Claire opened the drawers of a hand-painted

chest that they'd brought from storage and took out shorts and a top. She pulled them on and slid her hands through her hair. "We were having a lot of fun. Friendship kind of fun, and then I slopped coffee on my top and he felt bad and I felt silly, and then we argued over the check and it was then that — I don't know, everything changed. It got tense and suddenly it felt too personal, too intimate, and I backed off. He got very distant, as if I'd suddenly turned into a stranger. It was very unsettling. Anyway, he left and I was getting ready to. Then to make it even worse I got a summary of his likes in women from Muriel."

She filled Olivia and Lexie in on what Muriel said.

Lexie unfolded herself from where she'd flopped on the bed, stood, and crossed the room to the windows. "So you're upset and feeling like a jerk because he was headed toward a maneuver to get you into bed —"

Olivia interrupted. "That's a pretty big leap, Lexie, from coffee to sex."

"But that's where you thought it might be going, right, Claire?"

"I was uneasy and, well, yes, worst-case scenario."

"Or best case."

Claire sagged onto the edge of the bed and covered her face. Clearly Lexie had hit a button.

"Hey, you in fact said no," Lexie said, finding the point that Claire seemed to have lost. "Shouldn't that make you feel smart and confident that you stopped something before it got messy? Instead, you're angry because he took your brush-off seriously. What piece am I missing here?"

"Lexie!" Olivia admonished.

Claire looked at Lexie and then at Olivia and nodded. "She's right, Livie. I should be relieved and glad he walked out."

"And you're not."

"I like having coffee with him. I enjoyed his company. He reminds me of Dennis Roche, a neighbor in Lake Moses. He's a widower and with Jeff gone so much, it's lonely. Dennis and I have wine together once in a while." At Olivia's raised eyebrows she added, "It's nothing — two neighbors, that's all. Then, when Trent asked me for coffee, it seemed like the same type of thing. But then suddenly, going again tomorrow — I don't know, it just felt different — like I said before, more intimate. I was afraid if I said yes, I would have crossed some line."

Olivia said, "Your instincts kicked in and you followed. I'd say that's pretty smart."

"Then why am I so weepy and miserable?"

"Maybe you're the one who wanted more than being just coffee mates," Lexie said softly. "Maybe you're just lonely and horny and with Jeff off sailing the seven seas, and

173

Trent a few streets away . . . a little playtime with a sexy guy from your past . . . you wouldn't be the first woman who felt justified to wander a bit." Her words bounced around the room with a spring of truth. Olivia caught her breath and Claire covered her face with her hands.

Lexie slid her arms around Claire and hugged. "Come on, Claire. You're lonely and Trent was showering you with attention, it's no wonder you responded."

"I love Jeff. I do. I really do."

"Then you should be with him, not left alone to slug down wine with a local widower or eat breakfast with some guy from the past."

Claire pulled away, then knelt down to pick up the clothes strewn on the floor. "You're right, of course," she murmured, which sounded a tad too conciliatory to Olivia, but she let it lay. Then, after a bumpy silence, Claire said, "It doesn't matter about Trent anyway. According to Muriel, he won't have a problem finding another coffee mate."

You want him, don't you, Claire? You want more than morning coffee and conversation and now you're disappointed. Olivia didn't voice her conclusion, however. They'd ridden this hobbyhorse long enough. "You know what I think?" Olivia said. Claire looked as if she were steadying herself for a blistering lecture. "That we should put all men out of our minds and go through some of the boxes and then treat ourselves to a nice lunch down at the Dock."

Lexie nodded. "Sounds like a plan."

Claire's smile began small and then got bigger. "Lead the way."

"Helene is such a sweetie to let us in before the sale," Olivia remarked as they approached the back door of the Attic.

A few days had passed since their leisurely lunch at the Dock, where they stayed away from topics involving men, except for Olivia's confession about breaking up with Daniel. Given that no one at the table was high on men, Olivia figured it was a good time and would avoid any lengthy discussion. Claire and Lexie both liked Daniel, but to their credit, they'd never poured on advice in regards to anything more serious than whatever Olivia wanted.

Besides, with Daniel showing up and helping, all three women were very aware that his feelings for Olivia hadn't changed. As for Olivia's feelings, well, she wasn't going to linger on those. She had enough mental conflict with deciding whether to rent the house.

Now Helene, small and sweet with a distinctly French elegance, opened the squeaky wooden door, pulling it back against a stack of packing cartons. "*Bonjour!* Oh, please do come in and let me look at all of you."

Lexie, who'd been here just days ago, pushed Claire in first, which gave Olivia a chance to bask in the wonderful scent of old furniture and walls and cubbies seasoned with history and the ever-so-familiar stir of French perfume. It was so light as to seem almost indiscernible, much like the peek of lace on Helene's sleeves.

Unlike most women who wanted to appear younger, Helene seemed to relish embracing maturity; she was as vintage as her surroundings. She wore clothes from another era, her hair braided and pinned into a figure eight at the nape. Her hands, clean of polish or jewelry, fluttered as she touched Claire's cheeks and then took her hands, enfolding them. But it was Olivia who brought tears to her eyes.

"Ah, *chérie,* it has been so long since you've come to visit."

"I know."

"Sad memories for you here in Bishop, yes?"

"Some."

"And you are happy now? You found a man and a pretty shop to display all those treasures your mother collected? You always talked of having your own place someday. I remember well you sitting on that Victorian settee and telling me you were going off to a brand-new town and have a shop. I was in my late twenties with a baby and so much

176

responsibilities, I envied you your sixteen years."

"Seventeen, actually." Olivia lowered her head. "It seems like a hundred yesterdays ago."

"Oh, dear, I have made you sad."

"No, no. It's just that seeing you, being here — there's so many reminders." She didn't say that none of those young hopes and fanciful dreams had come true.

"Well, I've made *café*. We can drink and enjoy and then you can look for what you like."

The next half hour was relaxing with lots of catching up. Helene hoped to leave just after Labor Day, and revealed that an offer had been made on the shop, but the new owner was going to sell surfboards. "I am so upset at seeing the little shop being changed, but I do want to go home, and his offer has been generous. He's wanted the corner and plans a very modern building —"

"He's going to tear down the Attic?" Lexie asked, obviously stunned. "You only told me you'd sold the shop. I had no idea. . . . Oh, Helene, this is terrible."

"Did anyone else make an offer?" Olivia asked, her mind racing with thoughts and possibilities that sprang as if full grown into her conscious. They were wild, irrational, and probably stupid, but the thought of surfboards and vinyl in place of all the lovely character and memories of this old shop saddened her as much as the mirror that had been broken in her upstairs hall.

". . . not ones I could afford to take," Helene was saying. "As I said, his offer was very generous."

"What about other places? Maybe you should advertise in some of the trades," Claire said, thinking of all the auction and treasure tabloids she glanced through every month.

"It's too late. I've already signed a — what do you call it? Oh, yes, a purchase agreement."

"Helene, how generous was his offer?" Olivia asked.

Lexie's head popped up and Claire's eyes widened.

Helene, however, said, "Three hundred thousand."

"Holy sh— oh, sorry," Lexie apologized. "That's amazing, Helene. I had no idea real estate in Bishop was that expensive. Olivia, your house must be worth a half million."

Helene stood. "Oh, let's not talk about it anymore. It's so disturbing and I hate seeing this little place —" She stopped, her expression pained. "I'm glad I won't be here to see it torn down. Now, come. There are lots of things I know you all will want. Claire, I have some Depression glass that you will like."

And with that, they all rose and followed Helene into the main part of the store. While Lexie and Claire looked around and picked out pieces they wanted, Olivia wondered whether it was too late to reinvent herself.

Chapter Ten

Olivia pushed the key into the lock of her cottage in Parkboro and opened the back door. Over her shoulder were her duffel and her handbag, which she dropped on the counter; the duffel hit the floor. She opened the windows to air out the stuffiness.

She'd made a couple of quick trips home since she'd temporarily moved to Bishop three weeks ago, but this time returning wasn't to pick up the mail or send back those summer English essays she'd finished reading and grading, or to gather a few of her yard sale finds, specifically that green glass plate, to show to Lexie and Claire. No, this time was for a wedding that she'd promised three months ago to attend.

Ben, the groom, was a colleague, and Diana, the bride, owned a boutique that focused on imported soaps and candies that smelled wonderful and cost the moon.

When she'd sent in her acceptance the plan had been that she and Daniel would go together; she'd accepted for both of them. He hadn't mentioned it to her on his last trip to Bishop, so she assumed he'd probably forgotten. She had until the previous night.

She and Lexie and Claire had been looking through all the things they'd bought at Helene's, one of them being an early 1940s wedding album filled with black-and-white photos. Looking through the grainy pictures had the three women curious as to who would have such disregard for such a personal memento. Yet the more perplexing and sadder question was who would allow the album to be sold or included in an auction box lot? Helene said she'd learned that sad fact from the Brimfield dealer she'd purchased it from. All those thoughts had segued into wondering about the bride and groom and what had happened to them, their family, their children.

That conversation had triggered the reminder to Olivia of Ben and Diana's wedding. It would be rude to cancel at the last minute, plus she really wanted to be there to wish them well. So the next morning she'd tossed some things into her duffel and driven home. Lexie and Claire promised to keep Jimmie moving on his carpentry work, plus the painters were putting the final coat on the living room walls. Olivia planned to be back on Sunday.

Now she walked through the cottage feeling closed in and crowded after all the rooms in the Bishop house. Already she missed the long windows, the high ceilings, and the wide rooms, the hauntingly familiar scent of history permanently consummated in the house's footprint. Then there had been the relaxing pleasure she'd taken in her father's study, where she'd begun reading through old treasure-hunt articles he'd published in *Antique Monthly.*

The wonder was that she'd found a serenity in the Bishop house that had not only surprised her, but brought a deep, soothing sense of rightness. What did it all mean? She wasn't sure, wasn't even sure if she wanted to try and figure it out. What she did know was that a change of some dimension had taken place within her.

Funny, she thought now as she glanced around the cottage. This had been her home since she'd abandoned Bishop to come here to teach and live. And yet after the few weeks away, the cottage now felt strangely distant and sterile, like a temporary rental. *Just because you've been gone and preoccupied. That's all. Once you're back here and back to work all will be as it was.*

No doubt much of her pleasure in the Bishop house sprang directly from the time with Lexie and Claire. Once they returned to their homes, Olivia wondered if the house would revert to being a huge, expensive sieve on her wallet, a monstrosity where she'd once lived and cared for her parents.

Now she scooped up the mail on the floor inside the front door, flipped through the pile, tossing some and putting the bills into her bag to take back to Bishop with her.

In her bedroom she listened to messages, while she pushed off her shoes and wiggled out of jeans and pulled her tee over her head. The fourth one caught her attention.

"Olivia, this is Jeff. I've been trying to reach Claire, but with no luck. She told me she was getting together with you and Lexie, and since I can't get Lexie, either, I'm assuming you're all together somewhere. If you get this by Saturday, have Claire call me." He then left his number.

Claire had never let Jeff know she was going to Bishop? Apparently not. Olivia tried to think back and realized Claire had said little about Jeff except in the most general of terms. And there was that whole thing with Trent. A little payback by Claire? Perhaps.

Olivia relistened, took down the number with a California area code, and then called Claire.

Lexie answered and then went to get Claire.

"Olivia, what's wrong?" Claire asked, sounding a little breathless.

"I don't know. But Jeff called me looking for you."

"Oh? Did he say what he wanted?"

"No."

"Did he sound upset?"

"Short and irritated."

"Really. He leaves me for weeks on end and rarely calls, but I'm supposed to be at his beck and call and now he's irritated that I'm not."

"Claire, didn't you tell him where you were going?"

"Yes, I told him, but as usual he pays little attention. He was too busy complaining about jet lag, bad food, a botched-up deal that cost the company a few million and some idiot with a carry-on filled with firecrackers on his LAX flight." She paused. "Now he has time to realize I'm not home and expects me to reassure him and call back. Damn him anyway. I'll call him when I get good and ready."

Olivia sighed. This wasn't her fight, and Claire's fury over being neglected and then to have Jeff be the one who was irritated . . . Well, Olivia didn't blame Claire. No wonder the attentive Trent held so much appeal. Since she didn't know what to say, she said nothing.

"Olivia?"

"Yes?"

"Thanks for not giving me a pep talk or a tedious lecture."

"I'm the last one to be giving lectures on men. See you Sunday."

They hung up and then, standing in white

cotton panties and a lace bra, Olivia sorted through her closet looking for the navy blue dress with the white trim. She found that in a dry cleaner's bag, pulled her white slides from a shoe holder, and put the items aside. Then she opened a hatbox and took out a wide-brimmed white hat trimmed in navy with a thin red stripe. She pulled out clean underwear and began to sort through her jewelry.

The box with the ring that Daniel gave her lay where she'd tucked it, and with its presence came a pouring of memories and feelings that she'd tried to keep restrained and in perspective. She was very fond of Daniel, and he certainly hadn't been an embittered ex-boyfriend, which made her warm and fuzzy reaction to the ring a dilemma.

Now she opened the box, hesitated, and then slipped the ring on her finger. It fit perfectly and she loved the way the ruby stones caught the light. It would indeed make a unique and special engagement ring. If she'd wanted to be engaged. *Oh, Daniel, why couldn't we have left things as they were? Why did you have to push me?*

"Olivia?"

She jumped, swinging around, knocking the ring box onto the floor. How bizarre. Here she was thinking about him and he appears. She wasn't at all sure what to make of that.

She knelt down, feeling for the box, but to

185

her consternation the item had scooted way under the dresser.

"Hey, where are you?"

"In here." Then realizing she was nearly naked, she dashed for her discarded clothes, snatching them up, calling out, "I'll be right there."

But when she looked up, it was too late. He was already standing in the doorway, his gaze skipping and touching and coming back to her face. He wasn't in the room, but he so filled her vision, he might as well have been a mere foot away.

"Now, this is an unexpected surprise," he said softly. The *this* she knew absolutely was her state of undress.

She drew in a breath, eyes wide, cheeks flushed, holding her clothes tight against her as if she'd been caught doing a strip in front of the mirror. This was ridiculous. It wasn't as if Daniel had never seen her in her underwear. Obviously he assumed she'd be embarrassed. Well, she wasn't going to give him the satisfaction.

She dropped the clothes and then kicked them aside. This was her house and if she wanted to parade around in a bra and panties, who was he . . . ? "Stop looking at me with that 'I like what I see' look."

"I like what I see." All amusement and patience and tease. Typical Daniel.

"How did you know I was here?" she demanded, then moved to the other side of the room, trying to add some distance although she had no idea why. He wasn't boring down on her; in fact, he hadn't moved even an inch. Nervous, that's what she was, but the why annoyed her more than the reaction.

"Your car was a bit of a giveaway," he said sagely. He wore jeans and a Red Sox T-shirt and his hair had been freshly trimmed. "I was driving by to make sure the house was okay."

Why don't you stop looking at him like you want him?

"You were?" Had she asked him to check on the cottage? No, she had not.

"Vacant houses invite vandalism," he offered.

She started to say something and then closed her mouth. That would be a dumb — chiding him for wanting to prevent here what had happened to the other house. Why did he always seem to be two steps ahead of her?

Nonetheless, his timing seemed all too co-incidental. "I don't believe you, Daniel Cafferty, and even if it's true, you had no right to use my key to just walk in here like, like —"

"A lover who's missed you?"

Some inner voice whispered: *Really?* He'd said it as if it were present and not the past. A deliberate point, she guessed. She narrowed her eyes, ignoring the flutter of delight

187

that did a feathery sweep around her heart. "Don't try to flatter me."

"Not flattery, all true. But I should have knocked and been a gentleman."

This was too easy and he was too agreeable. "So how did you know to come here?"

"Not gonna buy that I was guarding your house, huh?"

"Nice try."

"Guess I'll have to fess up."

"There's a thought." She was feeling better, calmer, more on top of his unexpected visit. He was quiet for a few moments, and Olivia decided he was trying to get whatever his excuse was into reasonable believability.

Then . . . "I called Bishop to see if you were coming for the wedding. Lexie told me you were on your way and mentioned what time you left. Now, being fairly proficient in math, I figured you'd be here in the area of eleven." He glanced at his watch. "Not bad — it's eleven-twenty and here you are. As for me, I merely waited until a little past eleven, drove by, and like magic your car was in the drive. Amazing how it all worked out."

Olivia stared at him. It sounded simple because it was. He hadn't forgotten about the wedding, and calling her in Bishop would be perfectly natural. . . .

"Sounds like the planning process of a stalker," she said, sounding churlish, over the top, and not even caring.

"Yeah, it does, doesn't it," he mused cheerfully. "By the way, I did try your cell."

"I didn't —"

"— have it on, yes, I know, Olivia. You never do."

Feeling more than a little mentally bruised because he was, always was, amused when she was serious and far too accommodating when she wanted him to rant like other men she knew. He never got insulted or offended, and he was always too agreeable.

She turned toward the bathroom. "The wedding is at one. You better go home and change. I'll get ready and we can meet back here at twelve-thirty."

"Twelve forty-five."

"Whatever. What are you doing?"

But she knew what he was doing. And so did he. He came toward her, his steps slow, measured, and unhesitant.

Olivia wanted to back away, move sideways, flee to the bathroom and close the door, but her feet melded to the floor like they'd been dipped in warm wax. She knew where this was going, and even more unsettling was that she *wanted* where it was going. Her tummy turned and dropped, her mouth tasting of the sweet moisture of desire.

By the time he put his arms around her and slid his palms down her back to slip under the lace of her panties, she was kissing him and locked against him like a garden of wilted flowers plunged into a new spring of water.

He tumbled her onto the bed, hands seeking, mouths searching, bodies joining. Clothes were disposed of quickly and with messy efficiency. Olivia wrapped her legs around him, pulling him closer, deeper, wanting to marry their bodies with an energy she'd willed herself not to think about these weeks they'd been apart.

"Daniel, this is so crazy . . ." But when he slipped inside her, all thoughts spun away and in a profound and dazzling moment, her climax tore through her with such depth that later she would wonder if he truly had the gift of wizardry when it came to satisfying her.

"Sweet, sweet," he murmured, his sigh spiraling up and then stretching out and rising and falling as they both descended down into a puddle of satisfied silence.

And in the streams of late-morning light, they lay quiet, their breathing slowing and their heartbeats returning to normal.

"I'm glad you came," she whispered.

He chuckled. "In more ways than one. I love you."

"I know you do." She cuddled in closer. "There's something a little wicked about this."

"I figured it was better done here than having to ravish you at the wedding."

She kissed him, refusing to think about

complications or what would happen next. "Oh, darn, here I was hoping for a ravishment in the cloak room."

He dropped a kiss on each breast and then slid off of her.

She reached to pull him back. "Don't go."

He grinned. "That good, huh?"

"You know you're good."

"We're good." He leaned down and kissed her deeply. "I'll be back in half an hour."

"You should have brought your clothes," she groused.

"I didn't want to push my luck."

She watched him pull on his clothes, then leave the room while she listened for the back door to close. She lay sprawled, panties on the floor, bra tossed to the nightstand, body warm and pleased, basking in the soft breeze coming in the window. She sighed in contentment. She'd missed him. She'd really, really missed him.

And with that thought came the recognition that at least for today, he was back in her life, filling her heart, and she intended to enjoy it.

The garden wedding was held at a local country club and could have been a layout for *Bride's* magazine. Bows and trellises of flowers, huge bowls of white and red roses intermingled with a buffet that would have fed most of Parkboro. There had been dancing and the traditional throwing of the bride's bouquet, which Olivia avoided by wooing Daniel off to an ivy arbor for a long, deep kiss.

"This is nice," he murmured, nuzzling her neck.

"What? The arbor, the kiss, or me?" She giggled, knowing full well she'd had too much champagne.

"The arbor," he deadpanned, and then winced when she pinched his rear end.

"I'll have you know, Daniel Cafferty, I don't just kiss anybody."

"Gratitude overwhelms me."

"If you want more than kisses, you better flatter, cajole, and say sweet wonderful things to me."

"For more than a kiss, I'll extol all your virtues and remind you that you're gorgeous and sexy and always clear my mind of anything but you."

"Okay," she said, giggling. "Where?"

"Lead the way, sweetheart. I'm your humble servant."

"This is only for today," she said sternly, taking his hand and walking across the wide lawn that embroidered the country club.

"Couldn't be better if I planned it."

"I have a feeling you did."

They were headed toward the massive parking lot of cars. Daniel had parked near a grove of trees so that they wouldn't have to get into an oven when they were ready to leave. His foresight had paid off, for the interior was merely stuffy.

"You're going to ravish me," he said, opening the windows while she her fingers worked at his belt buckle.

Olivia grinned. "Of course."

"May the day never end."

And their mouths met in a long and hungry kiss.

Later that night they were once again locked in each other's arms and leaning against Olivia's back door. "I want you to stay," she whispered, her mouth and her thoughts and her body so full of him that the idea of going to bed alone made her feel bereft and cold just thinking about it.

"I think we're making up for lost time," he said as he slipped her key into the lock.

"I'm going back to Bishop in the morning," she murmured, working at opening the buttons on his shirt.

"Maybe. Maybe not."

Somehow the back door was relocked, and they stumbled their way to the bedroom, their desire so intense, their bodies so parched, Olivia would never have guessed they'd already made love three times, not counting that first time in her bedroom.

And this time was no less startling and dazzling, and as she curled up in his arms, she wished she could just release that demon inside her that didn't want marriage, didn't want the responsibility, the lifetime commitment. And while these hours with Daniel were as perfect as any woman would want, the fear remained vigilant.

One thing she had noted through all the haze of kisses and satisfaction, he hadn't mentioned marriage once nor had he noticed that she'd worn the ring he gave her.

Then she remembered that Daniel always noticed everything. Just because he'd been silent didn't mean he was clueless. She smiled as she stretched and entwined their hands, her ring snuggled against his fingers. Tomorrow she'd deal with her conflicts and anxieties; once he was gone she'd be more practical and less emotional.

Lexie knew how to dress for success. She knew to be businesslike, to ooze comfortability that meant confidence, but not arrogance. She knew about poise and showing an innate curiosity about the job she wanted; she could quote the standards of office etiquette. She knew it all and more. So why did she feel like a college graduate on her first major job interview?

She sat in the outer office of WBIS ten minutes early for an appointment with Bill Riggs, the station manager. He wasn't the one who did the hiring, but he signed off on any new employees. Lexie had a leg up, she believed, because her aunt Marion knew Bill Riggs and his wife; he lived a few doors away. Their relationship had been neighborly, friendly — house watching, a borrowed item here and there, sharing an overabundance of summer vegetables, plus her aunt sending over food and condolences when Bill Riggs's brother, a local fireman, had died in a fire.

A few times when Lexie had been in high school, she'd baby-sat for the Riggs kids. There'd been a close community harmony that made neighborhoods work and flourish like a huge extended family.

Lexie had no problems using connections; she knew that in the communications business, who she knew would get her a lot further than a flawless résumé. Her work, in the end, spoke for itself, but giving it a nudge in the direction she wanted to go seemed more than prudent.

"Lexie, it's been a long time." Bill Riggs, fit and lean and strikingly handsome, had a full head of dark brown hair streaked gray and enough creases around his eyes to indicate he spent a lot of time in the sun. He came forward, offering his hand when Lexie rose to her feet.

"Mr. Riggs —"

"I think we can make it Bill. You're not the teenager who used to baby-sit for the kids anymore."

"I wasn't sure you would remember that."

"Not remember Lexie James who went off to the big city and made a name for herself? Not likely. You seemed to know what you wanted and went after it. I've always admired that kind of determination."

His praise overwhelmed her. It had been so long since anyone credited her with any business savvy; she sopped up the unexpected gusher of confidence.

He held the door, ushering her into an office that was plush and comfortable, but with a working desk and computer setup that very solidly indicated he did more than think about his days off. On the walls were sailing prints, and filling one corner was an intricate sailboat replica sized to fit a wide backlit shelf. Now she knew where he got those face creases.

"Sit down. My assistant is away from her desk for some errands, so what can I get you? Iced coffee, iced tea?"

"Iced coffee would be wonderful."

He nodded. "My passion, too." He made them at a buffet with a small refrigerator beneath. He handed her a tall glass and a napkin, and then, with his glass in hand he sat down in a chair opposite her. Not behind the desk, she noted. Maybe he thought this was a social call.

"So what brings you in to see me? Is my ex hounding your aunt again?"

"Excuse me?"

"My ex-wife, Julia. You remember her, don't you?"

Lexie recalled a tall pinched-faced woman who wore a perpetual scowl of reproach whenever anyone appeared to be having any fun. The contrast to her husband, even in Lexie's foggy memory — it was over twenty years ago — had been startling. Obviously Bill Riggs got tired of living with a sourpuss. Hunting through her own experience with Mrs. Riggs, Lexie said, "I do remember she made the best Christmas cookies."

He smiled, one eyebrow raising. "I'm glad you had at least one good memory, or you're being very kind." He paused, leaning forward, his face growing tense. "After we separated, Julia was calling your aunt with questions about me and who I was dating. Ammunition for the divorce, no doubt. She was living in Westerly and I stayed here in Bishop. She got nothing on me because there was nothing to get — at least nothing that she could find." He winked, a smile matching the twinkle in his eyes. "My attorney spoke with her attorney and she stopped. Then there were a few more calls after the divorce. I confronted her, saying I'd have her back in court on harassing my neighbors. I thought it was all straightened out." He leaned back, watching her, the scowl coming slowly. "Uh-oh, by the stunned look on your face, my ex isn't the reason you're here."

"No. I'm sorry. I didn't know you were divorced."

"Your aunt didn't tell you?"

The statement seemed so typical of the smallness of Bishop, where everyone assumed their history, foibles, mistakes, and accomplishments were served up to every visitor with relish at the morning breakfast tables.

"Actually," Lexie said, "I'm not all caught up on the local news. Plus I'm staying with friends. Aunt Marion doesn't know I'm here to see you. She's been busy planning her annual trip up to Maine. She leaves tomorrow."

"And you would prefer she not know you're here?" He looked a little puzzled, and she had to admit even to her that seemed a little weird.

"It's just that she worries about me and already she's feeling guilty for leaving while I'm in Bishop."

"I think I'm confused. I don't understand why your coming here to see me would worry her."

Lexie took a deep breath. "I didn't mean to sound so clandestine."

He looked a little dazed, and she wanted to kick herself for getting into this verbal quagmire. "Let me explain."

"Please." He gestured with his hand that he was listening.

Here goes. Don't look desperate. Don't act

nervous. Make it clear and simple and don't blink.

"Actually, I'm planning on moving back into the area, and I'm very interested in working at WBIS."

"Interesting. Tell me more."

She went on to detail her years at WCG-TV in Chicago, the stories she'd covered as a beat reporter and as an investigative one. She knew she sounded like a self-appointed cheerleader, but she was proud of her qualifications and believed she could bring a new perspective to WBIS. She finished her spiel with "I received the Bulldog Award two years ago."

"That's the one for dogged in-depth reporting."

"Yes. It's a national award that usually goes to the big-city affiliates."

"Pretty stiff competition, I'd say. Quite an honor."

"It was. I'm only the second female to ever get it."

He nodded, and she continued, "I love doing investigating reporting, but I'm more than willing to cover school committee meetings, too."

"That's quite a range. Why the move from the Chicago market?"

She needed to just tell him and quit circling around it. "To be upfront and straight with you, I was let go when the station was sold and new management brought in."

He sipped his iced coffee, then set the glass down on the napkin. Lexie's hands were hot despite the cold glass.

"I'm surprised that one of the other affiliates didn't pick you up."

She'd been not just surprised, but angry and embarrassed, especially when a protégé of hers had been hired within hours after her layoff. Bill Riggs's comment was shrewd, and Lexie quickly recast it into what he really wanted to know.

Why didn't anyone want her?

Why hadn't she been snapped up by another station?

Why, after all these months, was the Bulldog winner still unemployed?

All were expected questions, but instead of firing them at her, he'd couched his question in a general curiosity.

The easy side of her appreciated his politeness, but the hard-nosed reporter side knew truth worked better when it was all laid out early and complete.

And so she told of her involvement in a local protest for better housing, and then in an AIDS protest that got out of hand with bottles being thrown at the police and her picture on the front pages of the *Tribune* and the *Sun-Times* trying to evade the cuffs a cop was trying to put on her. WCG INVESTIGATIVE REPORTER ARRESTED. It had *not* been one of her shining-star moments.

He listened, but without any reflection in his expression that she could detect. She'd probably blown it, but at the same time she couldn't lie and she wouldn't evade a direct question.

Then, without even referring back to her confession, he focused on her being let go. "It happens when new blood comes in. New management, new ideas, a fresh direction. We've done it here a few times. However, we're not doing any hiring of the caliber of your résumé."

"A résumé doesn't feed me or pay the rent. I want a job, Mr. Riggs." She couldn't call him Bill, not when this was about hiring her. This was business, not personal. "I work hard, and as I said, I'll do committee meetings."

She waited, staying quiet, hoping he would give her just a pinch of hope that he would hire her.

"Let me check into some things, Lexie. I'll let you know in the next few days."

Lexie nodded slowly and got to her feet. "Then I guess that's that."

He opened the office door for her. "Say hello to your aunt for me."

And that was *definitely* that. No reaffirmation that he would call, that he'd grease all the bureaucratic hiring gears for a former Bulldog Award winner.

Outside, it had begun to rain. Depressing weather, depressing day. She'd promised Aunt Marion she'd stop and say good-bye, and after that . . .

She knew if she went back to the house, Olivia and Claire would be there, and right now she was in no mood to see anyone she cared about.

She was in the mood to feel sorry for herself, and she intended to do just that.

Chapter Eleven

When Claire was lonely or bored or angry or sad, she cooked. As a result, when the family found a bulging refrigerator and a full complement of desserts, the first question was "What's wrong?"

Tonight, as she sprinkled chocolate chips over the chocolate brownies, she decided she was all of the above. Lonely for Lexie, who'd been gone all day, and Olivia, who was still up in Parkboro. Claire was also bored with her life, angry with Jeff, and sad about the state of dissolution she found herself in. She slid the brownies back in the oven just long enough for the chips to get glassy and soft, then she pulled them out and, using a knife, smoothed out the chocolate so that it formed a thin glaze.

Setting the pan aside to cool, she began filling the dishwasher with bowls and utensils. Then she wiped the counter down, tied up a bag of trash, took it outside to the garbage, then swiped the beads of sweat from her face and neck.

"No wonder I'm hot," she muttered, noting that the earlier rain had not lowered the still over eighty degrees temperature though the sun had long since set. "What'd you expect — it's August and what sane person runs an oven on a hot night?"

No answer was forthcoming, and the silence of the house reminded her too much of the all-alone nights she spent in Lake Moses. Lexie had gone somewhere around midafternoon, offering only a vague "got an appointment" for an explanation. Something was going on with her, and although both Olivia and Claire had tried to pry loose whatever problem their friend was concealing, they'd had no luck.

With Olivia, her absence wasn't so mysterious; she'd stayed longer in Parkboro than she'd originally planned, and Claire was delighted. Then, as if her thoughts about Olivia had made it to her friend, she called.

"Now, don't tell me Daniel doesn't have something to do with this," Claire said, amusement lacing her words.

"Daniel isn't even here."

"Don't split hairs, Livie. You know what I mean."

"It's ridiculous and I'm going to be sorry and I know it."

"You love him and you want to be with him. What's to be sorry about?"

"I don't think I can make it work, Claire."

"Sweetie, you don't have to make it work all by yourself."

"I just get claustrophobic whenever I think about — oh, never mind, it all sounds so silly and selfish and stupid. If Daniel were only a worthless jerk —"

"Then you'd be here sorting linen with me."

"I'm sorry, I did promise you —"

"At least you have an excuse. Lexie took off and I thought she was coming back, but no sign of her."

"Where'd she go?"

"Just said she had an appointment in town. Clearly she didn't want me to ask questions."

"I wonder what's going on. She's not been quite herself, has she?"

"I love her dearly, but sometimes I want to shake her. She's got a big-paying job, a guy who's crazy about her, and no responsibilities but to herself. I just want to tell her to wake up."

"Obviously, I've been too involved in the house," Olivia said, realizing in these past few days with Daniel, she'd wasted little worry for her friends or the Bishop house.

"We're here because of your house, Livie. That was the whole point, so don't go making excuses for Lexie. Let's not talk about it. It will probably all work out. Maybe I'm just feeling melancholy. By the way, the sage green paint in the living room looks per-

205

fect. Really makes the white woodwork pop."

"That's a relief. Oh, by the way, have you called Jeff?"

"No."

"Oh, Claire."

"You know what? I'm weary of being expected to just respond whenever he wants something."

"It could be important," Olivia ventured, noting a fierce obstinacy in Claire.

"Important to Jeff, as in why isn't Claire where she should be?" Claire snipped. "He could find me if he really wanted to. Lara knows where I am, and in fact, I talked to her a few days after I got here. She has the number here."

Olivia sighed. "Okay, I see your point."

It had been the perfect and nonarguable point. And every hour that went by without hearing from him just irked her even more.

So much for urgency and importance, she thought now as she glanced at the clock. It was close to eight-thirty, and she suspected Livie would be arriving in a few hours.

Claire was convinced that Livie loved and wanted to be with Daniel — if she could just get past her fear of being trapped. Funny, Claire thought. She was in the exact opposite situation. She wanted to be secure and folded into her marriage and couldn't find a way to convince her husband that she was tired of being left behind and ignored.

Leaving the stuffy kitchen, she took a bottle of wine from the refrigerator, grabbed a glass, and walked outside to the patio. Dusk grew deeper and the evening air finally was marginally cooler, although the wind was but an occasional whisper. Claire poured a glass of wine, kicked her sandals off, and leaned back in the chaise and closed her eyes.

Like at nighttime when she climbed into bed and tried to sleep, Jeff filled her mind. The Jeff that she loved and married, the Jeff of long walks, building a rope swing for Lara, and coaching Tony's Little League team . . . The Jeff of five years ago who turned down a last-minute trip to the West Coast that would have kept him from his family at Christmas, the Jeff who once viewed his career as a means to provide, not the reason for living.

And this last turn had spilled into every sphere of their marriage, of their family. The frank fact was that Jeff was rarely home, and when he was, he was planning his next trip. Trying to slow him down got her a fierce look and mumbles about the importance of a retirement-rich 401K, the lure of extra bonus cash for new software development, or some other excuse that meant more travel and more absences and more money.

She'd never had a problem with nagging if she felt it served a good purpose. Although she thought of herself as more of a pesterer than a nagger. Perhaps it was a matter of the end justifying the means, but when it came to her family, she wasn't about to be strangled by complaints over methods. And with Jeff, she was trying desperately to pull him back to the closeness they once had.

But her methods, no matter how well intentioned, had the unintended consequences of driving him farther and farther away, and so a few months ago, Claire had stopped pestering and cajoling and pleading.

He had his life and she had hers, and sometimes hers included her friendship with neighbor Dennis Roche. No cheating or betrayal unless that one brief kiss could be called immoral. A light brush-the-lips kiss, nothing deep and hot and trembly. And compared to what some women in Lake Moses were doing, Dennis's kiss was almost chaste.

Call her needy, call her petulant, call her silly, but Claire liked to be appreciated. She liked being praised, and she liked Dennis telling her, "Having wine with you in the evening is the perfect coda for the end of the day."

Perfect coda, she thought now, thinking that no one but a music teacher like Dennis could have carried off such an expression so naturally.

She sat up, thoughts of Jeff returning the frown lines to that narrow place between her eyes. What was it she'd advised Olivia about her fear of marriage — it wasn't just up to her to make it work, it was up to Daniel, too?

And therein lay the frightening reality of her own marriage. She and seemingly Jeff simply didn't care if it worked or not.

That was magnified in Jeff's shallow attempt to get in touch with her and her dismissal of that attempt. The Claire of last summer would have returned his call immediately, all apologetic that he'd been worried.

But the Claire of the last year had slowly and regretfully eased away from making Jeff's world work and strived more diligently on making her own life satisfactory and full. She poured some more wine, leaned back once more, and closed her eyes.

She must have drifted off to sleep, for when she opened her eyes at the sound of a vehicle in the driveway, it was very dark. She stirred, deciding it was Olivia or Lexie, and closed her eyes again. Then came the footsteps on the back walk. Too heavy to be either of her friends.

She turned, some unease bubbling when she saw a male figure emerging out of the light of the back doorway to the dimmer area of the yard. Now she got to her feet, her wineglass forgotten beside the chaise. Then she saw who it was and braced her hand against her heart.

"Trent." Relief poured through her.

He drew closer, filling her vision. "You look lovelier than I remember," he whispered.

The softness and sweetness of his words sounded so natural, she was briefly speechless. "I thought it was Olivia."

"Then you're all alone," he said, as if relieved and pleased. "I saw Lexie at Ricky's — 'bout five guys all pushing to buy her drinks, so I expect she'll be busy for a while."

"I guess she will." Since he was in his uniform, he was obviously working. "What are you doing here?"

"I'm on a break." He held out a flat white box with a yellow ribbon around it. "This is for you."

"I don't understand."

"You will. Go ahead and open it."

She took the box, pulled the ribbon, and lifted the lid to find, nestled in white tissue, a light blue knit top with tiny roses embroidered around the scoop neckline.

"Since it was my fault you got coffee on the other one —"

"How sweet of you, but the slopped coffee wasn't your fault."

"Don't tell me you can't take it. Please. It's the least I can do after the way I walked out as if you didn't matter to me."

He was sorry? She mattered to him? She smiled and it was broad and genuine. "All right. Thank you. It's very pretty."

Then the silence fell between them. He'd folded his arms, and she couldn't help but notice how authoritative he looked in his uniform, but at the same time there was a touch of ill-at-ease standing here in the dark with her, talking about their last meeting at Muriel's.

"I wasn't sure on the size. It's a small, but the lady said you could exchange it."

Claire grinned. "Very smart, Trent. Small is always a safe size."

"Yeah, I found that out when I bought a dress for Tanya one Christmas. She burst into tears when she saw it was a bigger size than she wore. She asked me if I thought she was fat. I didn't, honest, but I figured out that when it comes to sizes women get very sensitive, so ever since then, I always buy small."

Claire laughed. "I applaud your sensitivity."

"Well, it was more not getting my head bitten off."

"That works, too." The raised lettering on the box read Tenley's; they were known for their boxes, which were as elegant as their contents. It was also the most expensive women's store in three counties. He couldn't afford such extravagance, and she was touched that he'd wanted to show her that he could.

"Would you like some wine? Or beer?

Lexie's a beer drinker. Oh, sorry. You're on duty. Iced coffee?"

"I have to go."

"Oh," she said, feeling a stab of disappointment. "Thank you for stopping by and for the pretty top."

He nodded, then added, "I'd like to take you out to dinner, Claire."

"Oh."

"Tomorrow?"

This was all moving too fast.

"I don't know if that's a good idea," she said, grimacing at her fraidy-cat answer. Curiosity and flirtatious danger had just blended into an emotion she didn't recognize.

"It's just dinner. Please?"

For heaven's sake, she was almost forty years old. She'd known Trent for years. If she couldn't handle a dinner with an old friend — flirty or not — she was in serious need of a social upgrade. "Yes," she said softly.

He smiled and she saw it as genuine relief. "I'll pick you up at seven tomorrow."

She managed a nod, feeling as if the only thing keeping her on her feet was the gossamer softness of his words.

And then he was gone, the cruiser starting up, headlights throwing light across her eyes, backing out of the drive, and speeding away.

She let out the breath she'd been holding.

Oh, boy.

★ ★ ★

It was near midnight when Olivia returned to Bishop. In the kitchen an under-the-counter fluorescent had been left on. A plate of brownies had been covered with plastic wrap with one of Claire's precise and detailed notes propped against it: *Got too sleepy to wait up. Lexie, don't eat all the brownies if you come in first, and Livie, forgot to mention it when we talked, but Peter called with yet another family who is very anxious to look at the house. He wants to know when you're going to let him show it. I told him you'd call in the morning. Sweet dreams, Claire.*

Since the brownies were untouched, Lexie hadn't come home. Olivia set her bags down by the front stairs, flipped on some lights, then returned to the kitchen where she took two brownies, tore off a paper towel, and poured herself a glass of milk.

Carrying her food, Olivia walked into the main part of the house and went to the living room eager to see the new paint. Definitely a "wow" reaction widened her eyes and made her grin. It was perfect, exactly what she'd wanted; the smoky sage green simmered with dramatic intensity.

She'd discovered the color quite by accident when she was tearing off the vandalized wallpaper. The room had been painted a cream beneath the paper, but Olivia found a strip beneath one of the windows where the cream hadn't covered a previous color.

Carefully, using a small putty knife, she worked under the plaster to get that swath of green off the wall. At the paint store she asked them to match it. They'd used a computer color matching that was so exact, Olivia almost believed she'd discovered three cans of the original paint.

She walked the parameter eyeing the walls from all angles; the night shadows, she knew, gave a false drama, but that made the room even more interesting.

The storage unit held much of the furniture from the house, and she was itching to move it back. And then there was that Victorian sofa at Helene's that she'd recklessly bought with her fingers crossed that the greens in the tapestry covering wouldn't scream with the walls.

"If it's wrong, *chérie,* I will give you your money back."

"You certainly will not, Helene. You're not going to get anything out of your sale if you keep offering such deals."

"But what will you do if the color is wrong?"

"It won't be," she said, sounding more sure than she felt. "Don't worry. If it is, I'll put the piece in another room. I have a big house."

Helene clapped her hands together like a delighted child. "Oh, you sound like your father. He would tell me that if you love it, you'd better buy it. And if it didn't go in one place, then there was another place it would fit even if you had no idea where. He was like that, saying that anything kept was kept for love and that loved items always had a place."

Olivia had listened, too aware of the nudge in her heart. The feeling that she'd abandoned her father's house, that gripped her right after the vandalism, returned with a vengeance. *Anything kept was kept for love.* Perhaps love, the simplest of all reasons, was why she'd held on even after she'd walked away.

She gave the surprised Helene a hug and promised she'd have someone pick up the couch in the next few days.

Now, with the painting finished in the living room, she would see Helene tomorrow and make arrangements. Maybe she could get Daniel to drive down and get the sofa for her. . . .

Thinking now about the house, and Claire's note about the realtor, Olivia felt a definite tug of conflict.

Well, actually, the tug had been tiptoeing around her thoughts since she'd returned to Bishop, but she'd chalked it up to old-fashioned nostalgia that was based more on what might have been than on what really was.

The truth, however disconcerting and disturbing, was that for most of the last years she'd lived in this house, she'd felt trapped. Being honest wasn't necessarily pretty nor consoling, but denial of her deeper feelings had been too much in evidence for too many years. She'd felt stifled in Bishop, and moving away had been smart, progressive, and freeing. She'd returned for an interlude event, and she would soon go back to her regular life. The house would have a new family, and that would be that.

And yet.

She sat down on the third stair, picked up the glass of milk, and washed down the brownie. She could hear the house in the deepening night. The settling down to sleep, the fading smells of the day making way for old scents of time and history.

She rose and again walked around the room, hugging herself. She loved it and she couldn't wait to add window treatments and furnishings and loving attention.

"With the living room done, you should be about finished, huh?" Daniel had asked her earlier that day when she told him that Claire raved about the paint.

"The work wasn't as long or as bad as I thought it would be," she'd told him.

"So you're going to put it back up for rent?"

"I'm thinking about moving in permanently."

It was the first time she'd put that thought into words, the first time the idea gelled with clarity.

"Commuting to Parkboro? That's crazy." He slid his hands in his pockets and leaned back against the kitchen counter. His hair was still damp from his shower. They'd made love, bittersweet in that there remained questions that weren't answered and answers that weren't expressed. Olivia didn't want to talk about any future between them, and Daniel had acted as if he'd never even considered the idea.

"Commuting *is* crazy and I have no intention of doing it."

He'd stared at her. "You're going to quit your job."

"I'm giving it some thought." She braced for an argument, a long list of reasons on why that was foolish or reckless, even a question like, "What are you going to do for money?"

"Then do it."

She blinked, getting ready to argue. "You don't think it's a dumb idea?"

"It's your house in the town you grew up in, and even I could see how being there suited you. You obviously have strong ties and great affection for it."

The sweetness of his affirmation of a decision she hadn't really been sure she'd make overwhelmed her.

Then he added, "Let me know when you want to haul stuff; we can probably get most of it in my truck. What we can't, I'll get one of the kids with a truck to help."

Thinking back now about Daniel not once pushing her and about the house and about moving back here, she decided life couldn't get much better.

Chapter Twelve

The three women had gathered at the kitchen. Early morning showers had left a sheet of dampness on the lawn and droplets on the garden flowers.

Olivia, in shorts and a lightweight sweatshirt with sleeves pushed to her elbows, was eating yogurt and a bowl of fresh peaches. Claire, impeccable as usual, wore white belted jeans and the blue top Trent had given her. Silver hoops dangled from her ears. She sipped from a mug of coffee and munched on one of the chocolate-frosted brownies she'd baked the previous night.

Lexie, well, Lexie looked as if she'd been rode hard and hung up wet. A description she'd applied to herself just moments before. Holey sweats, wrinkled sleep shirt with Mickey Mouse on the front, snarled hair, well beyond her usual tossled tangle, pale skin and half-shuddered eyes. There was a long scratch on her arm.

"Lexie?" Olivia said her name gently, trying to ignore Claire's obvious annoyance with their friend. Based, Olivia knew, on Lexie pulling away from the both of them. Friends confide in friends, Claire had said more than a few times. Of course, the fact that Claire hadn't been forthcoming when it came to Trent tended to undercut her irritation with Lexie. Olivia took that into account, once again finding herself taking a middle ground.

Lexie covered her ears amidst a jumbled mumble of words that sounded like "leave me alone."

"Not a chance, kiddo. Tell us what happened and where you got the scratch." Olivia put down her unfinished yogurt and focused on Lexie. "Come on, this is more than just a bad hangover."

"I should have stayed in bed," she grumbled, shuddering when Claire cheerfully offered her the plate of brownies that under normal circumstances she would have reached for immediately. Lexie had always had a weakness for sugary breakfasts.

"Did something happen with one or all of those guys who were buying you drinks in Ricky's?" Claire asked, startling Olivia. She hadn't heard this and how did Claire know?

Lexie's head came up, her eyes questioning.

"Trent told me," Claire said, brushing crumbs from the table and into the trash. "He saw you there."

"And just where did you see the informative Trent?" Lexie had straightened and tensed up. "Another secret meeting?"

"It was not a secret, and so that later I won't be accused of 'sneaking' out, we're having dinner tonight." Claire drew her defense line, eyes narrowing as if daring Lexie to offer advice when her own choice of companions hardly came from a monastery.

Olivia started to intervene, then didn't. Nothing like some air-clearing to shake out some true feelings.

Lexie rolled her eyes. "A dinner date? How very quaint."

"It's not a date."

"Oh, sorry, that's right, you and Wonder Cop are just old friends — breakfast companions. How silly of me to forget." Lexie's ability to command the offensive when by all rights she should be the one explaining hadn't been affected by either her hangover or whatever was bothering her. She lived by the rule of Don't carry a knife to a gunfight. And while the image was a bit over-the-top for an argument between friends, the principle remained.

The color drained from Claire's face. "You don't have to denigrate him."

Obviously realizing she'd stepped from prickly into a brier patch, Lexie softened, "He doesn't deserve you, Claire. And knowing that you're headed for some big-time hurt makes me want to shake you for being so gullible."

"I can take care of myself," she blurted out, arms rigid at her sides, hands clenching into fists. And in that moment Olivia saw just how vulnerable Claire was. And how dug in she was with defending her relationship with Trent no matter how questionable it might be.

"Come on, you two. Let's slow this down. We're friends here."

Lexie finally muttered, "Friends tell friends the truth even when it burns."

"Excuse me," Claire snapped, turning her back to walk out of the kitchen.

"Claire, wait," Olivia called.

"For what? More demeaning of me and my choices? I've had enough. Trent has done nothing but be kind and attentive, and she's treating him like he was some hustler."

"Bingo," Lexie mumbled.

"Lexie, knock it off." Olivia then grabbed Claire's arm. "And you're not going to leave."

"I'm not listening to any more trashing of Trent." She pulled free, her cheeks flushed, anger clear and present. "I'll see *you* later, Olivia," she said, clearly not including Lexie. With that she left the kitchen.

Olivia debated whether to go after Claire or deal with Lexie. Here she was, once again, in the middle, Olivia thought wearily. Where she seemed to end up too much of the time. Between her parents, between wanting Daniel and fearing marriage, between her friends . . .

Lexie said, "Could you hand me that bottle of aspirin?"

Olivia did so. Lexie swallowed three, washed them down with a few sips of warm water.

Her eyes caught Olivia's worried look. "I know. I owe her an apology."

"That might not be enough this time."

Lexie shrugged. "She's always so damn perfect that when she slips off that pedestal, it's too tempting to call her on it."

"You don't mean that. You're not a gotcha friend."

"Okay, maybe I pushed it a little too far, but somebody has to nudge her." Anger gave way to contriteness. "We tried reason and logic last week. You think I'm getting off on hurting her or making her cry?"

Olivia sighed and started clearing away the dishes. "No, I don't think that. You're just a little too tough and blunt."

"So who died and said she was excused from the tough, blunt world? Jeff has coddled her far too much. She doesn't have to work or worry about money or wonder if her husband is doing threesomes in the neighbor's shower." Lexie glanced away.

"Ah, so your own nasty experiences were the reasons for the jugular cut to Claire," Olivia said, remembering how humiliated Lexie had been when she'd gone to her neighbor's apartment, on an innocent errand, and found her second husband, Gary, the neighbor, and another man in the shower.

"I lived the embarrassing and depressing aftermath," Lexie said grimly.

"And came out stronger and better than most anyone I know," Olivia said softly, slipping an arm around Lexie's shoulders and giving her an encouraging squeeze.

For a few moments the two women were silent. Lexie recalled how much her two friends had meant to her in those days that followed. Claire and Olivia had flown to Chicago to be with her.

Olivia, too, remembered. She remembered how Claire had been so fiercely protective of Lexie. Screening phone calls and visitors and once going toe-to-toe with Gary when he showed up to get his clothes. Claire had withered him with her outrage — like a mother, Olivia had noted at the time — and he'd slunk away like a whipped rat. Lexie had clearly been impressed, the incident fusing their friendship even closer.

"I remember, too," Lexie said. "Gary didn't know what hit him. He always thought Claire was meek and mousy."

"She loves you and she's worried about you."

"That goes both ways. Claire needs to wake up. Maybe she is mad at me, but maybe she'll also consider that I'm right.

Trent isn't sniffing around because he has gaps in his social life."

"Besides the obvious, what?"

"There is no *what* besides the obvious."

"Claire is not going to go to bed with Trent."

Lexie looked at her, her eyes clear for the first time since she'd come downstairs. "Has she called Jeff? Is she going out on a date with Trent? Let's see, should the next question be? . . . after dinner and wine and he's made her feel wanted and sexy and wonderful, is it possible our sweet perfect Claire might just welcome a sweet seduction?"

"You make it sound like the natural progression, as though Claire were just his puppet."

"Livie, she's clearly attracted to him. And all the upheaval with Jeff makes that attraction too similar to years ago when she and Jeff had that falling out and she ended up dating Trent for a few months."

"Surely Claire is aware of that similarity."

"Maybe. Maybe she simply doesn't care."

Olivia turned her yogurt cup around and around. "It would be a disaster, Lexie."

"Yes, it would. She'll be ashamed and filled with Catholic guilt and roll herself in remorse. She's too innocent to play in this arena. If I could stand the sight of him, I'd prove to her what a scum old-friend Trent is. He wooed her and once he had her, the chase became possession and he lost interest. So off he went after someone else."

"I didn't know that."

"Of course you didn't. You were too busy trying to make him notice you. You were the lucky one."

"So who was the 'someone else'?"

"Me."

Olivia knew her jaw literally dropped. "You and Trent?"

Lexie made a disgusted face. "Yes."

"I don't know what to say."

"There's nothing to say."

"Does Claire know?"

"No."

"How can you be sure?"

"I can't. Not absolutely. But if she did know, she has never mentioned it to me." Lexie rose, poured herself a mug of coffee, and then stood and stared down at the steaming liquid. "I hated myself for letting it happen because I knew he was seeing Claire. I was going through a bad time — it was right after my father took off and I guess I justified hooking up with Trent — charming guy giving me lots of attention when I was feeling lost and abandoned. It's a lousy excuse, but there it is. At some point I probably justified doing it because I didn't think of Trent and Claire as being in some serious relationship. She was in love with Jeff and said so many times that Trent was just a good friend. Remember?"

Olivia nodded, thoughts so muddled and conflicted she didn't know what to say. Not for a moment did she believe that Lexie's motives had been to steal Trent from Claire, or even to play in her backyard.

Lexie had indeed been devastated by her father preferring a vagabond life with his motorcycle and the open road to his wife and daughter. It sounded romantic and care-free, Lexie had said when he'd talked about it, but the reality had been a devastated family that was left to struggle and depend on others. Her mother had never recovered, dying quietly one night as if she'd simply decided she didn't want to live anymore. Lexie had moved in with her aunt, but the loss of her parents had been a defining experience that had sown the seeds for Lexie's resolve to succeed, but even more a determination never to be vulnerable, to always be self-contained.

Now Lexie poured her untouched coffee down the drain. "Look, I think the best thing for me to do is to leave. I've got enough of my own problems to figure out; I don't need to become one with my friends."

"Lexie," Olivia said her name as she moved away. "This whole topic got started because you have a hangover and something was bothering you."

Instead of a stonewall that Olivia expected or an airy dismissal, Lexie folded her arms against her body. The pose emphasized a thinness that suddenly looked startling. Was it just the sloppy, oversize clothes or had she, Olivia, been so wrapped up in her own activities that she'd never quite taken close notice?

"If I tell you, I don't want pity," Lexie warned.

"I would never pity you." Olivia leaned forward and laid her hand on Lexie's arm. Yes, definitely too thin, but she could feel her pulse pounding. She didn't like this. Lexie was savvy and street smart, but the friend standing in front of her was shaky and small and so vulnerable, Olivia felt her throat go raw.

"Tell me," she whispered to Lexie.

Lexie glanced up, her eyes aching and her body wincing as if she'd taken about thirty punches. "It's been a bad few months, and yesterday it all caught up with me." Lexie took a deep breath, and Olivia felt her pulse climb.

Then, in an even almost disengaged voice, she began, "Eric dumped me for a woman I mentored and brought up through the ranks at the station. What really sucked was that I got dropped when the station was sold and she did, too. Then one of the other stations immediately hired her, and rumor is they're grooming her to anchor."

Olivia was stunned. "Why didn't you tell us? All this time you've been keeping all this to yourself. Why?"

But Lexie didn't act suddenly grateful for the lack of pity that she'd requested. She pushed away from Olivia, her voice crackly, her words harsh. "You think I want to admit what a mess I've made of my life? And telling you — both of you — would do what? Get my job back? Make Eric less than a cheat? Make me feel like less than a total blowout failure?" She began to pace the kitchen. "I've thought, dissected, denied, excused, and generally looked back on all of this six gazillion ways. No advice you're going to offer is going to change anything."

"But how is all of this connected to last night?" Lexie asked.

"I got wasted, okay? Picked up a guy, then changed my mind. He got pissed and I scratched my arm on his car door. No big deal. And no, I don't know what his name was, because I didn't ask and I didn't care."

"You could have been hurt," Olivia said, even as she winced at stating the obvious.

"You think I don't know that? You think I even give a rip shit?" She held up her hands, backing up, eyes sheened. "I don't want to hear it."

Olivia took another tack. "You didn't answer my question. How is last night connected?"

"You're a tenacious pain in the ass, you know that?"

"I learned from the master."

"Yeah, sure." She sighed. "Yesterday afternoon, I went to see Bill Riggs about a job and I didn't get it. It was humiliating."

"He said no?"

"He brushed me off with a don't call me, I'll call you."

"Then he will."

"Yeah, right."

Olivia wasn't quite as cynical. Bishop wasn't a big city, and Bill Riggs was a local guy. Yet trying to convince a cynical Lexie when from her point of view it was simpler to believe the worst than risk hope of what she wanted to happen and be disappointed. "So now what?"

"You mean when my head quits feeling like a leaded gas bag? I don't know. Maybe I'll stay here. Worse comes to worse, I can live with my aunt, although I shudder at that thought. I love her, but she makes me crazy if I'm with her longer than five minutes. Too much hovering and fussing. Hey, where are you going?"

"I'm going to get Claire. She needs to know this."

Chapter Thirteen

And a few days later . . .

"Three thousand dollars a month?" Olivia was aghast. "Peter, you must be mistaken." Olivia watched her usually reserved real estate agent bob his head as if it were unhinged. His potentially hefty commission caused his smile to split as wide as when his wife had been the grand-prize winner in a national baking contest.

"It was the most amazing thing," Peter said, eyes sparkling. "Three different couples wanted the house. It was like watching a hot vintage-toy auction where everyone wanted the mint Superman lunchbox. Then there's this." He paused as if waiting for a drumroll. "The couple with the three-grand offer want to buy and are hoping you'll be willing to offer them that option."

Her head was spinning. "But I'm not even sure I want to rent."

"Not rent? You mean you want to sell?"

She shook her head.

"Olivia, listen to me." Peter voice dropped

into his all-business tone. "This is very serious money even considering that all the rents in Bishop have tripled in the past year. The Whitestones have had their eye on the house when the last renters were there. When they first called, we were committed to the Marlowes, but even then the Whitestones asked about you selling after the Marlowes' lease was up. When the Marlowes cancelled after the vandalism, I called the Whitestones. I told them no on selling, but that you might be interested in renting. Guess word got around that the house was still empty. The other two couples are from this area. When the others showed interest, the Whitestones drove by your house and saw how much you've had done, and came immediately here wanting to rent with an option to buy. I did call the other two couples and let them know the house was spoken for, and that was when the counteroffers started to fly." He spread his arms wide as if multiple clients bargaining with cash was the ultimate dream of every realtor.

But instead of the flurry of excitement Peter expected, Olivia said, "I'll have to think about it."

"Are you crazy? What's to think about? This is a no-brainer."

"Yes, if I wanted to rent, but I'm considering living there myself."

His look was speechless incredulity.

Poor Peter, he just didn't get it. Maybe she didn't, either — at least not entirely. What she did get was that she was drawn here — to Bishop, to her memories, and to the house where she'd grown up. She glanced out the window where Bishop bustled. A charming busy town that she'd once viewed as claustrophobic and too self-contained. How strange that the very traits that had once repelled her now appealed. Very strange indeed. But there they were, a covey of feelings that had been slowly sharpening, and most important, they'd been laying the groundwork for today.

She had plans for when she left here — a visit to the Attic to let Helene know the Victorian sofa was going to be perfect, then getting some food items at the market, plus a trip to the police station to ask about the vandalism investigation. All pretty ordinary errands, and yet she looked forward to them with an unexpected enthusiasm that she embraced.

"How, pray tell, are you going to live in Bishop and work in Parkboro?"

"I'd do it by moving back here."

"But you —"

"Live in Parkboro."

"And you teach —"

"In the Parkboro school system, yes. Last I looked there are schools here in Bishop." She decided not to tell him she might give up teaching. He was already in shock over the potential money loss. No point in proving to him that she may truly — and happily — have lost her mind.

She rose, sliding her bag onto her shoulder. She was at his office door when she halted. What was she waiting for? Even Daniel, who she was sure would think she was nuts, had encouraged her. But even if everyone disagreed, this was her decision. Plus, if it turned into a disaster, she could always rent or sell the house.

She turned back to Peter. "Actually, I don't need to think about it. I've made the decision."

Peter practically levitated out of his chair. "Now you're being smart."

"Yes, actually I am. Very smart. I'm going to stay in the house." She would have smiled if he hadn't looked so deflated. "I'm sorry, Peter. You really have been patient, but I've been toying with this idea for a while — no, actually, since I came home to Bishop." She paused. "Not as consciously as now, but the seed of the idea was there."

He stared at her as though giving her an opportunity to reconsider. Then, with a nod to her silence, he came around the desk, resigned but not bitter. One reason she'd always liked dealing with him was that Peter put his energy into making his case, yet once it was lost, he let go and moved on.

He took Olivia's hands. "I'm trying to understand, Olivia —" He stopped as though her decision was *still* beyond his comprehension. "Just promise me that if you ever do decide to rent —"

"You don't even have to ask. The listing will be yours."

Outside Peter's office, Olivia slipped on her sunglasses and smiled with an almost girlish happiness about her decision. She'd gone into the office undecided about putting the house back up for rent. And that three-thousand-a-month amount had come very close to convincing her that only a very wealthy woman would turn it down. But she wasn't rich and she'd said "no, thanks."

She'd literally made a future-altering decision in an instant. She hadn't wrestled and thought and pondered or spent days angsting. How freeing that had felt. She wished she had a hat on so she could toss it in the air and twirl around à la Mary Tyler Moore.

And then she remembered the words of her dad: *You love this house, its walls, its smells, and its history. . . .*

"You were right, Dad. You were so right." She whispered the words, and she just knew he was as pleased with her acknowledgment as he'd been with her decision.

Meanwhile, three blocks south on the corner of Ocean View and Wave Avenue . . . at the Attic on the Corner, Claire was trying

235

to comfort a sobbing Helene. Trent had just arrived to check on Helene's daughter, Jessica, who was huddled in an upholstered armchair.

The teenager's clothes were torn and dirty, hair tangled. There was a bruise on her cheek, a swollen lip, and her bare arms were scratched. Scraped knuckles were visible from where she clutched her knees to her chest.

Claire had gotten involved purely by chance. She'd stopped in at Helene's to ask about where she might find a Bishop mug for Lexie.

Helene didn't have one, but promised to call some other consignment stores, but the scarce mug was soon forgotten when she saw a distressed Helene and a weepy Jessica.

Claire hadn't seen Jessica since she was an adorable toddler with big blue eyes and a headful of dark ringlets. In fact, Claire had assumed the teenager was away, as Helene had made no mention of her when Claire had made other visits to the store. Claire wondered now, if like her reluctance to talk about Tony, Helene's worry and disappointment in her daughter mirrored Claire's feeling about Tony. Much like if there's only distressing news to tell, why say anything? That had been Claire's approach in Lake Moses. Part of this was protection, a need to hold a rebellious child away from any criticism or pity-generated glances. It all made perfect sense to Claire.

Looking now at a ragtag Jessica, fresh from a catfight with another teenager, reinforced for Claire the absolute uncertainty of good parenting. She had Tony and her own mistakes; Helene had an even greater burden — the responsibility of a rambunctious daughter with no father.

She'd raised Jessica alone after the man who'd fathered her disappeared when Helene learned she was pregnant.

From what she could glean from Helene, she'd postponed returning to France so that Jessica could finish school with her friends, then there was the selling of her business, which had taken longer than she'd anticipated. Helene had to be thinking that if only they'd been able leave a few months ago, all of this would be moot.

Now Trent came over to Helene and took the hand she extended to him. Claire stood and moved away to allow Trent to crouch down beside Helene.

"She's okay, Helene," Trent soothed her, speaking softly. "I'm just sorry I wasn't close by to put a stop to it."

Helene touched his cheek. "No, you've been wonderful. I can't expect you to be watching her all the time."

Trent, who'd just come off a special detail, had been keeping an eye on Jessica for more than six months after Helene had caught her with an older man; naturally Helene was concerned. Then the police spoke with the man, mentioning laws about minors and what could happen to him should he get involved with Jessica. Apparently the warning had made an impression, for he hadn't been seen in Bishop in recent months. Trent, while not wanting to make his presence overly intrusive, had kept an eye on Jessica because of Helene's continued concern.

Now Trent was saying, "This kind of dustup is like hair-pulling and spitting but with a few big-girl punches. Most of the hurt is to egos."

"I just don't understand why girls do this sort of thing," Helene said.

"Sure you do," he said gently. "Jealousy is a pretty common motive between girls or women when there's a guy in the middle."

"I need to go be with her."

"Good idea." Trent rose and Helene went over to her daughter, who clutched her mother with such intensity it almost brought tears to Claire's eyes.

Trent started to turn away when Claire touched his arm.

"Can we talk?"

"Claire, I'd rather not —"

"About Jessica," she said quickly, curious, yes, but also wanting simply to speak with him; she was determined not to dither around like she had at Muriel's. That time he walked out. Not this time. "Please, this won't take long."

For a moment he looked skeptical, then said, "Let's go outside."

She nodded, stepping in front of him when he indicated she should go first. She whispered to Helene, "I'll be right back."

Outside, the day was bright and sunny. Despite the fact that the shop had been sold and Helene was waiting on paperwork and the new owner's financing, she'd found a new enthusiasm for making the items she had as presentable as possible. Lexie, Claire, and Olivia had diplomatically suggested the shop was looking a bit junky and dusty. Claire had noticed the changes inside, but outside was most inviting.

Helene had placed a distressed wooden church pew bench against the building with plump blue-and-white striped corner cushions. Window boxes filled with red geraniums posed beneath the narrow windows.

Now Trent indicated Claire should sit down, which she did, sliding one of the pillows behind her back. He remained standing, dark glasses in place, his long frame physically near her, but definitely she didn't feel any emotional closeness. Well, once she apologized, explained that she wasn't upset about the other night, and still wanted to be friends . . .

But first ". . . What happened with Jessica?"

"Basically," he began, "the police were called to an afternoon beach party where Jessica had gotten into a fight with a girl who Jessica said had been sneaking out with her boyfriend. Jessica's best friend tried to stop the fight and was hurt. Someone dropped a dime and an officer responded. Rescue came and took the three girls to the medical center. Helene was called and Jessica was evaluated and released."

All very factual, straightforward, and police-officer professional, Claire decided. When he appeared to be on the verge of bolting, she asked, "And what about the other girls? The two who were also hurt."

"The one Jessica was fighting with seems to be okay. Her mother took her home. The other girl — I don't know. Probably picked up by a parent, also. Excuse me." He turned away, going back inside, leaving the door open. Claire could hear him as he spoke with Helene and Jessica. His voice was low and even, and she was impressed by his concern for Jessica, but mostly for his kindness toward Helene. Her struggle to raise a teenager wasn't unique, but the very fact that it was a struggle rather than just hoping Jessica would grow out of her problems was an area Claire could relate to.

While waiting for Trent, Claire tried to busy her mind, watching a skateboarder zoom by and a pair of pedestrians window shopping. Carefree, she thought, a state she longed for. She'd come to Bishop to help Olivia, to be with Lexie, to enjoy her friends and be, well, carefree.

Instead, she'd become embroiled in a mild, friendly — okay, also deliberate flirtation with Trent, that now had taken on gigantic meaning that spilled far beyond a little fun. The dustup with Lexie was just one example of how entrenched she'd become — and for what? Logically, a serious connection to Trent, when she was married, was silly and impossible — yet she felt enveloped.

Despite attempts — halfhearted at best — to "move on" from their disaster of the other night, she felt like all her emotional gears were stuck. She didn't want to think or angst or even care about Trent or what had *almost* happened between them on their dinner date, but try as she might, the event had lurked and lingered and simmered almost without relief.

They'd gone to dinner, and he'd been a perfect gentleman. The atmosphere had been pleasant and relaxing, the wine and food all excellent. Claire had thought at one point how much the evening had been a reminder of those special dates with Jeff. No intrusive hassles of life, no arguments over disagreements concerning the kids, no debates about anything of substance. Just sweet interludes that had been only about them and how much they loved each other.

That Claire found herself, supposedly solidly married, in just this kind of intimate scenario with another man had been eye-opening. She didn't want to consider that the situation was a measure of just how much trouble her marriage was in, and how much emotional mutiny she could potentially create.

Trouble that she didn't believe was her fault, and because Jeff apparently felt no compunction to use the phone numbers she knew he had, Claire was, well, righteously angry and itching to do something, anything, to prove that she was her own woman, that her annoyingly absent and silent husband had no right to expect her to wait and wait and wait. . . .

And so the evening with Trent had been delightful and immaculate and gave her a sense of safety and, yes, even a sense of power.

He'd remained the perfect gentleman when the evening came to an end. No groping pass, no overtly sexy comments, not even an attempt to coax her into a kiss.

And if only she'd said good night and floated back to Olivia's. But no. Why stop and go home when she was feeling sexy and pretty and wanted? So she'd kissed him.

Kissed him boldly and brazenly and with a kind of recklessness that for a few scattered moments had her believing she could do anything and damn the consequences. Only later had she wondered if she'd totally lost her sense of reason and responsibility.

Of course Trent hadn't pushed her kiss away; he'd taken her mouth fully and deeply and slipped his hands over her breasts and whispered dark words of desire and want. That aroused combustion broke the dreamy trance she'd slipped into.

Calling a halt hadn't been pretty.

She was partly ashamed, partly embarrassed, and immediately furious at Jeff. This debacle was his fault, and she was determined to ignore the tiny voice inside that whispered: *No, no, no, Claire. This is of your doing and none of Jeff's.*

"Claire?"

Startled, she pulled herself out of her conflicting thoughts to find Trent standing in front of her.

"I didn't hear you. Are they all right?" She nodded toward the still-open door of the Attic.

"Yeah." He paused, glancing off toward the street as though wishing he were on the other side of town. Finally he added, "I have to go."

"Wait," she said, rising and stepping close to him.

"What?"

"We have to talk about the other night."

"Why?"

"I want to explain —"

"Just leave it, Claire."

"No, I owe you an apology."

"Fine. You're sorry. I have to go."

"You have to listen," she said, feeling a little desperate. "I am sorry, I really am. It just went too far, too fast for me." She took hold of his arm, and he glanced at her hand as if debating whether to shake it off or shake her.

Instead of doing either, he gripped her shoulders and walked her a few steps backward to a corner between the bench rail and the building so that any conversation wouldn't be overheard.

"It went exactly where you wanted, Claire. You flirted and played pretty and kissed me and when I kissed back you got all turned on — uh, yeah you did," he said when she started to object. "Then you freaked into the no-I-can't female. It's called a tease-and-freeze and for some guys that's a lethal combo. Neither of us are twelve-year-olds experimenting with hormone overload. You wanted me and when I wanted to give you what you asked for, you suddenly got cold feet."

"I know. But I'm married —"

"And you just remembered that?"

"No, of course not. I wanted us to be friends. You've been kind and attentive and we were getting along so well. I just didn't want that to change."

He looked at her for a long time, and she had to force herself not to start explaining all over again. How could it be that she could want him and *not* want him all at the same time?

He folded his arms, his words precise, his tone coolly neutral. "It changed at Olivia's, Claire. It changed that first day when you agreed to meet me for breakfast. You knew that and you went along so you could play at the edges of some asinine fantasy."

"Trent, I —"

"You want to hear mine?" His eyes gleamed, daring her to say no. "Sure you do."

And she did. God forgive her, but she did.

"I want you, Claire. I want to make love to you. I want you in my life and in my bed. I don't want to be your friend, I don't want to be a breakfast mate, or get a once-in-a-while visit when you come to Bishop."

Claire's eyes widened with the immensity of what he was saying, what he wanted. There was nothing teasing and light and fun about this. "You want to have an affair?"

"I want to have you. You can call it anything you want." He touched her arm, trailing his fingers from her elbow to her wrist. "Call it Trent and Claire's fantasy adventure. I'm not a big fan of cheating, having been on the bad end of that gig with Tanya. In fact, I don't want to share you at all — you could dump the ever-absent Jeff and I'd say good riddance." His thumbs were sliding and gliding and making her think too much about the way they would feel in places she didn't want to think about.

"Trent, please . . ."

But he didn't stop touching, didn't stop talking. "If you want to play house in two different places, fine. But don't come on to me dressed in some phony friendship armor. No dice."

Whatever she'd been expecting from him — this was definitely not it. "You've certainly made this black-and-white."

"Call it simple and straightforward and honest. That way we both know where we're going."

It was certainly *not* simple, and the ramifications had more spirals than a multitude of pinwheels.

"Here's the choice so there's no mistake. Either we're together with no barriers, or we're apart, as in I'll wave if I see you walk past me."

"No barriers," she repeated, absorbing all that he meant.

"None. You think about it. You know where to reach me."

And with that he sauntered away, leaving Claire with a decision that should have been obvious. Should have.

When Olivia, on her way to see Helene

about moving the Victorian sofa, turned the corner onto Ocean View, coming toward her was a black truck that looked exactly like Daniel's. As it came closer, she saw the Massachusetts license plate.

She waved and he cruised to a stop.

"I didn't expect you to come today to move the couch." Caitlyn was slumped in the passenger side, and Daniel's attention was definitely on her.

For a moment he looked confused by her comment. "This is something else. We were on our way to see you."

"Oh?"

Caitlyn turned toward her and Olivia saw the tears. "Sweetie, what happened?"

She shrugged.

Olivia immediately went around to the passenger door and pulled it open, touching the girl's arm. The teenager's pretty blond hair was snarled and damp with sweat; her right cheek was swollen. She also saw that her arm was scuffed as if she'd fallen against something rough and hard.

Caitlyn winced. "I'm okay."

"You're not okay. You're hurt."

Daniel answered. "She got in the middle of a fight."

"A fight with who? Never mind. Time enough later for questions. You need to get some medical attention."

"We just came from the clinic. They called

me when she and the others were brought in. She's been checked over and nothing's broken. They gave her an ice pack for her face."

Olivia hefted the ice pack, one of those clinic-issued plastic temporaries that after fifteen minutes became useless. "Come on, let's go to my house and get some real ice, and we'll get you cleaned up."

Olivia got into the truck, putting her arm around a weepy Caitlyn, and Daniel drove to the house.

No one was home, but there was a note from Lexie saying she'd gone for a run.

In the downstairs bathroom Olivia used warm water and gently bathed Caitlyn's arm and face. She sent Daniel to the refrigerator for some ice. "Put it in a plastic bag," she called.

"Sweetie, who did you fight with?"

"Nobody. My best friend did and she was getting hurt. That other girl kicked her in the ribs, and I went after her."

Olivia sighed. Girls physically fighting had been happening at Parkboro High in the past few years. More than a few times she'd separated a couple of rivals. It was almost always over a boy. "How's your friend?"

"She's okay, I think. She left the clinic with her mom. Can I call her? I mean, that other girl should have been the one wasted in the sand. She's a loser and a cheat."

"What did she do?" Olivia rinsed the cloth in warm water and again applied it to Caitlyn's arm.

"She was doing Jessica's boyfriend." She started to say something more, then lowered her head, shaking it, new tears forming. "Dad's super-pissed at me."

"Because of the fight?"

Daniel returned. "No, because she has something to tell you and should have done it days ago. Here's the ice."

Frowning, Olivia wrapped the ice in a soft terry towel. "Here, I want you to hold this against your cheek."

"You're gonna hate me!" she wailed.

"Don't be silly." But she couldn't ignore Caitlyn's distress and Daniel's scowl. Olivia said, "Why don't we go outside where it's cooler. I'll get some iced tea. Caitlyn, you want tea or a soda?"

"Just ice water."

In the yard Caitlyn settled into the chaise near the willow tree. Daniel remained in the house, scowling and just generally looking uneasy.

"Okay, fill me in. What's going on?" Olivia asked, putting ice in tall glasses and pouring cold tea and water.

He related the details of a beach party when a friend of Caitlyn's, Jessica Duprey, got into a rolling brawl with another girl when Jessica had learned the other girl had been having sex with Jessica's boyfriend. Caitlyn tried to break it up and ended up as punched as the fighters.

"Good for Caitlyn for sticking up for Jessica. If her last name is Duprey, she has to be Helene's daughter."

"Whatever."

"I haven't seen Jessica since I got back — no, wait, maybe I did. There was a Jessica working at the drugstore food counter that first day I was here. I wonder . . ."

"Caitlyn said she had a summer job taking food orders."

"But how would they know each other well enough to be best friends?"

"Caitlyn met her in an online chat room of local kids. Guess they hit it off, and when Caitlyn learned she lived in Bishop, the two girls decided to meet. They did that same day I dropped Caitlyn off to see her boyfriend on my way to your house."

"Okay, that all sounds pretty straightforward," Olivia said. "The girls have become friends. Caitlyn sticks up for Jessica when another girl tries to hurt her. So far, I'd say Caitlyn is indeed a very good friend. So what are you angry at her about?"

"The fight isn't the problem."

"Then what?"

"She'll tell you."

Outside, Olivia gave Caitlyn the ice water, then sat down opposite her. Daniel sprawled in another chair, dark glasses in place, mouth set in a grim line. Silence shimmered around them as intense as the summer heat.

Caitlyn concentrated on her water, chewing small pieces of ice. Olivia waited.

Daniel warned, "Caitlyn."

"I am, I am." She took a gulp of the water and then pressed the icy bag against her face. "There was this party —"

"She already knows about that," Daniel interrupted. "Tell her what you told me."

"I have to tell her some other stuff so she knows why," she said, looking a little desperate.

Olivia took her hand. "You tell me in the way that's easiest for you."

Daniel sighed and nodded.

Caitlyn began. "I came down to see Jessica and we went to the party and there were a bunch of kids whispering about her boyfriend and Sadie somebody or other. Sadie started it by trying to look cool and possessive and then telling Jessica she could do Christopher anytime she wanted. Even that she'd already done a French head."

Daniel slopped his tea, swearing.

"What? You think I don't know this stuff?"

"I'd hoped you didn't. Not yet."

"And you don't want to know I know it."

"You're fourteen."

"And I've known since I was eleven." She softened her voice, looking at him as if she

251

was the wise one and he was the one with the virgin mind.

He pulled his glasses off and hooked them onto his shirt placket. He rubbed the place between his eyes as though to press away an oncoming headache.

"Dad?" When he looked at her, she scooted forward, her voice almost soothing in an attempt to reassure. "I never did that to Brian. Even when he wanted me to — I — I didn't." At his deep scowl she stopped and said quickly, "I'm not doing any of that, if that's what you're thinking."

Daniel let that sink in, his expression somewhere between wanting to believe her and the skepticism that comes from knowing teenagers don't like to admit to sexual forays. He rose, looking down at Olivia. "You got anything stronger than tea?"

"Jack Daniel's. In the cupboard by the sink."

To Caitlyn, he said, "Get to the point and tell her."

When Daniel walked away, Caitlyn sighed dramatically. "He's harder than my mom. I mean, it's like he wants me to be six forever."

"He loves you very much, and he doesn't want you to get in trouble or get hurt."

"I can take care of myself."

Olivia touched her hair. "No, you can't, sweetie. All of us need good advice and warnings about bad people and bad things that can happen. He doesn't want to cramp you, but he doesn't want to look the other way and pretend there's no trouble for you to get into." When Caitlyn didn't respond, she said, "Think of it this way. As a teacher, if he knew something bad could happen to his students and he said nothing, plus looked the other way, he'd be fired. As a parent, his responsibility is even larger, and because he loves you very much, it's not possible for him just to shrug off what he knows could be potential trouble. All of this isn't about making you unhappy, but making sure you have the instincts to know when something is wrong. In fact, I'd say he's already done a pretty good job. You jumped in to help Jessica when others did not. I'd say that shows good instinct and loyalty and caring more about her than yourself."

Caitlyn stared down at the melting ice in her glass, saying nothing, and Olivia wondered if what she'd said had rushed right past the teenager.

Then she looked up and said, "I know who trashed your house."

Chapter Fourteen

Lexie beat out a sandy twenty-something girly-guy for the last umbrella table on the Beach Club deck. She dropped her sling purse onto the table along with the newspaper, where she'd circled some job possibilities and potential apartments.

Wearing sandals, a short denim skirt, and a red tank top, she sank into the cushioned PVC pipe chair and sighed with relief at the cool breeze off the water. A waiter appeared with small studs in both lobes and a summer buzz cut. His gaze slid over her, and his smile broadened.

"I know you," he said in a chirpy voice.

"Congratulations. I'll have a cranberry and vodka."

He grinned. "Bet you can't guess who I am."

"Tom Cruise."

"Hey, you think I look like him?" He curved his smile for a smoky smolder. "Pretty cool, huh?"

"Keeno-classo."

"Huh?"

"Before your time. Could you just get i order?"

But he didn't move.

"You're Lexie James." His look was all anticipation, and she knew she was expected to act wowed and surprised.

And because he was cute and enthusiastic and she was bored, she shook her hair back and sighed with a bit more drama than necessary. "Okay, sweetie, I give up. How do you know me?"

"You used to baby-sit for me and my sister. I'm Jesse Riggs," he said with a puff of know-it-all pride.

Lexie was indeed surprised. She figured him to be connected to one of the workmen at Olivia's and knew her because he'd heard her name mentioned.

Now she took off her sunglasses and really looked at him. Not as tall as his father, he had the litheness of youth and the bravado of too much confidence. The last time she'd seen him he'd been four, with sticky fingers and a penchant for disobedience that got him kicked out of three nursery schools. She'd predicted after a particularly exhausting evening that Messy Jesse, as she usually referred to him, would be lucky to escape childhood without a stint in juvenile reform. To see him working at something as benign as waiting tables almost made her smile.

"Well, hello, Messy Jesse Riggs."

He actually blushed. "Geez, I forgot about that."

"It described you well. I saw your father a few days ago."

"That's when I saw you. I was on my way out when you came in. I'm going be working at the station starting in September. I knew you right away — guess that's because I used to have a big-time crush on you."

"At four?"

"Nah, when you were in college. And I kinda followed your career — sort of. I always thought you were cool. Dad told me you'd been in to see him." His grin widened. "We both decided you were gorgeous."

For all the silly reasons that had to do with ego and self-pride, she soaked up the compliment like water in sand. "Well, thank you, Jesse. That's very nice to hear."

"So you staying in Bishop for the summer or forever?" He grinned. "I vote for forever."

If he was asking that question, he obviously hadn't heard anything from his father about her being hired. Either that was good and Bill Riggs liked to make his own news, or it was bad because there was no news to make.

She let her voice fall to a whisper, "Why, Jesse, I believe you're flirting with me."

"Big time. Is it working?"

"I'm getting turned on with the wonder of it."

He gulped and she almost laughed. Big-league play, sweetie, weeds out the weenies.

He started to say something else when the bartender yelled, "Hey, Riggs! Order for table six!"

"Be right there," he called back. Then to Lexie, he said, "Cranberry and vodka — back in a sec." Then he was gone, weaving his way through the crowd toward the bar and leaving Lexie to watch him with some amusement.

Well, that was an entertaining distraction. She'd probably scared him back into diapers.

Yet the exchange had given her a lift. Bill Riggs, as professional and businesslike as he'd been during the interview, had taken note of her looks and formed a consensus with his son that she was gorgeous.

In feminist parlance she should be miffed about such a sexist evaluation, but she wasn't. She'd already had success because of her brains, but anyone who thought that her looks didn't contribute to the TV hire-factor was truly misguided.

She'd been told many times that she was attractive, but Lexie was astonished at how *this time* she'd welcomed Jesse's words like some homely single who couldn't buy a man. Neither man — Jesse in his early twenties or Bill in his early fifties — were in the range where she usually dated. Not that either was asking, but still, she couldn't help musing the possibility.

Boats cruised through the water, some pulling skiers, some filled with party groups. The beach below the deck was littered with kids and moms and teenagers giggling and flirting. Lexie took it all in with a distant curiosity. Despite having been born and raised in Bishop up until her early twenties, the years since she'd moved away were where she'd made her mark. Sitting here, she felt as much of a stranger as a visitor just off a plane from Nebraska.

Except that a stranger would have brought the baggage of vacation clothes; she'd brought her failure status arrayed in depressing tedium.

She had no job, she had no boyfriend, or any hope of one unless she counted Jesse's flirty interest. She'd caused rancor with Claire, and no doubt she'd come up with some way — if she hadn't already — to piss off Olivia.

If she was smart, if she was really a friend, she'd go back to Chicago and take her feckless future with her. . . .

And then what? Live where she couldn't afford? Take guys home she didn't like? Settle for work doing interviews at supermarket openings?

She physically shuddered at those possibilities.

Jesse came with her drink, setting it on a small napkin and adding a basket of pretzels.

She took a sip and nodded. "Just right."

"Let me know when you want a refill." His eagerness to please was obvious and flattering. As he once more moved away, she turned her attention back to her own dilemma.

To stay here wasn't looking much better as an alternative. She could sublet her Chicago apartment — a definite necessity until her lease ran out — if she planned to rent in Bishop. She could barely afford one place; no way she could handle two. While staying in Bishop held a nostalgic ease that had never existed in Chicago, she still needed money and a job.

A young couple took an empty table beside her. Totally absorbed in each other, they looked young and fresh-faced — happy and oblivious to those around them. No cares or problems — just the intensity of each other on a pretty summer day. How well she remembered that feeling. Even a cursory glance at the other occupied tables showed most were couples except for her and one other frazzled woman with two unruly toddlers.

Lexie watched the couple next to her with a wistful moodiness, turning her glass and feeling very much alone in the male department. Most of her life there'd been a guy — a boyfriend, a husband, a lover — but she'd been in Bishop for a few weeks and there'd been zilch. All those guys the other night including the jerk she almost went home with were already a fading memory. Lexie James hadn't had sex since that forgettable night with Rob or Bob — whatever. Her dilemma had always been who, not when. Claire, on the other hand, had wasted no time with Trent, and of course, Olivia had Daniel.

Weird, she decided, signaling Jesse for another drink. She was the party girl and she'd flat-out run out of invitations.

Then there was her own lack of interest in any of it. Had she gone out looking since coming back home? Had she cruised the bars? Checked out the summer crowd for some fun? No, no, no.

Once again she was at some mental crossroads between her career and her personal life. And neither offered her the usual energetic excitement of a new adventure. Maybe she was too old, too cynical, or just plain too scared.

Conflicts, challenges, and choices. Suddenly they all sucked the energy from her. She felt mired in a thicket of indecision. Making one choice meant abandoning another, but of late she was bereft of choices worth the barest of attention.

She watched Jesse come toward her with her drink and when he set it down, she said, "What time do you get finished here?"

"Nine," he said without a flinch, a hesitation, or a gulp. Maybe he wasn't as much of a kid as she'd thought.

"Maybe I'll stop by."

"Cool. I'll wait by the front steps."

His eagerness rattled her. "Don't wait for me," she warned in a brush-off manner. "I probably won't show."

But he only winked and moved away. She sat back, letting out the long breath she hadn't realized she'd been holding. Well, now you've done it. So hard up for some male attention that you're trolling the beach club for boys barely old enough to drink.

She lifted her drink and sipped, watching some sandcastle construction and trying not to think too hard about how needy she was. For needy she must be. Why else would she even be thinking about Jesse Riggs?

Olivia blinked, her eyes widening. "You know who the vandals are?"

"Uh-huh. That's what Dad wanted me to tell you."

"But I don't understand. You don't even live around here; how would you know?"

"Jessica told me and made me swear I wouldn't say anything. Then after the fight she was so mad she said she didn't care who knew. It's her boyfriend and his creepy friends. My boyfriend, too. Well, ex-boyfriend now — the creep," she said, lowering her head with the pink color of shame. "I thought Brian was an okay guy, but when I

261

heard he was in on wrecking your house — forget it. Another guy who's been so cool and nice to me — he really likes me, but he's kind of an outsider and Dad would flip if he saw him. But once when Brian was pushing me around cuz I wouldn't do a French head, Ray heard me begging Brian to not make me. Ray punched him and then took me back to Jessica's."

Olivia didn't think Daniel would object to a boy who'd rescued his daughter, but she imagined there was more than just his good deed that Caitlyn worried about.

"It wasn't just your house they trashed. They did some others, too."

"Other houses? I just heard about smashed mailboxes."

Caitlyn pressed the ice to her cheek, wincing. "Jessica said it was some kind of bet by a couple of guys from down on Brace Street. Somethin' about 'Rich kids had no guts.' So they wanted to prove they were tough, figuring that if someone ratted to the cops, they'd all clam up and get lawyers so that nothing would happen. Guess they were right, cuz nothing has."

Olivia mulled that over, aware of the current tendency of kids to do things without a logical motive. She'd seen it as a teacher, and it was not only frustrating but frightening, for it tended to show lack of conscience and a sense of doing illegal things because they could. And yet, she wasn't quite sure why a motive such as kids looking for valuables to heist for cash brought a sense of "now I understand why" while "just for the fun of it" was so disconcerting.

Probably because no one was ever safe if there was no reason behind the crime. Then again, doing bad things to prove courage probably was a strong motive, albeit more than a little warped.

Daniel came across the lawn, hands jammed in his pockets. Before he could say anything, Caitlyn said, "I told her."

"Good. Next stop is the police."

Vehemently she shook her head, sliding deeper into the chair. "No, you can't make me do that. You can't! Jessica knows I was going to tell you, but to go to the cops — she didn't say that was okay. I don't want to get her in trouble. I did what you said and told Olivia."

Daniel scowled, then nodded, which surprised Olivia. She'd been sure he would insist Caitlyn go to the station and tell the police what she knew. Then, as if the whole issue was yesterday's news, he said to Olivia, "Let's go and get your couch while I'm here."

"All right," she said, trying to ignore a raft of questions tumbling through her thoughts. "Caitlyn, why don't you stay here and be lazy. We'll only be about a half an hour."

She nodded. "Can I look in the little house

over there?" She indicated the playhouse that Olivia had wanted to clean out and use, but with so much to be done in the big house, the small building hadn't been touched.

"Sure. I'm afraid it's not very appealing filled with tools and junk. It used to be my playhouse until I grew out of it. Let me get you the key."

Ten minutes later she was in Daniel's truck on her way to the Attic. He was quiet and had barely looked at her.

"You okay?" she asked, reaching over and touching his arm. It was hard and tense.

"Fine."

"Come on, Daniel. I know this thing with Caitlyn has upset you."

"You think?" He glanced over, and although his sunglasses were firmly in place, she could see the strain around his mouth.

"I wasn't trying to be flip."

"Noted."

Olivia sighed. "The way I see it, Caitlyn was honest and straightforward — she probably didn't have to say anything about the vandalism, but I imagine she was having an attack of conscience. I don't think you can ask for much more."

"I'm not annoyed with her. In fact, I'm very proud of her loyalty to Jessica. I'm pissed at myself and what I've allowed to happen by not living closer to her. While I'm not angry with her, she shouldn't have been in this kind of situation. Her mother seems unable or unwilling to exercise any control or set any boundaries. I'm too far away to make anything I say stick, so here we are. Caitlyn talking about French head, fighting, and who knows what I haven't heard about."

Olivia pressed her lips together, forcing her own silence. What could she say that wouldn't sound either clichéd or patronizing? Even though she was a teacher and dealt with plenty of teenage incidents and issues, she wasn't a parent and to presume to have behavior answers for Daniel . . . she didn't and she wasn't going to insult him by offering meaningless words. "I can't even imagine what it must be like for a parent in this crazy world."

"Try *terrifying.*" He made a right turn and drove around to the back of the Attic. Then, as he backed up to the door, he added, "For a while I've been toying with moving to Greeley, but now, after this . . ." His voice trailed off and Olivia was struck by how out of touch she was with what was going on in his life. Oh, she knew that Daniel hadn't liked Caitlyn being so far away, that he'd been troubled for some time about what he felt had become an emotional as well physical distance between him and his daughter. Cell-phone parenting, he'd once called it.

"You never said anything about leaving Parkboro," she said softly, trying to take in all the implications of Daniel moving away and probably, by inference, out of her life. "I know you've felt out of touch and constrained by the distance, but I had no idea you were going to do this."

"Olivia, I'm as out of touch with you as I am with her."

It hurt to hear him say it, but he was right. What he wasn't right about, however, was blaming himself. This was her fault. The fact that Daniel hadn't halted his friendship or his advice or his kindness toward her was more a credit to him than to any of her efforts. If she looked squarely at her own actions since she broke off their relationship, she could only cringe. She'd told him goodbye and then let him come to Bishop and spend his time helping her, he'd listened to her gripes, he'd offered opinions she hadn't liked, and yet continued to be her friend and companion.

She had done nothing worthy; she'd done nothing period. Oh, she'd taken and used and depended — maybe not in a deliberately selfish way, but she'd been selfish nonetheless.

Even that intimate unplanned weekend — he hadn't tossed that in her face or accused her of wanting him without commitment. She'd taken and enjoyed and memorized those hours of pleasure. As she guessed Daniel had, also.

Now Daniel rested his crossed wrists on the top of the steering wheel. "That was a lousy shot, and it sounded like I'm blaming you. Hell, maybe I am." He paused and she could see the pulse pumping in his neck. "I know I was pushing you when you didn't want any commitment like marriage. I've probably been as pushy with Caitlyn." He drew in a long breath. "My old man was big on making sure I followed *his* plans for me. No screwups for his son, no risk that didn't end with a reward, no easy jobs when I should be working at something that contributed to my future. I remember one summer I wanted to lifeguard at a local pool. I'd gotten certified, made the cut, and he freaked out because I wasn't clerking in his law firm."

"He wanted you to be an attorney?"

"Wanted?" His laugh was short and humorless. "Try *ordered.*"

Her heart turned over. It was so easy to imagine the excitement of a young Daniel with a summer job he'd worked to get and then having his happiness broken like a snapped sapling. Olivia couldn't help but compare it to her own parents' attitude toward her. They'd been more lackadaisical, and yet she'd felt compelled to please, obligated to live in Bishop with them when her heart longed for freedom and new places.

"But you didn't become a lawyer."

"Actually, I did. I just didn't take the bar

exam. Call it the ultimate rebellion. All that law school tuition as good as shredded paper. I was dating Marsha, got her pregnant with Caitlyn, and instead of walking away and leaving her with a big check and an appointment for an abortion — the old man's solution — I married her. My father didn't speak to me until Caitlyn was christened. In a small town he was not looking too good when he wouldn't see his only grandchild."

"Marrying Marsha was the right thing to do."

"Don't give me too much credit. My motives weren't all that honorable. I wanted to let the old man know he could no longer order me to do what he wanted. He took great pleasure in saying 'I told you so' when the marriage collapsed."

"Daniel, I'm sorry."

He looked puzzled. "For what?"

"That I've taken you for granted, always spouting off about what I wanted and about my problems, instead of thinking about what's important to you. I've known you for a long time, and I never knew about this relationship with your father."

"Few people do. He's been gone for a number of years now, so there's really no need to drag him into conversations. I only brought him up because I saw myself repeating with Caitlyn what he did with me."

"That's why you dropped the issue of her

going to the police?"

"Yes. Maybe I don't agree wholly with her reasons, but they are hers and as worthy of consideration as the more obvious ones."

"Did you and your father reconcile before he died?"

"Were there tears and apologies and turned corners? No. We never discussed the past, we simply started again after Caitlyn was born. I think he loved her — at least he seemed happy when he was with her. He left a sizable estate that included a trust fund for her, so if money is a sign of love, then yeah, I guess he loved both of us." He opened the door and glanced back her. "We'd better get in there before Helene begins to wonder about loitering trucks in the alley."

Olivia nodded and exited the passenger side.

It took only ten minutes to load the Victorian sofa into the bed of the truck. Using nylon rope, Daniel tied it to the rings on the truck's sides so it wouldn't slide and get bumped.

On the ride back to her house, Olivia again raised the issue of him moving. "If you move, what about your teaching and coaching in Parkboro?"

"Obviously that has to change."

Olivia was amazed at how fast all this had come about.

Daniel said, "Just after our weekend I had

a call from Webb Lopes, a friend who lives in a town a few miles from Greeley. Webb also collects old history books. He was looking for an obscure World War I diary, and I told him about the book you found for me at a yard sale. That led to him mentioning a late-summer tag sale at a private school and asked me if I wanted to come up for it. In the course of the conversation, Webb mentioned that the school was looking for a history teacher. The current one was in a boating accident. The guy was hurt pretty bad, and it's not known if he'll be able to start the fall semester. Applying for the job seemed too obvious a possibility for me just to pass up. I have to speak with Fisler about leaving, and work something out with the assistant football coach."

He stopped for a runner crossing the street, while Olivia thought of how the likelihood of seeing Daniel at all had just grown smaller, when he added, "Since you and I had broken up, there wasn't a lot to keep me in Parkboro, plus the idea of living closer to Caitlyn . . . that has been on my mind for a long time."

Olivia listened to all of this with a sense that she'd been totally out of touch. With all that had been going on in Bishop and with her own "should-she-should-she-not" decisions, she'd paid little attention to what was going on with Daniel. "It sounds as if you've made up your mind."

"About the move? Pretty much. About the teaching position, nothing is final. I spoke with the head of the school's advisory board and he was interested. This close to school starting has them in a bind, so I'll probably be offered the position."

"Then you decided before today, before this incident with Caitlyn?"

"I was eighty percent decided; today cinched it."

"And if they don't hire you?"

"Then I'll look for something else in the area." He reached over and squeezed her hand, a benign gesture that seemed all but vacant of the passion they once shared. Then, in case she'd been overreacting, he confirmed she was not, when he said, "You know, given what's happened, it's probably just as well that you turned down marriage to me. Your happiness here in Bishop is so obvious that you'd balk at moving to Greeley. Frankly, I wouldn't blame you, so it looks as if things have worked out for the best."

Olivia wasn't sure which shattered first, her no-commitment phobia or her heart.

Chapter Fifteen

"You're crazy."

"Nah. I've done crazy things before."

"Not like this."

"Hey, if I knew I was going to get all this grief from my best friends, I wouldn't have told you."

Lexie, Olivia, and Claire were in the living room with glasses of wine and a firestorm of disagreement over Lexie's announcement that in a few hours she was meeting Jesse Riggs.

While the silence circled and thickened, Lexie looked at both of them. Curled on the newly acquired Victorian sofa, Olivia and Claire reminded her of professional scolders. Of course, she was pretty adept at scolding, too. She'd certainly done her part to Claire about the annoying Trent McGraw.

It was late afternoon and they'd just finished an early supper of pasta salad, sliced cantaloupe, and chunks of a serves-four deli sandwich that Claire had picked up on her way home.

Claire and Olivia had changed to cooler

clothes; Lexie still wore her denim skirt and red tank top. If she was really going to do this, she needed to get showered and dressed. Then again, letting him wait a bit wasn't a bad thing. Somebody, somewhere once told her she was worth waiting for. On better days she tried to remember that.

"You both are way overreacting," she said, sipping her wine and considering what to wear. Her blue sundress looked great with her tan. Then there was the yellow halter-top dress that contrasted even better. She waved her glass in a no-big-deal flourish and continued, "We'll go out for a drink, he'll try to kiss me and cop a few feels, hoping he might get lucky. I'll let him play some tonsil hockey, cool him down, and tell him I never have sex on a first date and that will be that." Did she really sound that brutal? Silly girl. It wasn't brutal; it was the way things were.

"But why would you do this?" Claire asked. "He's a kid with stars in his eyes and hope in his heart about you."

Lexie rolled her eyes. "Claire, this is the twenty-first century. No guy in his twenties thinks like that. The only thing on his mind is how fast he can put it where he wants it."

"I think you're wrong," Claire said stubbornly. "Maybe they don't say it, but I bet deep down guys still want to believe in real love with the woman of their dreams. Human nature hasn't changed that much."

Claire of the storybook romance. God love her. "Okay, I bow to your wisdom."

"No, you don't. You're just trying to get me to stop making you uncomfortable," she said with an air of philosophy. "You don't want me to stir up your conscience."

"Me? With a conscience about men? I shredded that a husband or two ago. Livie, see if she's just drinking wine."

Olivia leaned down and sniffed Claire's glass. "Just wine."

"Never mind," Claire said, giving Olivia a withering glance. "Lex, you do have a conscience, so just shut up trying to deny it. As for Messy Jesse — yes, I remember that's what you called him — he's probably looking for a sex treat from you — the ultimate from a sexy older woman —"

"Who should know better? Who shouldn't act so desperate?"

"I didn't say that. I don't think you're desperate as much as bored."

"Yeah, well, no argument there. Olivia? No supporting comments? No serious lectures about using him, or telling me I'll hurt him?"

Olivia had been only half listening unless she was directly addressed. Claire had always been the vocal moral warden, and Olivia was quite glad to let her continue.

"Lexie, you're going to do what you want, so I don't see why we're even discussing this.

Who knows, maybe a younger guy with stars in his eyes is just what you need."

Lexie grinned, then stuck her tongue out at Claire, who muttered, "I give up. Just remember what Olivia and I know about you. You aren't the type to deliberately hurt anyone no matter how hard you try to act like it doesn't matter."

"Maybe it doesn't, maybe getting hurt makes a person tougher. Maybe spending all your life wringing your hands about how others feel is a waste of time. Maybe it's time I did what I like when I like and do it just for me," Lexie said slowly, digesting what she was saying as the words tumbled out of her thoughts. She wasn't usually as vocal about internal musings. Then she'd had those two drinks at the Beach Club, now she was finishing her second glass of wine. Tipsy, no, but definitely too talkative. But as long as she'd driven into this, she might as well make the trip worth the effort. "As for hurting men, they don't seem to have any problem hurting me."

Now Olivia was alarmed. "So this is some kind of get-even payback?"

Suddenly all her wordy bravado dissipated into a blob of weariness. She set her glass down and ran her hands through her hair. "I don't know. I don't even know if I want to go. It was one of those moments, and it just seemed a little wicked to be meeting up with a kid I once baby-sat for. Besides, for once I'd be going on a date where I'm in control." She paused, still piqued at Claire's throwing a kink in her planned evening. "That's the trouble with conscientious friends — they don't let you fool yourself. And speaking of men and boys, I'm not the only one fooling myself." She zeroed in on Claire. "Can we say unhappy friend is doing some solace sex?"

"I have not had sex with Trent!" Claire's hand flew to her mouth as though she'd revealed some private fantasy.

"But most definitely thinking about it?" Lexie asked affably.

Claire looked away, trying, without success, to stop the sudden color in her cheeks.

When she didn't offer a denial, Lexie said, "Ah, those wordless answers." Then she turned to Olivia. "At least you know a good thing when it comes along, but I have to say, I'm puzzled that Daniel is still around."

Olivia didn't try to duck Lexie's comment or her probing stare; instead she raised her glass in a toast. "Here's to good things. As far as Daniel being around, he's not. I've lost him.

If anything could have flipped Lexie from her friendly skewering, this did.

"What happened?" Lexie asked, her expression softening.

Olivia explained about Caitlyn, and Daniel's announcement that he was moving to Greeley to live closer to his daughter. "Actually, I don't blame him. I'm amazed he hasn't moved sooner. The kicker was when he told me that it was just as well we broke up. That I didn't expect. I think I made a huge blunder and yet, the alternative — damn, I don't even know if there is an alternative anymore. I feel like such a selfish hypocrite. I wanted him but not on his terms. Now his terms no longer exist for me to even ponder, never mind reconsider."

"What are you going to do?"

She shrugged. "Right now I'm numb. It's so strange. It seems like I no sooner made a few definite decisions about staying in Bishop than Daniel hit me with this."

"Okay, color me confused. If Daniel is moving to Greeley and you're staying here, how is that different than you here and Daniel in Parkboro?"

"In miles, not much. But in where we were as a couple, it's world's apart."

"But, Livie, you didn't want to be a couple. You broke up with him."

"I know that. But because I came here, on the exact day, by the way, it always felt more like a separation. And when Daniel didn't nag or pressure me, it began to seem like we'd started again. He's been so good and thoughtful and not pushed me. Like I thought he'd be against me deciding to stay here, but he was enthusiastic and supportive. I was beginning to feel that I should reconsider, maybe try again. Then this."

"Did he say he didn't want you?"

"He didn't have to say it, but he's changed. The dynamics between us, the focus, even the tension is simply gone. I've lost him and I never saw it coming. One day we were going along, and then suddenly he's quitting his job, moving to a new place, and telling me it's a good thing we're not getting married and nice knowing you. It's like I woke up from a dream and years of life had passed and I missed them."

For a few moments no one said anything. Olivia still couldn't grasp the enormity of loss that she felt, but loss of what? This wasn't a breakup, and yet it grabbed at her with more force and distress than when she'd said good-bye weeks ago. What kind of sense did that make?

Lexie finally said, "Look, why don't you talk to him, tell him what you've told us?"

How simple and straightforward that sounded, yet it also seemed too little, too late. A bit like suddenly being surprised and sorry a faithful friend went away, when in fact she deserved to lose him.

"Livie?"

"I can't go to him. Not now. It will sound like I'm grasping for him now that he's gone. Anyway, he's making a lot of big changes, and the last thing he needs is me whining that I'm sorry and I want another chance with him."

"Are you afraid he'll tell you to go away?"

She was. She couldn't stand that. "Maybe."

"So don't try to get him back as a boy-friend, just offer to help him."

Olivia frowned. "Help him do what?"

"Find a new girlfriend," Lexie said sarcastically. "Wake up, girl. Help him move, help him fix up his apartment or house, be there so he has someone to talk to besides the blonde who will be itching to take him to bed."

"There's no blonde."

Lexie narrowed her eyes. "There's always a blonde, Olivia. Or a brunette or someone who will spot Daniel from a mile away and zero in like a one-woman swarm to a honey pot."

"I never even thought about another woman," Olivia whispered, as if saying it too loud might alert Daniel.

"Well, you'd better start."

Suddenly her pride reared up, fighting for something she hadn't realized she wanted. She sagged back on the couch, overwhelmed by the twist her life had taken in the past few hours.

While Olivia pondered what she should do, Claire toyed with her empty glass.

Lexie said, "Well, I'd better get upstairs

and get showered if I'm going to meet Jesse —"

"Wait," Claire said. "As long as we're discussing conscience and solving problems . . ." She stared at Lexie, pleading as if her friend had special powers when it came to figuring out complicated relationships. There was no pride in having knowledge if she couldn't figure out what to do with it. She needed advice and maybe a little help. "I'm not as good as you think."

"Uh-oh."

"Trent told me he wants me — like, you know, with lovemaking." Claire refused to demean her own ripening feelings by calling what Trent wanted just sex. "If I don't want to be with him that way, he as much as said, get lost."

Lexie said, "Actually, I'm impressed. Trent is saying it like it is instead of all that hokey meet-and-greet crap."

"So what should I do?"

It was Lexie's turn to be astonished. "You're kidding."

"What would you do?"

"Don't ask me that, sweetie. My moral compass and yours aren't even on the same dial. Despite the conscience you seem determined to push at me, I'd've done him after the first meet-and-greet just to find out if he was —" Then she stopped, and Olivia held her breath. Surely she wasn't going to tell

Claire that she and Trent had had sex way back when.

"Find out if he was what?" Claire asked.

"— worth the trouble, which I seriously doubt." Olivia relaxed and Lexie went on. "You've got a lot more to consider than sex with Trent. I know you don't want to discuss him because you're pissed, but remember Jeff, the guy you're married to?"

"I'm still annoyed at him," she said peevishly. "Of course, I've thought about him, which is more than he's done about me. I decided before I left Lake Moses that it was time to think about me. My life and my happiness. If Trent has done anything, he's made me realize just how lonely I've been. I'm terrified to go back to Lake Moses, where the only thing I have to do is cut flowers and read decorating magazines. Here with Trent has been fun and sexy and exciting." She turned to Olivia. "I guess I already know your opinion."

"Actually, I don't have any advice, Claire. I do think you should have tried harder to get in touch with Jeff —"

"— like he's tried to call me?" she snapped back, still stinging from what she thought was an outright rejection.

"Okay, let's not plow that ground again. But you're the only one who can make your life fun and exciting — I think you're giving Trent too much credit."

281

"This would be a lot easier if both of you said don't do it."

"That's the thing with a moral dilemma," Lexie said. "The one with the most to win or lose has to make the decision."

And with that last word from Lexie, she went upstairs to shower and Claire poured herself some more wine.

"I think I should have gone into a convent," Claire muttered, sipping deeply.

"We have managed to get ourselves into a quandary, haven't we?" And Olivia, too, refilled her glass.

An hour later, wearing her yellow halter dress and brown sandals, Lexie drove into the nearly full parking lot of the Beach Club. She found a parking space, and once the engine was off, she inspected her hair and lipstick in the visor mirror. The clock on the dash read 9:26 — a tad late but not so much that he would think she'd stood him up.

She'd pretty much decided what she would allow — for there was no doubt that Jesse would want more than a little hand-holding and some deep kisses. He was a guy after all.

Lexie always liked to face the obvious, and frankly she was excited about an adventure with a much younger man. In fact, she needed to be careful she didn't allow things to get out of hand. She wasn't feeling anywhere as cool and detached as she wanted him to think; she was damn close to second-degree horny.

She slid out of the car, took a deep breath, and slung the beaded strap of her summer purse onto her shoulder. She started across the lot, weaving in between cars and toward the front steps, where he said he'd wait for her.

Two couples were standing near the entrance beside one of the driftwood tubs of sea grass and beach roses that anchored the corners of the wide wooden steps. She couldn't quite make out whether the figure just behind the couple was Jesse.

Then the foursome, amidst laughter sprinkled through chatter carried in the evening breeze, moved on into the lot. Lexie affixed her smile as she drew closer.

The figure stood but didn't step forward to meet her as she expected. In the dark she couldn't see him clearly, but one thing was obvious, the build wasn't the slender leanness of Jesse.

Lexie stopped. What was going on? Some kind of date switch? Or had Jesse set her up for one of his friends? That possibility seemed incongruous to her. She was a lot of miles from naïve, plus she prided herself on being able to read men, and Jesse's enthusiasm sure hadn't indicated he was yanking some chain. She'd dealt with enough arrogant louses to know Jesse might be full of himself, but she doubted he was a total idiot.

The figure started toward her and despite an instinct to whirl around and run to her car, she ditched that idea. Whoever it was, she was having none of being intimidated. Not at her age and with her experience. Jesse wanted to play games? So be it; he'd just been trumped — big time.

Then the figure emerged full into one of the parking lot spotlights and Lexie went from surprised to stunned to horrified.

From about four feet away he said, "Hello, Lexie."

"Mr. Riggs." She was amazed she got his name out, her mouth was so dry.

"Bill."

"Yes." Well, this was a trip. "Hello, Bill."

"You were expecting Jesse, I know."

"I was — is everything okay? Nothing's happened to him, has it?"

"Jesse's gone home."

Which explained nothing.

"Oh." She couldn't think of what else to say. Lexie, who was rarely without either a quick retort or a salient response, drew a total blank. Her eyes were wide and riveted on him as he drew closer. Whether it was the backlight of the night, her own roaring heartbeat, or the sudden sense that she'd stepped into something a lot more complicated than Jesse standing her up, she couldn't pull her gaze away.

"Let me buy you a drink."

"I don't understand."

Then, because he obviously knew she meant his son's absence, he said, "I know, but you will."

He took her elbow but instead of going up the wide steps to the Beach Club, he was guiding her to a silver Lexus.

"Wait a minute." Lexie balked, pulling from his light grip. "Why aren't we staying here?"

He slid his hands into the pockets of tan trousers. He wore a brown cotton shirt with a collar and placket open at the neck. He wore his clothes well — no rolls hanging over his belt; his physique was solid and mature. She wondered if he worked out or ran.

"Jesse had told a lot of his fellow workers about his date with you. To walk in there with me would raise a few questions that could most likely embarrass him. I'd like to not do that if you don't mind."

It all sounded reasonable and logical and, well, just plain honorable. She'd always liked him, but there was something gracious about a man who would be that considerate of his son. All of that plus curiosity and a stirring of excitement swirled within her. "I don't mind."

He smiled easily, as though waiting for the opportunity. "Good."

He opened the door for her, and she slid

onto a butter-soft black leather seat. The door closed with that soft thud common in heavy expensive cars. The interior smelled of leather and a woodsy scent that she guessed was his cologne or aftershave.

He slid into the driver's side. "The Blue Lantern okay?"

"Sure." She hadn't been there, but she'd heard of it. It was an expensive tavern with patrons who mostly belonged to private clubs and moored their yachts in Newport.

Lexie didn't know what to say, but she was certainly intrigued. She could get used to this kind of dating, which suddenly was a far cry from groping with a kid who probably had none of the obvious finesse of his father.

In the dimness of the car she peeked at Bill's profile. Here was a man who had lived well and yet hadn't become bloated and puffy from too much rich food and other excesses. She began to relax as he drove down one street and headed up another. No radio, no talking, just the hum of all those powerful horses under the hood.

"When are you going to tell me what happened with Jesse?"

"Soon. Thought it might go down better over a sniffer of brandy."

"You do know how to intrigue," Lexie said, settling deeply into the soft seat.

Ten minutes later he was guiding her into the Blue Lantern. Dark wood, lots of glass behind a bar with rows and rows of glasses overhead. While they waited for the host to seat them, Bill told her the massive mahogany bar with a rolled lip had come out of an 1800s gentlemen's club in Boston. The room was lit by lanterns with blue globes that threw a shadowed intimacy over the room.

"Mr. Riggs. Good evening, sir. Sorry to keep you waiting."

"We're not in a big hurry, Gordon. Busy tonight, I see. How's the family?"

"Fine, sir. Your table is ready. Would you be wanting menus, sir?"

"Lexie?"

"Uh, I've already had dinner."

"Skip the menus, then."

Gordon led the way to a square corner table covered in white linen. In the center along with a lit candle was a trio of yellow roses in a blue bud vase. Bill held her chair for her and then took the one immediately to her right.

Gordon stood with his hands folded in front of him.

"Lexie, what would you like?"

She drew a total blank. "Whatever you're having."

He ordered two brandys and Gordon moved away.

"I've been meaning to call you about you coming to work for us. We'd like to sign you

for a year, then see how things work out."
He mentioned a moderate figure that two
years ago she would have laughed at. Tonight
she was just grateful.

"I thought you weren't interested."

"It's been a busy few weeks and I'm
backed up on phone calls. Since I was taking
Jesse's place tonight, I thought this might be
a good time to make the offer. I have the
contract in the car. You can take it tonight
and have your attorney or your representative
look it over."

What had loomed as a lost cause now was
suddenly solved. "I promise to get back to
you in a few days."

He nodded as Gordon brought the sniffers.
When he'd retreated, Bill raised his glass. "To
our future relationship."

Lexie nodded, knowing he meant work and
wishing he meant more.

After they'd sipped, Bill set his glass down.
"Now for that explanation."

"All right."

"I saw you this afternoon at the Beach
Club. I'd stopped by for a beer after a sail. I
was going to come over and speak when I
saw Jesse waiting on you. He's so obviously
and understandably enchanted with you, I
didn't want to interrupt."

"I have to say I wouldn't have recognized
him. He's turned out to be a fine young
man."

Bill's expression was stoic. "This last spring he was involved with a girl who tested positive for HIV."

If he'd told her alligators lived behind the bar, she wouldn't have been more stunned. "Oh, Bill, how awful. Is he okay?"

"We don't know yet. He learned about the girlfriend a few weeks ago. Like most kids, he was convinced he was immune. I finally got him to be tested last week. No results back as yet."

"The waiting must be horrendous."

"For me more than him. Jesse refuses to believe there's even the possibility he could have contracted it. When he told me this afternoon that you were meeting him tonight, I knew I had to do something."

For the first time in about a zillion years, Lexie blushed. She was glad the lighting was so dim. "I wouldn't have had sex with him."

"I couldn't take that chance. And I knew Jesse wouldn't tell you."

"So you intervened."

"It was necessary."

Lexie sat back in her chair, filled with a relief and a gratitude that she didn't believe she'd ever felt before for anyone. She didn't know what to say, so she simply whispered, "Thank you."

Chapter Sixteen

Olivia drove to Parkboro armed with a list of
things to do. She stopped at the cottage,
opening the windows to air out the closeness.
In her bedroom she dug through a desk
drawer and found a small manila envelope.
Then she went to her jewelry box, took the
ring Daniel had given her and his house key,
put the two items inside, sealed it, and then
folded it smaller, added a rubber band to
keep it folded so it would fit in her purse.

She'd waffled about doing this, but now
she was determined. Yes, she'd considered
Lexie's suggestions of going to Greeley, offering to help him settle in, look around for
suspicious blondes on the make. She shuddered at that last one. But even with the best
of intent, the approach struck her as shallow
and mechanical — beneath her, beneath the
honesty of their relationship. No, he'd made
it clear they were finished, and short of
something extraordinary, she would leave
things as they were.

Olivia wasn't angry at Daniel, but the

heavy sense of reality that had lodged in her chest since he told her it was a good thing they'd broken up allowed for no more "maybe tomorrow" vacillating.

Reclosing the windows, she got back in her car and headed for her next stop — the principal's office at the high school. She'd spoken with Fisler by phone, but she wanted to drop off her official resignation in person, plus say her good-byes.

"We're going to miss you, Olivia," Frank Fisler said, showing her to a chair and then sitting down behind a desk that dwarfed him. "I've notified the school board. They're disappointed, of course, that you'll be leaving us. Fortunately there's a waiting list of potential teachers."

Olivia was relieved. She didn't want to leave the school in a last-minute bind; resignations usually were submitted in the spring or at the end of the school year. "I know this is very sudden, and I would be glad to stay on for a while to make a smooth transition for my replacement."

"That shouldn't be necessary."

Olivia knew how the system worked, and especially at Parkboro. Leaving was never dragged out; she was already viewed as "the previous English teacher," and anything she offered now would be finalizing details.

"I will say this," Fisler said. "If you have lesson plans for the first semester, I'm sure those would be helpful, plus any student insight you could add."

She did, well . . . she sorta did. Her lesson plans had always been as vague as she could make them so she would not get boxed into some plan that put her students to sleep. As far as "student insight," she was not going to do that. It was unfair to prejudice an incoming teacher, or label a student. Her perceptions of class behavior and effort were her own, and since she'd had no budding dropouts or promising serial killers, she had little to pass on beyond encouraging the next teacher to urge them to pursue their dreams and potential.

But he wasn't finished. "In my days of teaching, when I went to a new place, I always found that kind of information helpful."

Info about students or class lessons? Since she wasn't sure, she didn't elaborate, either. "I'll put something together and send it here for you to pass on."

He nodded. "I haven't asked, and you aren't required to say, but I believed you were happy here, and I was a bit startled that you wanted to leave."

"It was a purely personal decision. No reflection on you or the school. I've began thinking about making a change since I returned to Bishop, but it didn't solidify until the past few days. I grew up there and my family home is there. After being back for a

292

while I realized, well, there were a number of personal reasons that convinced me it was where I wanted to be."

"Ahh, a going-home reason," he said with such empathy, she thought he really did understand.

"Funny," she said. "All the years that I lived there I couldn't wait to get away. Now I can't wait to get back."

He smiled. "You seem a little young for such a nostalgic philosophy. Are you going to be teaching?"

"I spoke with the principal at Bishop High, but only in the most general way. I wanted to make sure you were notified and that you could get a short-notice replacement before committing myself elsewhere."

"We appreciate that, Olivia. And the best of luck to you," he said, rising and coming around the desk. Then, as he was escorting her to the door, he said, "This seems to be the month for losing our best teachers."

"Yes, I've heard about Daniel."

He stopped, frowning. "Daniel? Daniel Cafferty?"

Instantly she knew she'd misspoken. Daniel hadn't notified Fisler. Why, for heaven's sake? He'd told her three days ago . . . unless he'd changed his mind. But she couldn't imagine that. Then again, he was under no obligation to keep her updated on his plans. He'd cer-tainly made clear his relief that they had no relationship and how much better that was than being entangled. What pricked at her was that when she made the decision, she'd believed that she was being kind and thoughtful of Daniel — not wanting to lead him on. But when he told her, she'd felt totally rejected. What kind of sense did that make?

Now she scrambled to downplay her words. "Perhaps I heard wrong," she said vaguely.

"Oh, you must have. Losing Daniel would be a huge blow, but fortunately that's not going to happen."

Olivia felt her stomach go into freefall, and she just barely managed to hold a neutral expression.

Fisler continued. "You must mean George Bonner, the sub from the math department. He's taking a leave of absence. So where did you hear this about Daniel?"

"Something was mentioned to me, and I'm afraid I assumed —" What was that warning about when you've dug yourself into a hole to stop digging? She managed a weak smile. "I must have assumed wrong."

"Well, I certainly hope so. I don't know how these things get started. I haven't seen Daniel but a few times this summer. Once where he seemed to be having a very animated conversation with Karen Clancey. I think it was around the time you left for Bishop. And then again a week or so ago we chatted at football practice. It was hot as

Hades, and Daniel sent the boys home." He paused. "Don't recall anything being said about his leaving any time soon."

Olivia didn't want to say anything more; she'd already said too much. She offered her hand, promised she'd get the requested material off to him in the next few days, and quickly exited the office.

Outside, the sun shimmered, making her very glad she'd skipped the panty hose and dressed for comfort. Next stop was the realtor from whom she'd purchased the cottage; she wanted him to list it for sale. But first she wanted to stop by Daniel's.

Claire, in what she called her perpetual state of indecision, procrastinated once again by stopping at the Attic to visit with Helene.

Earlier, she'd called Trent, and they arranged to meet at a garden shop just down the street from Helene's. What she was going to do from there . . . that was the decision.

"You didn't forget what I said, did you?" he'd asked when they'd spoken a few hours ago.

"No."

"Then why don't you come to my place?" He gave her the address, which she'd scribbled down on the back of an envelope. Just in case she ever needed it, she told herself.

The street, however, was some distance from Olivia's. By way of excuse, she said,

"Lexie has a bunch of errands, so she's taking the rental car. Olivia has gone to Parkboro."

"Then have Lexie drop you off. I'll take you home."

"It just sounds so —"

"Like you're coming for sex?"

"Yes."

"Aren't you?"

Maybe she was, but a little finesse and romance shouldn't be that hard for him to deal with. Her silence must have alerted him, for he quickly said, "Claire, that was crass. Of course, this is more than hopping into the sack. I'm sorry. I've wanted you for so long that sometimes my desire gets ahead of me."

She liked that he was honest, and she also liked that he wanted her so badly. She couldn't recall the last time Jeff had been so eager — Stop, she warned herself. This isn't about what Jeff didn't want, it's about you and what you want.

"Tell you what," he said "Let's meet this way. There's a garden shop on the lower end of Beach Street. I'll pick you up there about four."

She wasn't sure how this was different from going to his place, except it added an extra step. Nevertheless, the time and place was set, and while Claire had every intention of meeting him, she wasn't yet sure if she intended to do more.

Now, at the Attic, to her surprise, Jessica

was dusting shelves while Helene was re-arranging an array of red glass that Claire hadn't seen before.

"How's everyone doing?"

"Claire, how sweet of you to stop by and ask," Helene said with more enthusiasm than Claire had seen since she'd arrived in Bishop. The tears and worry over Jessica seemed to have dissipated. "We're doing just fine, aren't we, *chérie?*"

Jessica nodded. The bruises from the fight had faded or yellowed, but what Claire noticed the most was how calm and reserved she seemed to be. Much more like Helene than the volatile teenager her mother had worried over.

"You gonna tell her what happened?" Jessica said to her mother.

"In due time." Helene added a Ruby Flash bowl to her display and stepped back to look at it. "What do you think?"

Claire drew closer, studying the five pieces and the bowl. The five were small in different shapes — one a small cruet, a squat pitcher, a bud vase, a sleeping cat, and a ruby slipper. All the items were red, but in differing degrees determined by how the light hit them.

To Helene, Claire said, "It depends on how consistent you want to keep the red display. Jessica?"

"Me?"

Helene said, "Of course, you."

"I don't know anything about red glass."

"You know what attracts you to a display in a store. This is the same thing. Would you stop for a closer look or pass on by?"

"Oh. That presentation stuff you always talk about."

"Yes. What draws the eye and convinces the buyer to stop, admire, and decide she has to have the items. So much of this is selling the fantasy and showing the buyer what to do once the pieces are in their home."

"Okay." Jessica walked over, tipping her head this way and that, then backed up and frowned and again came in close. Claire and Helene exchanged smiles.

Finally Jessica said, "I like the bowl, but putting it with the other pieces — it, well, it looks awkward and clunky."

"Hmmm. Clunky in that it takes away from the delicacy of the smaller pieces."

"It calls too much attention to itself."

"She's right, Helene. At first, I thought it set off the others, but the Ruby Flash is so detailed, and although the piece is lovely, by contrast to the smaller ones, it looks gaudy."

Helene laughed. "I've never heard anyone call Ruby Flash glass gaudy." She looked over at her daughter, then removed the bowl from the display. "Any suggestions, Jessica?"

"I don't really know — now the small pieces seem lost."

"Then we need to spotlight them. What would draw you? Some contrast, maybe?"

She nodded and then quickly crossed the room and took a piece of lace-edged linen from a basket. "This is white and under the red . . ." But this time, instead of glancing at her mother, Jessica slipped the lacy piece under the delicate pieces of glass, and the entire display came alive. "Wow," she said softly.

"Wow, indeed," Helene said, so obviously pleased not just by Jessica's interest, but by her instinct. The Ruby Flash bowl was then placed on a sturdy oak side table and filled with some vintage lace ladies' handkerchiefs.

Then Helene excused herself and a few moments later returned with a pitcher of lemonade and three glasses.

Jessica shook her head. "I can't, Mom. I have to get to the drugstore. I told Kelly I'd cover for her until six. I'll be back then." She kissed her mother, said good-bye to Claire, and went upstairs to the apartment where they lived to change clothes.

"Jessica has done quite a turnaround, and I can tell you're very pleased," Claire noted as Helene poured the lemonade. The teenager had been so absent from the shop those first few times Claire, Lexie, and Olivia had visited, Claire had almost forgotten Helene had a daughter.

"Yes, and it's wonderful. Like night and

day. After you left the other day, she and I went to the police station and she gave them the names of the boys involved in that vandalism of Olivia's house."

"Really? Well, that's impressive. You must be very proud of her. And I imagine Trent was glad to have the names so he could officially charge the little creeps."

They carried their glasses outside and sat on the old church bench where Claire had waited for Trent only to have him tell her he wanted to be her lover, not her friend. In an hour or so she'd be embarking on an affair.

"So was all this good news about Jessica what you were going to tell me?" Claire asked, glancing at her wristwatch and pushing away the tangle in her own thoughts that suddenly felt like briers and thorns.

"The sale fell through."

Claire frowned. "You mean the sale of the store?"

"Yes."

"But I thought you had an agreement. Didn't he give you a cash binder?"

"Yes and yes. But it seems he got into an accident somewhere in Connecticut — drunk driving. No one was killed, but there were some serious injuries to two of his passengers. One of them is the son of a personal injury lawyer."

"Oh, my."

"Anyway, his father called me and literally

begged me to let his son out of the agreement." She looked at Claire. "I couldn't refuse. Poor man, he was desperate, so I said yes. I offered to return the binder, but he insisted I keep it. I'm still not sure I should."

"Of course you should. This has changed your plans, plus the shop was in that market transition so that you lost potential buying customers. You should keep the binder. Are you going to put it back up for sale?"

"I don't think so — at least not for a while. Not to say this young man's troubles are an advantage for me, but the sales agreement falling apart was actually a plus. I was having some regrets about leaving, especially after you three came home."

"Us? I thought we were all pretty chaotic, buzzing through the store and whining about how we hated that you were selling."

She smiled. "You just brought back so many memories of years ago when we all went antiquing before everyone in the world was doing it."

"It has become a popular pastime."

"And the Attic has been hurt by all the antique malls and those huge consignment centers. Used to be that everyone wanted authentic. Now they mostly want the look of authentic. I'd been discouraged by low sales and low foot traffic. When you three came, with all your excitement and enthusiasm, well, it was just a reaffirmation of why I loved this business. Going home to France has been a dream for so long that I hadn't even considered what I'd do when I got there. The past year when Jessica was acting out and I was so worried about her, taking her away became a solution and the reason for selling and leaving. My own need to return wasn't as strong as I thought, and yet I kept telling myself it was. Oh, dear, it all sounds so confusing."

"Actually, I think it's quite clear. Mixing up what we want to do with what we need to do is pretty common. And no one can blame a mother for wanting to protect her child from trouble."

Helene sipped her lemonade, then held the glass with both hands in her lap. "I began to have some regrets about the sale before Jessica had this change of heart." She gave Claire a warm look. "Again, those second thoughts were because of you and Olivia and Lexie. Watching you browse and ooh and ahhh over finding some treasures — oh, and speaking of treasures —" She set her glass aside, rising quickly, hurrying into the shop and returning with a small bag and handing it to Claire.

"The Bishop mug for Lexie," Claire said, taking a guess and being rewarded with Helene's wink. Anticipation and excitement filled her as she quickly opened the bag and unwrapped the tissue. "I just knew you'd find it for me."

"I called a friend who has a shop down in Newport. She didn't have one, but she said she knew who did. She was on her way north and stopped here this morning."

Claire examined it. "It's perfect. The other one had a tiny chip on the lip. How much do I owe you?"

Helene waved off her question. "It's insignificant. I was glad we could find one."

"Well, thank you. Lexie is going to be thrilled." She hugged her friend. "And I don't have to tell you how glad — and this is from Lexie and Olivia, too — that we all are that you're staying and keeping the Attic."

Claire lingered for another half an hour while Helene showed her some of the new acquisitions she'd purchased from an estate liquidation. They chatted about where to display them until finally Claire told her she had an appointment.

The two women said their good-byes, and Claire tucked the Bishop mug into her sling purse and started walking toward the garden shop.

She saw his truck parked in the front lot. He was leaning against the right front fender wearing boots and jeans and a dark blue T-shirt. A can of Coke was in his hand, his sunglasses in place, and he looked so sexy and, yes, eager to see her that Claire nearly stumbled as she approached him.

"Hi," she said, coming close, hoping her nervousness didn't show. Her excitement bubbled even deeper.

"Hi, Clary." Then instead of opening the passenger door for her as she'd expected, he slipped her bag from her shoulder, passed it through the window to the seat and then in one continuous motion, he hooked an arm around her neck and pulled her against him. He settled her intimately, the heat from his body circling around her like a cocoon.

He put one hand on her hip, the other casually cupping her neck, holding her as if the two of them had no other need but for each other; he was unconcerned that they were in broad daylight, that traffic cruised about jockeying for parking places. A few yards away, at the garden shop stalls, browsing customers wandered in and out of rows of newly arrived fall plants. The more curious glanced over; a few smiled, some frowned, but nothing and no one mattered to Trent.

Claire, however, was sure too many things mattered, how this looked, where it was going, and what she was doing here — perhaps a little late for an attack of conscience, yet the intensity rushing between them was alarming.

Then he kissed her.

A kiss that consumed her, enveloped her, sent her heart thumping and her mind reeling. Those tangled thoughts and fidelity stuff that should have mattered unraveled and flew away like so much fuzz in the wind. She could feel him on her and around her and in that heady instant she rode the uncoiling arousal soaring through her. . . .

"You can't say no," he whispered against her mouth. "You can't walk away from this."

"No . . . No . . . I can't."

And once again his mouth consumed her.

Lexie was seated on the chaise under the willow tree. Dressed in shorts and a halter, her tanned legs straddled the seat, glasses she used for fine print perched on her nose, and in her hands the contract from Bill Riggs.

On the ground within reach were the remains of a lobster salad, a cold can of barely sipped beer, and the phone.

She was on her third trip through the contract — They'd discussed the pertinent points when they'd changed their minds and decided to have dinner at the Blue Lantern, including her salary, which she'd negotiated up and then agreed to a compromise figure. The money offered wasn't as much she would have liked, but then, that was nothing new; she always asked for a high figure — the company came up a bit, she came down a bit, and they found an amount in between that was agreeable to both.

With Bill's offer, she'd taken in other considerations. A television station in a small market never paid what a big market paid. The position she was being offered — an on-location reporter — wasn't anywhere's near as lucrative as an in-studio gig.

But she had to consider the upside. She'd be working at what she knew how to do well, at a place where she wanted to be, and while flights of fancy about Bill being so impressed that a Bulldog winner from the huge Chicago market was now living in his midst and deserved big bucks, an anchor chair, and diva perks — well, she never really thought that would happen. Ego springs eternal notwithstanding. In fact she'd planned for a "thanks, but no, thanks" phone call, or even worse, no call at all.

Something intriguing occurred to her as she set the contract aside. This was the first time in her life that she wanted the job more than she wanted the money or special perks that in the past made a company's offer worth taking. This time the money didn't matter; she wanted to work for Bill. In fact, she couldn't recall ever wanting anything quite so much.

Such a hastily formed decision should have brought her up short, suggesting she take a step back and reevaluate what she was about to do, and yet at some level this all seemed just right.

She picked up the phone and punched out

Bill's number. When Amanda answered and she asked for him, identifying herself, his assistant said, "Ms. James, he was just asking me if you'd called. I'll put you right through."

Lexie grinned to herself. He'd been waiting to hear from her? How very cool.

Then he was on the line, his voice deep and just a little amused, and now she wished she'd gone to his office just so she could see him. She preferred to ignore her girl-with-a-crush reaction; she was too experienced for such silliness, and yet there was no denying either her eagerness or her infatuation.

"I've been waiting to hear from you," he said. "I hope you have good news."

Oh, I have good news and it's about you and me. "First I wanted to thank you for the other night."

"My pleasure. I enjoyed your company even though the initial reason could have been better."

"Have you heard anything about Jesse? Any test results yet?"

"Actually, yes. Jesse heard this morning. The test was negative for HIV."

"Thank God."

"My sentiments exactly."

A pause of silence.

"Bill, I have to say this. No man has ever done such a thoughtful thing for me. I'm still awed by it and that you cared enough about me to go to so much trouble."

"I'm just glad that Jesse mentioned his date with you."

Unsaid, of course, was that Bill assumed sex would be part of that date. While Lexie hadn't planned it, she wasn't so naïve as to think that intimacy absolutely would *never* have happened.

"Mostly," she said, "what you did says a lot about you."

"Jesse should have told you, and I made that clear to him. Denial on his part is one thing, but denial is a poor argument for his deliberate silence. Just because he didn't want to believe doesn't absolve him of responsibility. I think he understands that now."

Lexie didn't want Jesse to feel slighted, but now in light of hindsight, what had she been thinking? She was more than a bit annoyed at herself and at him for that charade of risky flirting. If she'd been a teenage mother, he could have been her son. And was there anything more desperate or pathetic than a woman in her late thirties dating a kid she'd once baby-sat? It even sounded obscene.

"Was he angry that we went out to dinner?" she asked.

"He'll get over it."

"Then he was."

"He thinks we had sex."

"Oh." And then, when he didn't say anything, she asked, "What did you tell him?"

"The truth."

"Did he believe you?"

"He better have. I've never lied to him before, and I'm not about to falsify something this serious." He paused, then cleared his throat. "I'm just glad that he's okay. It was pretty scary for a few days."

"I —" Then her throat closed around a sudden a wad of tears. Perhaps a delayed reaction of her own relief, but it was more the realization that fate or luck or salvation had tossed Bill into her life and her heart was straining to hear something from him that had to do with her and their dinner and a reminder of the tension surely he had felt as strongly as she. . . .

Then, as if he sensed her emotional conflict, he murmured, "Ahh, Lexie . . ." Another pause, then he added, "You're very pretty and I enjoyed our dinner. I'd like to spend some time with you. . . ."

His voice trailed off, the "but" screaming like a siren. In the past, Lexie would have leaped in and reassured if she was interested or reinforced the hesitation if the guy was a loser. But this time she fell silent, not wanting to topple what was so obviously fragile. Bill was struggling with what he wanted against how their being together had come about. Not because they'd casually met for a drink and dinner, but because of his son.

She changed the subject. "About the contract."

"Yes, the contract." She could hear the relief in his voice. "Any problems?"

"No, actually, it's quite fair. Do you want me to drop it off? I was about to go for an afternoon run, so it's not a problem."

"I have to attend an out-of-office meeting at four, but Amanda will be here until five-thirty."

"I'll make sure I get it there." She said good-bye, realizing the unspoken subtext that if she wanted to deliver it to him personally (translation: see him because he wanted to see her), it had to be by four.

She rose from the chaise, picked up the contract and her tray of leftover lunch. Running had never been so appealing.

In the house she went up to her room and changed into running clothes. She twisted her hair into a braid, and though she never in her life had done it before a run, she added a slash of lipstick.

She tucked the contract into her waistband lengthwise, tried a few moves to see if it would fall, and when it didn't, she patted her waist and proclaimed herself good to go.

Outside once again, she did some stretching exercises in the drive, waving to Flo and the girls as they assembled for afternoon iced tea on Flo's back porch.

"You sure are ambitious for such a hot day," Flo called.

"Guess it depends on what you want,"

Lexie said, waving again and heading out. She knew what she wanted; what she needed now was to be patient enough to wait for him.

Chapter Seventeen

On the Parkboro High School athletic field, Daniel wound up a two-hour practice having taken advantage of the lower humidity. Nevertheless, the boys were hot and eager to take a dunk in a pal's pool or drive over to Woodsett Lake. Daniel didn't blame them, and if he wasn't driving up to Greeley, he might have joined them.

Summer was dying, and with the new school year approaching, everyone seemed determined to cram in as many days of waning freedom with as much fun as possible.

Holding his clipboard with pages of notes and plays, he traced the lines of the football field with his eyes, mentally seeing the plays he'd been constructing; plays and moves the boys would execute this season.

He hadn't planned to be here — coaching or teaching — and in fact, he'd had dinner with the assistant coach last night to tell him of his plans. Then, within an hour of his arrival home, came the phone call from Marsha.

It was after ten o'clock and when Daniel heard her voice, his blood pressure must have shot up 100 points. His heart rate skipped right off the charts. "What's happened? Is Caitlyn okay?"

"Daniel, I swear you worry way too much," she said sternly, as though he were borderline paranoid.

Because you don't worry enough. "Maybe because she's seventy-five miles away and I don't like not knowing what's going on."

"Which is why I'm calling you — to tell you what's going on." Her voice had a swampy engulfing cadence that after a few moments always managed to convince him that drowning was preferable to listening. And to think that way back in his dumber days, he'd thought it chic and sexy. "Your daughter is being very stubborn and disagreeable about my plans."

His daughter? Her plans? Marsha's moments were always about her plans. Daniel relaxed. He was already on Caitlyn's side. "I can hardly wait to hear them."

"Are you going to be an ass, Daniel? If so, I'll hang up and call you after the fact instead of being thoughtful and considerate."

Daniel rolled his eyes. "My apologies. What are your plans that *our* daughter is so against?"

"Howie and I are getting married and we're going to move to Hartford. In Connecticut."

"I know where Hartford is."

"You don't have to be sarcastic. There could be other Hartfords —"

"Marsha, please. Get on with it."

Her tone cooled. "His family is there, plus there's a job waiting for him that pays much more than he's making here. Caitlyn refuses to go."

"And you want me to do what?" He wasn't sure what Marsha wanted to hear, but agreeing with Caitlyn probably wasn't it.

"Tell her she has to obey me."

"Marsha, look —"

But she wasn't listening. "I have custody, Daniel. She has no choice."

"*We* have custody," he reminded her though he knew to Marsha that meant he had custody of the bills.

"And she lives with me. Therefore she goes where I go."

Daniel sighed. "Try and think about this from Caitlyn's side. You're asking her to leave her friends and school and —"

"Oh, no, it's not that," she said, as if those reasons weren't even worth a discussion.

"Then what?"

"She doesn't want Howie as a stepfather. She told me she hates him."

Caitlyn, the truth-teller. He silently applauded, while cautioning himself. Then again, why in hell should he pussyfoot around this just because Marsha might do one of her temper snits? She'd never had a problem saying what she thought; he was the one who was always careful, always concerned that Caitlyn would get caught in some verbal crossfire.

"Did you hear what I said?" Then instead of allowing him to answer, she said, "Of course you did and I find it very hurtful that you have nothing to say about your daughter's rude and unacceptable behavior."

That did it. "Her behavior? Marsha, how about yours? You're the one bringing a new guy home every six months. Why should she think that this one is any different than the last three?"

But as usual, her response was all about Marsha. "And it's all your fault, Daniel Cafferty. If you were supportive of me being happy instead of tearing down my boyfriends to Caitlyn —"

"Now, wait a minute. I never did that and you know it. Let me speak to Caitlyn."

But he might as well have held his tongue. She railed on, and he could visualize her eyes hardening, her hand pounced on her hip, that nervous pulse in her neck throbbing. "I'm getting married, Daniel, and we're moving to Hartford. It will be wonderful and Caitlyn will have to adjust —" Then she yelled, "Caitlyn!"

"Marsha, wait a minute." He'd just had a brilliant idea.

"What?"

"Maybe we can work something out that will be good for all of us."

"Like what," she said, and he could hear the leeriness in her voice.

"Caitlyn comes and lives with me."

"No."

"Hold on. Just until you and Howie are settled and have had a chance for a honeymoon and some time to enjoy married life." It was all so much bull; Daniel didn't give a frigging hoot about Marsha's adjustment to married life. But he cared a great deal about his daughter. He continued. "Since we share custody, we can work this out. Just because Caitlyn has mostly lived with you doesn't mean you shouldn't have a break and let me take on the responsibility." Then he threw in his trump knowing that Marsha would think she was getting the better deal. "After all, I've been just having visits while you've had all the worry and angst and obligations."

"That's certainly the truth. Still, I don't know, Daniel. She's always lived with me. I've given her so much. I don't think she'll want to leave."

Daniel bit back the caustic remark that danced through his thoughts. "I know she'll miss doing things with you, and if she's really unhappy with me and wants to move to Hartford to join you and, uh, your new husband, then I'll drive her down." This he said because he knew there was not even the remotest possibility of Caitlyn wanting to go to live in Hartford with Howie.

"It would give us a chance for just us," Marsha was saying. "Wait a minute . . . Oh, Daniel, I can't. What would Howie's family think? Me letting my daughter go. It would make me look like I didn't care about her."

"On the contrary. They'd think you were a mother who wants her child to know her father and that you respect our relationship and you aren't afraid to share the time equally."

"They would?" Then, as if she finally got it, she said, "Yes, they would, wouldn't they?"

"And especially if you tell them."

"I will. That's just what I'll do." Then, "Let me get Caitlyn. I'll let you explain all of this to her, for I fear I'll probably break down."

Daniel just shook his head at the drama overplay. "I'll make sure she knows how much you love her."

And a few moments later Caitlyn was on the phone crying about how she wasn't going to Hartford and she hated Howie and she'd run away if she had to.

"How about running to here? Come and live with me?"

Silence skittered between them. "She'll never let me."

"She already has. It's all arranged."

"Daddy, really? Real and true?"

"Real and true. Get your things packed. I'll drive over and pick you up tomorrow afternoon."

"Oh, I love you! I love you so much."

Now her words from yesterday once again thrilled him. He was finally getting the chance to be a full-time father. Which reminded him, he'd better get home and shower and hit the road. He checked around to make sure the boys had put all the equipment away, then turned and headed toward his truck.

How quickly and wonderfully his plans had reversed. Three days ago he was talking of moving to Greeley, and now that had all changed.

Life was good. Yep, it was definitely good.

About twenty minutes later Daniel was home and downing a glass of cold water when his neighbor knocked on the back door.

"Hey, Jake, come on in."

"Thought you'd taken off for Greeley." Jake was spare and tanned and gnarled from years of hard work in construction. He'd retired after arthritis had crippled his hands, making wielding a hammer and running power tools too dangerous for his company to chance. He lived next door with his wife, Carol, and he and Daniel often shared a beer on hot afternoons.

"I'm off in about three minutes. What's up?"

"Olivia was here looking for you."

He set the glass down and wiped his mouth on his forearm. "She say what she wanted?"

He shook his head. "Didn't talk much. I told her you'd gone to Greeley." Jake knew this because Daniel had told him that morning when Jake invited him to Fenway for a nighttime Sox game. "So how come you didn't?"

"Football practice."

"Oh, yeah." Jake took his sports by season, and in his mind this was still baseball time. "So you think you got a winner with these kids?"

"We'll know by late October." Daniel took another long gulp of water. "I gotta run. Olivia want me to call her?"

"Nope. I got a feeling from the way she looked she figured you'd be here."

"Uh-oh, wonder what's going on."

"Want some advice? Say good riddance. Once you get married, you don't ever have to wonder what you did or didn't do wrong. She'll remind you every time she looks at you."

Daniel laughed. "I'll bear that in mind."

Jake turned to leave, then, when he got to the door, said, "Almost forgot. She left somethin' for you."

"Maybe I should call the bomb squad."

"Nah, too flimsy, don't tick, and I already dropped it, so scratch explosive."

"Jake, my dynamite expert," Daniel muttered, remembering that Jake had worked with explosives in Vietnam.

"It's in my kitchen. Be right back."

And when he returned, he handed Daniel a small manila package with a rubber band around it. Daniel stared at it, his stomach turning numb and sour.

"Gonna open it?"

"I know what it is."

"Don't sound like you're too happy."

He kept staring at it, wanting to be wrong, foolishly all these weeks counting on the fact that there was still hope because she hadn't returned it, hadn't sent it back.

Now he knew all hope was gone. Perhaps he went too far with that declaration that it was best that they weren't involved. He didn't believe that; he never had, but he'd thought that if he cut her loose entirely she'd change her mind. A kind of full freedom brings its own reward.

Daniel opened a drawer in the kitchen, slipped the package in, and closed it. "Remember what you said about saying good riddance?"

"Yeah."

"Well, she beat me to it."

Jake pressed his lips together, nodding. "Be

seein' you," he muttered, going out without offering any words. There were none to say, and besides, what would be the point?

Lexie arrived at Bill's office with little time to spare if she was going to catch him before his meeting. She was hot and sticky, hardly the condition to be in when meeting a man she wanted to get to know better. But if she was anything, she was deliberate and unconventional and certainly not trite.

To Lexie trite would have been a pretty dress, hair all casually tousled, a light scent, maybe a little musky, and high heels. Guys liked spikes.

No, coming here sweaty and hot would be the natural occurrence after a run, plus it was the approach of choice when one wanted to show that coming here was simply convenient. Just an ordinary event, and though she had every intention of timing her arrival to Bill being there, she didn't want to be blatant about it.

So when Amanda said he'd been unexpectedly called away from the office, Lexie was disappointed and a touch irritated.

"You're welcome to wait, although he didn't say if he was coming back here before his meeting."

She sighed, then pulled up her shirt and lifted the contract where it pressed between the band of her running shorts and her tummy.

Amanda's eyebrows arched. "Very clever."

"I told him I'd drop it off."

Amanda laid it on her desk. "I'll make sure he gets it."

"I have to go back to Chicago to tie up some loose ends. But I'll be back in plenty of time for the prep work before I start the fifteenth of September. If Bill needs to get me, he can call Olivia Halsey." She gave Amanda the number.

"Then we'll look forward to seeing you then," the assistant said warmly.

Lexie thanked her, then turned to leave when the office door opened and hurrying in was a hair-mussed, tie-loosened, and jacket-off Bill Riggs. Wherever he'd been, he'd beat feet back here in a huge hurry, despite the heat.

So as not to miss her? she wondered hopefully. Well, of course.

It was an overt gesture — Bill rushing back just to see her — and more than a little extravagant given that they were adults, but at the same time she found it charmingly encouraging that he was as interested in her as she was in him.

"Hi," Lexie said, hoping her grin had spread all the way to her toes.

"Lexie, hello."

"Mr. Riggs, are you okay?" Amanda looked alarmed. "You look as if you've been running, too."

"Usually, I wear other clothes for that, Amanda," he said ruefully, and Lexie pinched her lips together to not giggle. "I wanted to get back here in case Lexie had any last-minute questions about the contract."

The man was a master; he answered the question and opened the possibility of a running partner. At least it sounded that way, and Lexie was not one to pass an opportunity when it was smiling at her with such boyishness.

"You're a runner?" Lexie asked, her mind racing with the excitement of seeing him in a very natural way.

He grinned. "Mostly on weekends on the roads along the beach."

"I heard that area is pretty congested with bikers and traffic."

"Usually I go around six. Start at the top of Gull Beach. Early morning is the best."

Lexie nodded. "The best."

"Ah, something else in common."

And they looked at each other for a few moments, when Lexie finally smiled and said, "Oh, I gave the signed contract to Amanda. I didn't have any other questions."

"Good."

Then, because there wasn't much else to say and Amanda was signaling him about the time, Lexie said, "I should be going."

"Yes, I have that other meeting."

She left the office, her heart and pulse

racing with an exuberant energy. So much for going to Chicago this weekend. Mr. Bill Riggs altered those plans. Monday was soon enough. A nice weekend morning run by the beach was just what she needed.

"So did you get all that stuff on your list done?" Lexie asked Olivia later that evening.

"Mostly," Olivia said. "It all went okay except that teaching full-time here in Bishop isn't going to happen. They put me on a sub list, which is fine, but I can't live on a sub's salary. I'll have to look for something else."

The two women were in her father's den with Lexie in an oversize shirt and cotton panties, lounging on the daybed nursing a can of cold beer. Olivia had been sorting through the mail and came across an "unable to deliver" notice.

"Were you expecting something?" she asked Lexie, showing her the notice.

Lexie shook her head without looking at it. "Must be for Claire."

"Probably." She set it aside. "Sure wish Helene hadn't sold her shop. I'd love to work there."

"Maybe I could put in a good word for you with Bill Riggs."

Olivia glanced up and grinned. "You signed the contract." At Lexie's happy nod, Olivia went over and hugged her. "I'm so happy for you. A new start and a new job — this is so cool."

"And to think none of it would have happened if Claire hadn't nagged me about coming here."

"Claire, the mother of us all. So when do you start?"

Lexie filled her in on the details, adding, "Next up is looking for a place to live."

"Don't be silly. You can stay here."

"I don't know, Livie. For a few weeks in the summer is one thing, but it doesn't seem right. . . ."

But Olivia was shaking her head. "It's right for as long as it needs to be. Who knows, you and Bill might be an item in a few months and you'll be moving in with him."

"I hope so."

"You're really smitten, aren't you?"

"It's weird. When we had that first meeting, there wasn't any sense of attraction, no tension except my own fear he would flat-out say no to hiring me. Then that night when he met me — even before I knew why he was there instead of Jesse — it was like simmering fireworks. Oh, Bill said the test on Jesse came back negative." At Olivia's relieved look, she continued, "And then today, I was at his office, and it's like something is happening between us and both of us are trying to keep up."

"Sounds very exciting," Olivia said, very

happy for Lexie and wishing her own personal life had just such an energy.

"Did you see Daniel today?"

"I tried, but he was already on his way to Greeley. Probably house hunting."

"It's not over between you two," Lexie predicted.

"Ha." She held up her hand at Lexie's *but.* "Believe me, it's over."

"Okay, if you say so. My money's on another round in the near future. But if not, that's what you wanted, isn't it?"

"I thought so, but now that it's really true — I don't know, Lex. Maybe I want him like one wants a spare set of keys. You don't use them or think about them, but boy is it comforting to know they exist." Olivia sagged back in the old wooden chair of her father's. "That sure makes me look like a selfish bitch who uses a man who deserves much better."

"I think you're being a little tough on yourself. Given the way you were tied down for so many years with your parents, all the dreams you let go of, not wanting to be trapped, committed, or responsible for anyone but yourself sounds pretty normal to me."

"I got what I wanted, so how come I'm not shouting yippee and dancing through the rooms here embracing all my 'pretty normal' independence?" She paused. "I returned his ring today and his house key." She turned away, her eyes suddenly pained with tears she was determined she wouldn't cry. "He'll find someone. He deserves someone wonderful."

"As opposed to the woman he loves?"

"No more, Lexie, please. I'm just wrung out with it."

Lexie shrugged while Olivia stood and went to the window.

She had to stop thinking about Daniel, stop placing him in the same frame that she occupied. Starting tonight. It was over and finished. Her choice and his choice. A final breakup couldn't go much smoother. And never mind that her entire core was vacant, empty and cold.

Outside, the streetlights were on and she could hear voices coming from Flo's. The girls were there for their weekly canasta game.

She turned away and asked Lexie, "You hungry?"

"I thought we were waiting for Claire."

She glanced at the desk clock. "It's close to nine. Where is she anyway?"

"I think we both know."

"Wait," Lexie said. "I think someone just drove in."

Chapter Eighteen

From the center of the bed where she curled warm and soft — her back to his front — Claire felt dreamily enveloped. Overhead the ceiling fan whirled, squeaked, whirled, stirring the night air. His breathing was steady, reassuring, soothing, his heartbeat so strong it felt as if both of them were drawing life from one place.

Summer-evening sounds drifted through the open window — laughter from a late-running neighborhood party, a barking dog, the passing rumble of traffic, and the faraway call of a train whistle.

In Lake Moses she heard trains at night. Freight hauled along old tracks headed north; she'd always found the haunting blare solitary and comforting like being tucked into the folds of a family-treasured quilt on a chilly night.

Trains and quilts and family — all Lake Moses images, impressions sealed in moments that conjured up the things she'd always assumed were right and true and forever.

That she was here against a man who wasn't her husband, but had made her feel special and beautiful and more perfect than she had in years, had evolved from a hard-to-make choice yesterday to a committed dilemma tonight.

His hand, cupping her breast, slipped away now as he stretched out and rolled from the bed.

"Trent? What are you doing?" She turned over to watch him move like a naked shadow around the dim bedroom. The ceiling fan's slight squeak had her mindlessly counting turns, waiting for him to say something.

"I'm on duty in a little while," he said, as if they'd been together every night for the past year. "You staying here or you want to go back?"

She wished she could see him better, and reached over to switch on the table light. He seemed startled by the sudden illumination, and his expression flashed annoyance before he turned his back and began to take clothes from a drawer.

What was going on? What had she done? Or not done? Going to work was one thing; this came across as more like an escape.

"I should probably go back," she said, wanting him to argue, to come over and kiss her and tell her he wanted her here when he came home.

But none of that happened. Nothing happened beyond his saying, "I won't be long," and going into the bathroom. He closed the door, and seconds later she heard the water for a shower.

Claire blinked at what appeared to be the proverbial brush-off, or was it post-intimacy regret? Wasn't that supposed to be her role? Wasn't she supposed to be plagued with second thoughts, wrenching guilt, and wanting only to run from what she'd done?

Why had Trent assumed this role? Especially when this had all been his idea. She'd wanted friendship and some innocent flirting; he'd wanted sex and an affair. She'd more than met him halfway, although an affair seemed unmanageable given she had no intention of moving permanently to Bishop.

It had to be her, she decided, pushing the sheet back and wincing as she sat up on the edge of the bed. Whatever he'd expected from this coupling, she hadn't given him, which in turn led to . . . led to him . . . led to him doing what?

Obviously a question only he could answer.

She stood, searching for her clothes that were scattered about with the abandon of impatience and passion. They'd made love furiously and heatedly, and while she wouldn't put herself on a track with Lexie when it came to gauging a man's interest, Trent had been no slacker.

She dressed, found her bag, from where

she retrieved a hairbrush and some lipstick. When she had to dig beneath a wrapped package, it took a few seconds for her to remember that it was the Bishop mug for Lexie. Helene had given it to her just a few hours ago, and yet it felt like days.

She walked over to a bad reproduction of a dark wood highboy with an inadequate mirror. The dresser surface was cluttered with pocket change, wrinkled receipts, half rolls of Life Savers, his truck keys, an American flag in a Budweiser can, and a snapshot leaning against the beer can.

The photo was of a grinning Trent with a perfect-teeth blonde on his lap. The couple were on a boat, she in a skimpy two-piece pressed against a shirtless Trent in denim cutoffs.

Claire wondered if this was Tanya; she hadn't seen her in years and Tanya had been blonde. Or maybe that's what she wanted to believe — happier days with his ex rather than recent days with a girlfriend. Claire looked for a date on the snap but there was none.

Setting the picture aside, she realized what coming here and becoming too involved had wrought; an automatic intrusion and curiosity and even some seeds of jealousy that if this were a friendship, she would be only marginally interested.

No, correction. If this were a friendship she

wouldn't be here, she wouldn't be a little sore from the frantic sex, nor would she be nosing around the debris on his dresser. He was single, sexy, employed, and as Muriel had told her that morning at the coffee shop, he was, most of the time, hip deep in women, a situation Claire had no doubt that he enjoyed, encouraged, and would be unlikely to abandon. A photo of summer playfulness with a blonde was right in character.

The water stopped, an electric razor started, buzzed, as she mentally pictured him shaving stubble, then the razor stopped, and after a few more moments the door opened and Trent appeared.

By then, Claire was standing by the window, completely dressed, hair in place, purse slung on her shoulder, and but for the wariness in her eyes, she could have been waiting for a friend to go out for a late dinner.

"All ready?" he asked, sliding his belt into loops and buckling it. He pulled his wallet from last night's jeans, pocketed it along with his truck keys. He hadn't yet looked at her.

"What's the matter with you? And don't say nothing. You're not the same guy who practically had me undressed at the garden shop."

And to her amazement, the cool distance that had been there since he'd climbed out of bed simply dissolved. He drew in a breath and she wondered if her bluntness had caught him by surprise.

Finally, in a low steady voice, he said, "It's not going to work, Claire. I shouldn't have brought you here. And I never should have pushed you into making that asinine choice."

"Lover or nothing?"

"Yeah."

"You were sure I wouldn't choose lover?" At his nod she said, "And when I did you were stuck, and now you've decided I didn't measure up and you want out." She was astonished at how these pieces of logic bubbled out as though she'd known them all along. She was both amazed at the perfect sense it all made and disgusted that she'd been in such a haze of wonder just hours ago.

She walked from the window, prepared to leave; she would call the house and ask Lexie or Olivia to pick her up.

He grabbed her arm before she could get to the door. "You think you didn't measure up? Where the hell did you get an idea like that?"

"Perhaps from your less than loving approach to me since you got out of bed." *Well, Claire, when you mess up, you do it in a big, big way.* When he started to speak, she touched his mouth with her fingers. "Please don't. Don't spoil what we had. I'm leaving, which is what you probably want. You're right. My coming here was a mistake."

Instead of either the denial she *still* hoped to hear or the agreement she didn't want to hear, he said, "You were too good, Claire, and you were too open and willing and vulnerable. I hadn't counted on that. I figured we'd be hot and eager and then in a few months it would cool and we'd agree to go our separate ways, like usually happens. End of affair and we move on. No regrets, just a good time while we lasted. You were too intense —" He plowed a hand through his hair in frustration. "I'm no good at explaining this stuff. I just know that there was too much of your heart in the sex. I don't want anything as serious as you want."

Claire remained silent, absorbing not only the words but her own failed expectations. Maybe she should have watched a few porno videos to learn how to carry off unemotional sex.

But beyond "too much of your heart," as he called it, she concluded that Trent must have had lots of experience with both women who care and those who don't. That old adage that women promise sex to get love and men vow love to get sex wasn't even true for Trent. He promised sex to get sex.

She shuddered at this new realization. She'd been honest and flattered and very aroused, but now she recognized some deeper questions that she'd either ignored because of the moment or dismissed as fodder for later thoughts. *Where had she intended this relationship to go?*

Would she have fallen in love with him? Would she have left Jeff? Would she have been one of those women who, because of some loneliness, marital dissatisfaction, and more than a little boredom . . . simply walked away from years of marriage and started anew with an exciting lover who made her feel good?

"Claire?"

"I was considering what you said. I'm amazed that you've concluded so much about me, about us, from a few hours of love-making."

"I've been around, Claire."

"How reassuring," she muttered sarcastically.

But he continued on. "You're not the affair type, and while I probably knew that before, I wanted you and I knew you wanted me. It was just a matter of time. I've wanted you since we were together that summer you were fighting with Jeff. This time I wasn't going to let you walk away wrapped in some 'we're just good friends' comfort like I did back then. That's what happened twenty years ago, and no way was it going to happen again. So I gave you the ultimatum."

The more he explained, the more horrified she became. And all along, she'd been deluded enough to find his "lover or nothing" proposal challenging and more than a little flattering.

Now she didn't know whether she was relieved that she had indeed been more than he wanted, or furious that this dance of the past weeks had been more about what she hadn't done twenty years ago.

"Just so I'm really clear on this. You're telling me that because I wouldn't sleep with you years ago, you were determined that I would this time?"

"Come on, we have to go."

She pulled from his grip. "Answer me."

He swore, looking a little put out that he still had to talk and explain. Finally he said, "I wanted you then and I wanted you the past few weeks. I don't know what else to say."

Claire didn't, either. *He wanted? He wanted?* This was all about what *he wanted.* Well, she wanted some things, too. She wanted to rage, she wanted to cry, and she wanted to blank it all out as if it was a dream she could escape by waking up.

She pushed away from him and weaved her way around the apartment furniture looking for the door that led out. She'd been so wrapped up with him and around him when they got here, she recalled nothing but the taste and feel of his kisses and her own desire.

"This way," Trent said softly, pressing his hand against her back, guiding her toward the door. "I want to take you home."

She wanted to say no, but what did it matter? She felt disoriented and sad and, more than anything, humiliated and ashamed that she'd been such a vulnerable fool.

In his truck she sat close to the passenger door, at least a million emotions away from earlier when she'd curled next to him and he'd slid his hand around her thigh.

They didn't speak and when Trent stopped at the end of the drive at Olivia's, he said casually, "Looks like company and a party."

His friendly tone, as if he were dropping her off after a late date, enraged her, and for the first time in her entire life, Claire gave in to some primal anger, turned, and in one continuous motion, slapped him.

Trent reared back from the force, but Claire was already scrambling to open the door and get away from him.

Then he reached around her, unlatched the door, and briefly touched her shoulder. "Take care of yourself."

She said nothing, neither looking at him or answering, pushing the door open and sliding from the seat. She slammed the door and Trent wasted no time backing around. His headlights swept the house and yard, illuminating an SUV that was parked near the back door.

For a moment she scowled, wondering who was here while at the same time thinking she'd forgotten if Olivia or Lexie had mentioned company. She started up the drive trying to think of a way she could sneak in and get to her bedroom. Being sociable and smiley was *not* what she wanted to do.

Then Olivia came running out of the house.

"Claire, I thought you'd never get here," she said, reaching her and steering her toward the door she'd just come out of. "Lexie is running out of excuses. She saw Trent drive away and —"

The mention of Trent and knowing they'd probably guessed what she'd done suddenly overwhelmed her. "Oh, Livie, I've been so stupid and so awful. You and Lexie were right."

"We'll talk about it later," she said, then lowered her voice. She took her arms and shook her lightly. "Listen to me, Claire. Jeff is here."

"Jeff?" Then she blinked, looking back at the SUV and really seeing it. It was the same as Jeff's. "Jeff is here? No, no, please God, no, I can't go in there." She could hear her voice rising, a rush of coming hysteria drenching through her. "I can't, I can't —"

"Claire!" Olivia gripped her shoulders, stronger this time. "You need to get a grip and hear what I'm saying."

But instead tears sprang into her eyes and she tried to break free. "I can't, I can't."

It was then that Flo wandered over from

next door. She wore a flowered cotton robe and terry-cloth slippers; she was snapping the robe closed as she came. "Is she okay? What happened? I was in bed reading when I heard the truck leave and then your voices. I wasn't going to come out, but then I wondered if there was trouble." Before Olivia could come up with a reassuring response that didn't raise more questions, Flo said, "Did that Trent McGraw try something nasty?"

Olivia could have kissed her. "A misunderstanding, I'm sure, but Claire is upset."

"Hummph. I always did think he was too fast with the ladies. Nothing good about a man his age who isn't settled down. Good for Claire for not falling for his line." Flo patted Claire's shoulder.

"Flo, can I ask you a favor?" Olivia put her arm around her friend, letting her keep her head turned and her face hidden by the yard's shadows.

"Sure you can. That's what I'm here for and you never ask me any favors." There was a hurt pique in her tone that Olivia didn't miss.

Olivia smiled. Flo really was sweet, just a bit too mother-hennish, but now the mother hen in her was what Claire needed. "Well, consider this a favor, then. Can we freshen up at your house?"

Flo glanced at the SUV and then at the

house. "Well, of course. No one wants to greet company with blotchy skin and red eyes."

And so with Olivia's arm around Claire, the two women followed Flo into her house.

"You know where the bathroom is. Towels and washcloths in the cupboard. Can't find something, give a holler."

"Thanks, Flo."

Olivia took Claire into the bathroom, flipped on the light, and made her sit down on the commode lid. Claire had folded her arms tight, holding them pressed against her as though holding down a coming rush of nausea.

"You okay? You want to throw up?" Olivia asked, grabbing a towel in case Claire didn't move fast enough.

"No, I want to kill both of them. Trent for what I let him do to me, and Jeff for showing up tonight."

Here in the bright glare Claire's distress was clearly evident. Olivia took a washcloth and soaked it in cold water, wrung it out, and wiped Claire's face. Then she cooled it again, twisting the water from the cloth, watching Claire as she took it and pressed it against her face, taking deep breaths and finally beginning to relax.

"Claire, he didn't force you, did he?"

"I wish he had. This is worse."

Olivia couldn't think of anything worse

than forced sex. "Worse because you let him?"

"Because I was a fool."

Olivia sighed. "I get the feeling there's more here than post-coital regret."

But instead of nodding or attempting an explanation, Claire asked, "Why is he here?"

"It's a surprise."

"Well, he already accomplished that, and I haven't even seen him. So why is he here?"

"I can't tell you. And you sound like some hard-ass broad. Do we thank Trent for this, uh, change?"

"You can thank Trent for giving me a crash course in what women get when they cheat."

"Trent was the loser this time, Claire. He just doesn't know it. Come on, brush your hair, and maybe a little makeup. But we need to get over there."

She shook her head. "Jeff will know."

"Probably not. He's excited about seeing you. Time to rise to the occasion, Claire. And that is what you do best. Later we can rant and eat Trent alive."

Olivia looked through an array of Flo's cosmetics, some so old they were by companies no longer in business. All of them were too winter heavy and the wrong color for Claire, but they'd have to do. "Look up here at me." Using a cotton ball, she brushed some color on her cheeks, then took most of it off. She dabbed beneath her eyes where some mascara had streaked.

Claire rose, straightening her skirt. "I can manage the rest." Once again she brushed her hair, added some lipstick. She stared at her reflection, seeing sadness and harshness. Her eyes met Olivia's in the mirror. "What am I going to say?"

"That you were out with an old friend, and if you'd known Jeff was coming you would have canceled. You and the friend had dinner and drinks and you had a bit too much to drink. An acquaintance offered you a ride home and you took it. When you got here and saw the SUV, you wanted to look your best for him, so you took a few moments to get your head together."

Claire was wide-eyed. "How did you think of all that so fast?"

She grinned. "Scary, isn't it?"

"Yes, and it's all a lie."

"Of course it's a lie, Claire. Would you rather tell him the truth?"

"If I did, he wouldn't stay long."

"Well, that's a decision for later. Meantime, you're going to be yourself and at least act glad to see him." Claire flinched as if Olivia was suggesting necessary pain. "Okay, let's do it this way. Let me do the talking and you just smile, and well, you'll know what to do when we get in there."

Claire took her hand and squeezed. "What

would I do without you?"

"You'll have to thank Lexie. She spotted the truck and nudged me to find out if you were okay."

Claire managed a slight smile. "She's so smart, so quick. As long as we've all known each other, she's always the one who sees the trouble first. I keep thinking I'm smarter than I used to be, then something like this happens, and I see how really dumb I am."

"You are not dumb. Impressionable, maybe, but neither Lexie or I would have you any other way." She drew Claire into her arms. "Just remember, whatever happens, we're always your friends and you can always count on us."

"Oh, Livie, you're going to make me cry."

"Yeah, me, too." She opened the bathroom door. "Quick test with Flo," she whispered, pulling Claire with her as they walked back down the hall to where Flo was eating some ice cream in the kitchen.

"Well, well, you certainly look better," Flo said, smiling.

"Thanks for your kindness," Olivia said.

"Yes, Flo, I'm afraid I was a real mess."

Flo waved off their comments with her spoon. "Just you stay away from that Trent McGraw. He ain't made you happy, and we women shouldn't be wastin' time with men who make us cry."

They both nodded, and when they were

outside, Claire said, "Flo summed it up, didn't she?"

Olivia nodded as they approached the back door. "Ready?"

"No."

"Trust me, you're going to be very happy when you get inside."

And before Claire could mold her frown into a question, Olivia had her walking through the kitchen and into the living room.

Claire came to a dead stop, hands flying to her mouth before she was running across the room to embrace the young man who rose to his feet.

Chapter Nineteen

"I don't believe you're here!" Claire cried. "I thought you were out West and — oh, Tony, y-you look s-so wonderful a-and —" Claire didn't know she was sobbing her words more than speaking them until her son drew back and then patted her awkwardly.

"We wanted to surprise you," Tony said. "Guess we did. As for the wonderful, yeah, well, I don't know about that. Mostly I'm just glad I'm still here."

"What do you mean?" she asked, not so euphoric now that her maternal worry quotient had gone immediately on alert.

Tony answered vaguely, saying, "Lots to tell you."

"And I want to hear it all." She couldn't take her eyes off of him. The "why here" and "what happened" were for later. Right now she wanted to simply bask in the realization that he was here and she couldn't have been happier.

At that point Jeff slid an arm around her shoulders and hugged her lightly. She was struck by how naturally routine and secure the gesture felt. His body, his scent, the familiarity of years of marriage, and when he bent to kiss her, she relished the maturity and the sweetness. Funny, it had been a long time since she'd had such philosophical thoughts about their relationship. She wasn't sure if it was this timely "family" visit or the contrast to those hours with Trent. Perhaps it didn't matter. Then again, perhaps it did.

"And you sure were surprised, weren't you?" Jeff asked, his eyes warm, his smile pleased.

"I'm dumbfounded."

Then it was Lara's turn for a hug and kiss.

"Mom, I've missed you." Tanned and looking so pretty and poised, Claire wanted to weep. Her family, all here to see her, all waiting for her, and where had she been? The guilt that she'd thought she should have felt earlier now trickled in, bringing with it an unexpected chill. Claire drew her daughter to her for warmth and because she just needed to hold her.

"Now, how could you miss me with all the fun you were having in Richmond," she said to Lara, trying to lighten the moment.

"Yeah, well, actually I haven't been in Richmond for a couple weeks."

"You haven't?" Claire's chill turned to alarm. "Where were you?"

"With Dad." She paused, glancing at her brother. "And Tony."

"This is beginning to sound like the plot of a mystery," Claire said, trying to relax. Tony had sat back down on Olivia's Victorian sofa, notably missing from their trio.

Now for the first time she saw an unsettling distance that seemed to encircle him. He seemed quieter, self-conscious, anxious, not the usual talkative, fearless, and restless young man she'd watched through his late teen years. This change jarred Claire by its marked conspicuousness, and yet she sensed genuineness, as if he'd embarked on something that held meaning and purpose.

Obviously the "something" was the mystery, and apparently having a united front was paramount, otherwise why would the three of them trek clear to Rhode Island? Certainly not just to surprise her.

Then there was the always tense issue of Jeff and Tony barely able to say a civil word to each other for the past year — what had changed that? When Tony refused to interview for a job that Jeff had set up, then took off on his cross-country adventure, Jeff had been so furious that he'd ordered her not to send him any money. According to his father, Tony was irresponsible, impulsive, and self-indulgent — now he was here and Jeff was smiling at him as if he'd become a hero?

Even as wildly pleased as she was by these seeming changes, Claire knew that to get from a splintered family to this unity, there had to have been compromises and concessions. Jeff caving and suddenly embracing his son? Or had Tony had some kind of prodigal son epiphany?

She went over and sat beside Tony, taking his hand and lacing her fingers with his. Lara sat in an upholstered side chair, and Jeff took the window seat.

Near the edge of the room, stood Olivia and Lexie. They had already eased out of the Fitzgerald family reunion, wanting to leave Claire to hear all the news and bask in the togetherness of her family. Except no one was saying anything, and Claire, edgy from the continued silence, began to talk.

Watching the four of them and yet out of earshot, Lexie whispered to Olivia, "So what happened?"

"Don't know except she's done with Trent."

"Hallelujah." Then Lexie scowled. "He didn't hurt her, did he?"

"Not physically, but he did some kind of emotional number on her."

"Bastard," Lexie spat. "Tell me she didn't have sex with him."

Olivia nodded her head. "Wish I could. Something happened afterward that has convinced her she was dumb and ignorant. I mean, I don't ever recall seeing Claire so hard and rough on herself about anything. There was almost a loathing."

Lexie's eyes narrowed. "The jerk should be hanged."

"I'll get the rope," Olivia offered.

"Or how about a nice long knife and he could join the soprano section of one of the local choirs."

"That works, too."

The two friends giggled.

"And to think you once were wailing away because he never noticed you," Lexie said, raising her eyebrows at Olivia.

"Yeah, well, guess I was the lucky one."

"You think?"

"Okay, okay. But I got over that longing pretty quick. When a guy can't remember your name from one hour into the next, that's pretty telling."

"Hmm, now if you'd just stop being so stubborn about Daniel."

Olivia sighed. "I told you. Daniel's made it clear we were better off with no relationship —" She stopped, sending a glare Lexie's way. "Even when we're talking about Claire, you drag Daniel in like you've got some agenda to get us hooked up."

"I do," she said without pause. "You love him and he loves you. Clean, simple, and ready for you to do something about it."

"And I see it as a big fat dead end —"

"That you created, my friend."

"I know, you don't have to remind me." Olivia deliberately changed the subject. "And speaking of Trent and Claire —"

"Yesterday's bad news. Now, as for you and Daniel —"

"Lexie," Olivia warned.

"Okay, okay. What about Trent and Claire?"

"We haven't heard his side of the story."

"Who cares? He hurt Claire, which automatically makes his side worth either a rusty knife or a double-knotted rope," Lexie said dismissingly.

"You're right." Olivia paused. "When I told Claire that Jeff was here, she practically hyperventilated."

"Lousy timing."

"Actually, I think it was good. Otherwise we might all have been planning Trent's deserved demise. And this news they're going to tell her will sweep away all the night's nastiness."

"Come on," Lexie said, turning toward the kitchen. "Let's you and I get another glass of wine and go into the study. Claire can find out why her family is here, and you and I can commiserate about the current men in our lives."

Olivia glanced over at the family group. "Claire seems to be doing the talking, so maybe the others are nervous with us standing here."

As the two women slipped away, Claire finished her rambling account of her weeks in Bishop, minus any mention of Trent. She guessed they wanted Olivia and Lexie to leave, but no one was going to be so rude as to say so.

Now, as she watched them disappear around the corner, she wanted to know what was going on. Her family hadn't driven all the way up here just to say hello and listen to chatter about vandalism, house restoration, and Helene.

Then the real possibility that their hesitance was about bad news worked its way through her. Had something so terrible happened that they wanted to tell her in person?

"As wonderful as it is to have all of you here, something prompted this trip."

"No lecture on why I didn't call you?" Jeff asked.

"I wasn't happy about that," she said, giving him a direct look. "And I was determined I wasn't going to break down and call you. We can discuss that later," she said, not wanting to get sidetracked. And a later talk would also include her frustration and hurt after too many years of being the one trying to track him down, being the one who worried and fretted, and being the one feeling guilty if she didn't promptly return his calls.

"Yeah, I got that impression when you never called after I left that message on Olivia's answering machine. As for after that, you can blame my silence on your son." But Jeff's words weren't harsh or accusatory. In fact he almost sounded proud, which astonished her even more. He continued, "I wanted to call a number of times, but Tony squelched it and made me promise not to sneak. He made Lara promise also."

At Lara's nod she turned to Tony.

"Go ahead," Jeff said. "Tell your mother."

Tony wouldn't look at her, but he began to talk. Slowly, carefully, and in an unemotional monotone that seemed determined to state only the facts. "That last money you sent me, well, I used it for drugs. Had a good time with some guys — we all got high and then someone brought more stuff. The next thing I remember was waking up in a hospital. They said I OD'd. Later I was told some old lady found me and called 911. Guess they tried you in Lake Moses, and when they couldn't get you, they called Dad. I was pretty much out of it, but even in my stupor, I figured Dad would never come and I'd be in the clear." At her puzzlement he said, "Like you guys wouldn't know what happened, you know, I'd get away with it. I'd get out of the hospital and do just what I'd been doing."

Claire listened, eyes wide, and color draining from her face as she too vividly envisioned the scene he was unfolding, and its ramifications.

"Except Dad screwed up his theory and came. Thank God," Lara said before Claire could muster any thoughts into words. "After Dad saw what had happened, he called Olivia's. Since he didn't want you to freak, he didn't leave a message that Tony had OD'd. Guess he thought you'd call him back."

Claire visibly shuddered with the reality of her own prideful stubbornness. While she'd been busy ignoring Jeff, nursing a prissy anger to prove some silly point about him making a better effort to call her, her son was fighting a drug overdose. She should have been there, and the realization that . . .

"You could have died," she whispered to Tony, as if saying the horror too loudly might make an instant death reality.

"I think I did for a second or two because when I woke up — yeah, I felt rotten, but I also felt like I'd climbed out of some dark hole."

"You very likely did," Jeff said somberly.

Her hands gripped Tony's arm, fingers noting his thinness. Her eyes swam with tears. "Oh, Tony, I don't know what to say. I'm so grateful that you're okay."

And for the first time he smiled at her. "I am, too, Mom."

She gulped, swiping at her damp cheeks. "But why didn't you want to call me?"

"Because I was always calling you to bail me out, always expectin' you to. This time, I don't know, it seemed like a second chance, like I could prove I could make it. I wanted to do it without runnin' to you like some loser kid. I wanted to prove I wasn't a total freakin' failure who needed you to get me out of the latest mess."

She knew she was supposed to understand his reasoning. And on some level perhaps she did. "Son wants to prove himself" was hardly an unusual concept, but still, as his mother . . . if he'd died — no, she wasn't going to think about that. He was here and he was fine, well, almost fine.

There had to be more, something ongoing. Surely he wasn't "cured" because he'd survived an overdose that scared him off drugs. Right now he was still in the throes of turning that corner. But long range? She'd read and heard enough about addictions to understand that those trying to recover needed a plan.

"Claire, are we overwhelming you?" Jeff asked.

His question gave her a nudge of irritation. That sense that Jeff on more than a few occasions thought that unless the subject was flower arranging or setting a pristine table, she was besieged and unable to cope. However, this was not the time to point that out to him, but she made a mental note for later.

"I'm not overwhelmed, I'm very grateful," she said. "Where did all of this happen?"

"In New Mexico," Jeff said. "I called Lara after Tony was in the clear, and she flew out so she could see him. She wanted to know why I hadn't called you, too. I almost did because I was so glad he was alive and getting better. But Tony was absolute in his determination that the next time he saw and spoke with you he'd be clean and sober." Jeff nodded to Tony. "Fill in the details, son."

"The hospital let me go and we all flew home to Lake Moses. I'm starting in a rehab clinic on Tuesday. I'm still a little shaky and not having anything to take the edge off has been rough."

Now she knew why he seemed so anxious.

"But I wanted to see you and I wanted to see you before I started in rehab. I guess to prove to myself that I could take some control and function even though I'm scared shitless. So Dad said we should just drive up here and surprise you and here we are."

Claire leaned back, relaxing for the first time in hours. First that disaster with Trent, then arriving home only to be trapped in a fear that Jeff would take one look at her and know, followed by the revelation that while she'd been debating — these past days — having sex with Trent, her son had come very close to dying.

Jeff stood and stretched. Lara wandered over to look at a Victorian vignette that Claire and Olivia had placed on an antique desk.

Tony folded his arms together, brows

knitted deeply, voice so soft, Claire could barely hear him. "Mom, do you think I can do this?"

"I know you can," she replied with a sureness as definite as tomorrow's sunrise. "I'm so proud of what you've already done."

"Yeah, like today is a new beginning."

"Yes." But she wasn't just thinking about Tony. She was also thinking about herself, and if there could be a new beginning with Jeff.

A few hours later, after Tony and Lara had gone off to bed — Tony on the study daybed and Lara in a small sewing room upstairs, Claire and Jeff were alone in the living room. Olivia and Lexie had disappeared somewhere, and Claire knew they wanted to give her space and time alone with Jeff.

Between the disaster with Trent and this near tragedy with Tony, Claire was in no mood to be either meek or silent.

"It's terrific about Tony, isn't it?" Jeff asked, breaking the silence. He'd taken her place on the sofa, and she was standing by the windows.

"Yes. And I wish I could say we're terrific, too."

She heard the sigh.

"No warm-up, huh?"

"No."

"I know you're annoyed I didn't call —"

"It's not that. Not now. Now I know why.

And if it was just that, I'd be pretty petty to be holding it against you." She paused and then looked at him directly. "I'm weary of being ignored, Jeff. I'm tired of being left home while you are more married to your job than you are to me. And while I'm very happy that you and Tony are once again father and son, that new relationship hasn't changed ours. You and I have no relationship beyond being parents and being legally married."

He didn't say anything, looking beyond her as though there were answers outside in the starry night. "What are you saying? Do you want a divorce?"

The question startled her. "Is that your solution? Let's not try to work things out? Let's just toss away almost two decades of marriage?"

"I don't want a divorce." He rose to his feet, slipping his hands in his pockets. "I love you. I can't even imagine not being married to you. I know I haven't been the most attentive husband. Despite you thinking that I never noticed you were unhappy, I did. I just didn't know how to fix it. Work was crazy and whenever I tried to pare down or ease off, there would be another crisis that needed solving." He held his hand up. "I know what you're going to say. Our marriage was also a crisis that needed solving. I plead guilty. I guess it was just easier to believe it would all work out between us. Also, it was easier to solve work problems than our problems. Work stuff was pretty cut and dry. You and I, well, it was just too complicated."

Claire listened, a little more encouraged by his words. At least he knew there were difficulties and admitted to not having any solutions. That was a good first step. Still raw in the back of her mind was the issue of Trent and the realization that if she and Jeff had had this conversation months ago and had begun work on their relationship, she would have never gotten involved with Trent.

Maybe she was seizing on any excuse for what she'd done, but there was no doubt that the timely arrival of her family had jerked her back into reality with a massive punch.

"Jeff, perhaps the best place to start is to uncomplicate us. Get back to talking to each other, to making a few sacrifices. I mean me as well as you."

"Look, I know this isn't going to be solved with a few conversations and one or two suggestions, but we have to start somewhere. How about we start by making sure we're together more?"

"Already I like it," she said and really meant it.

"Good." He walked over to where she was seated. "What about you coming with me on some of these business trips? We could probably eek a few days away together — do some antiquing that I know you like. Do some sightseeing, which I like."

"Sightseeing?" Claire scowled. "You hate to sightsee."

"Actually I was going to say sex, but sightseeing seemed more in keeping with the tone."

"Sex is more honest." She smiled and slipped her arm around his waist. "And much more fun."

He grinned. "Hey, no argument from me."

"Or me, either."

"I'm scheduled for a trip to Hawaii in September. I've also got some vacation time coming. What about we plan to stay an extra week?"

"I'd love it."

"Then we're all set. . . ."

And as they walked upstairs, Claire knew that their problems hadn't been all neatly solved, but at least they were talking and looking for solutions. A first step and a beginning.

In Olivia's bedroom the overhead fan whirled above the bed. Lexie sat cross-legged at the bottom with Olivia sprawled on pillows against the headboard. Between them was a just-delivered pizza to make up for the dinner neither had had. It was just after two-thirty in the morning.

"Is this private or can anyone join?" Claire

asked from the doorway.

"On one condition," Lexie said with a grin. "You have to go downstairs and get the beer."

"And napkins," Olivia added. "I don't want pizza stains on my good white sheets."

Claire nodded. "Can I ask why you guys aren't in the kitchen?"

"Because the walls between the kitchen and Dad's study are thin and Tony is sleeping in the study."

"That makes sense. Be right back."

And she was with three cans of cold Coors Light, a handful of napkins, and a package wrapped in brown paper.

"Jeff is asleep."

"We guessed. Are you all right?" Olivia asked. "I mean, earlier I was really worried."

"Don't know what I would have done without you guys."

"Never have to find out," Lexie said, taking the cans, popping the tops, and handing them out.

Claire smiled at her friends, sipping from the can and reaching for a piece of the pizza. "Guess you want to know what happened."

"Every detail," Lexie said, working on a second piece.

"But first . . ." She handed Lexie the package.

"What's this?" She opened the paper, then unrolled the tissue-wrapped item. When she saw what it was, she almost squealed. "A Bishop mug! Oh, Claire this is so terrific! Wherever did you find it?" Her face was shiny with delight.

"Helene got it from a colleague who owns a Newport store. I meant to tell you, Livie, that I had it, since both of us were trying to locate one."

Olivia waved away her forgetfulness. "I'm just glad you found one. I even stopped at my favorite consignment store while I was in Parkboro. She usually has everything, but no luck."

"Well, thanks. Can't think of a nicer present."

"Oh, and speaking of Helene, she told me she wasn't selling after all." Claire explained about the potential buyer's drunk driving and accident as well as the father calling and asking if she'd be willing to cancel the purchase and sale agreement. Claire continued. "Helene agreed, and said she was just as glad. With things going so well with her daughter, she said she realized that returning to France had more to do with getting Jessica away from bad influences than her own need to return to her homeland."

Lexie said, "And what were you saying earlier, Livie?"

"That I wished Helene wasn't selling."

"Hmmm, let me see . . . do we see prospective employment in your future?"

Olivia laughed. "Sure hope so."

Lexie turned to Claire. "Okay, kiddo, fill us in on the Trent details."

"First some good news. Jeff and I had a talk, and I think we're going to work out his work and me home alone problem." She told about traveling with him and the upcoming trip to Hawaii.

"Claire, that sounds wonderful," Olivia said.

"It does, and thank God you got rid of the odious Trent."

"So you don't want to hear what happened with him?" Claire asked.

"I absolutely do," Lexie said with a sniff. "Just so I can find more reasons to trash him."

Claire amazed even herself with her change in attitude. Compared to what had happened with Tony and then the fresh steps with Jeff, talking about what had gone on with Trent just seemed so pointless and nonproductive. Hours ago she was humiliated, heartbroken, and furious. Now she felt next to nothing.

She told them all that had happened, from his giving her a choice between lover and nothing, her decision to have sex with him, and then his rejection of her that followed.

"I wasn't the one filled with guilt and second thoughts."

Lexie stared at her. "Trent was? That's hard to believe."

"Oh, it wasn't as straightforward as an attack of conscience — his second thoughts were more about getting himself out of ever having to see me again."

"Claire, on its face, that's a little hard to believe. The guy's been sniffing around you for weeks. And as far as your ability in the sack, not one time have you ever said sex was an area of trouble with Jeff."

She recalled Jeff's comment about sex over sightseeing and how wonderfully uncomplicated it all seemed. "Trent told me I was too serious, that I wanted more than sex, and that he wasn't into 'long-term,' and therefore, it was over."

Olivia and Lexie absorbed that, while Claire was beginning to think she should be thanking Trent for saving her from herself.

Finally Olivia put down her pizza, swallowed, wiped her mouth and fingers with a napkin, and said, "I'm impressed."

Claire almost choked. "Impressed! Impressed by what?"

Lexie chimed in. "You must have done a number on him, Claire, as in rattled his 'as long as I get my way' view of women." Then to Olivia she said, "Guess that eliminates our rope-and-knife plan."

"Definitely."

"Maybe a commendation of some sort for the boy."

"For doing the right thing at the last minute?" Olivia asked with a heavy dose of sarcasm. "I don't think so."

"You're tough."

"Yeah, well. He should have done the right thing before he had sex with her. This way he got what he wanted — Claire into his bed and then out of his life."

"Hmmm, maybe we'd better go back to the rope-and-knife plan."

"All right, enough," Claire declared, not even trying to follow their chatter. Right now Trent seemed so yesterday. "What are you two talking about?"

"Just this, sweets," Lexie said. "Trent did you a big favor by blowing you off."

"Probably. But I sure did feel rotten."

"Because you're usually a saint and you did something very unsaintlike. This is a situation where you got to be a bad girl with no bad-girl consequences."

"Olivia's right, Claire. Trent revealed one redeemable quality in that he didn't want to lead you on into an affair, long distance, or otherwise, because he had no intention of marrying you when you decided to leave Jeff for him."

"I never said I was going to leave Jeff."

"But you thought about it." And when she started to deny it, Lexie shook her head. "Come on, Claire, this is us. Even if your thinking was abstract and vague, you did consider it."

Finally she nodded. "Okay, maybe I was."

364

"And it's moot now anyway. The reality is that Trent knew you wouldn't be content with just sex romps no matter how hot you two were for each other. He figured — and he was right — that eventually you'd want more."

Claire was quiet, staring down at the beer she'd barely sipped. "Nothing stands still," she whispered, beginning to understand that yes, in time, she would not have been content with just illicit sex.

"Yep, life is full of changes and choices. Tonight I'd say you got a bucketful of both."

"So I should thank Trent for telling me to get lost."

"But you're not lost, Claire. Your family is here, and what we saw while you were all talking was a deep reservoir of love and oneness. Jeff and Lara and Tony; your son wanting to prove himself to you, all of them coming here as a surprise, plus you were spared something quite unexpected."

She was agreeing right up until the spared something unexpected. "What was I spared?"

"Yeah, I'm curious, too," Lexie said, leaning forward.

"If you'd called Jeff a few weeks ago, if you'd flown to New Mexico, which you would have done, then all of this with Trent would have remained a what-if fantasy. You would have wondered and considered and maybe followed through at a later time. All the choices you made plus the merging of two events — Trent saying get lost and your family saying we love you and did this for you . . . Claire, I think it's all quite extraordinary."

Claire blinked, realizing that in a perverse way she'd come out of this debacle with Trent a wiser and stronger woman. Certainly the beginnings of honesty and a new direction for her marriage had evolved. Tears slipped down her cheeks, and she swiped at them slowly. "I feel so grateful to have both of you."

Lexie crawled over and hugged her, and Olivia scooted over, too.

"Is this a group hug?" Lexie asked, her disgust with such machinations obvious.

"Nah," Olivia said. "This is a friendship bond."

And they all agreed with that.

Chapter Twenty

Mid morning on Monday, Olivia wandered through the silent house. She loved being here — the largeness of the rooms, the furnishings, her own personal touches in the color and fabric selections. But as important as all those tangibles were, what really mattered was that she was home — home in the house she'd avoided as if just being here was a punishment.

Yes, she'd felt trapped in the last years she'd lived here, and yes, coming back hadn't been in her plans. But she'd come and she'd stayed and she'd reunited with her best friends — that in itself had been priceless. Instead of trying to figure out how quickly she could get the repairs done and leave, she'd happily rearranged her life so she could stay.

She was pleased and content and — well, almost she was. Yet Daniel was a closed issue and she wasn't going to allow herself to be blue or sad or infested with *what-if* regret.

Now, wearing dark green shorts, a white scoop-neck top, and sandals, she toured the rooms sipping from a glass of iced coffee. She opened the windows wider on the west side, where a cool breeze was a reminder of the coming change of season.

Just moments ago she'd said good-bye to Claire and her family, with Claire promising to return in a few weeks for their annual trip to Brimfield. The trip to Hawaii was the last week, so that wouldn't interfere.

Lexie had left, also, taking the rental car to Rhode Island's T.F. Green Airport, where she had a late-morning flight to Chicago. With a potential relationship with Bill Riggs looking more and more likely, plus her new reporter's job, Lexie had been feeling upbeat and excited. The Chicago trip was to tie up loose ends, such as a sublet on her apartment until her lease ran out next spring. She also intended to make arrangements for getting her furniture shipped to Bishop — and into temporary storage.

"Thanks for the invite to stay with you," she'd told Olivia after her Sunday night run with Bill Riggs, of which she'd returned nearly giddy with excitement because they'd shared a glass of wine and a good-night kiss. "I'm going to get my own place."

Olivia understood; Lexie wanted privacy.

Which, Olivia decided as she glanced around the empty rooms, was what she had in more abundance than she wanted.

In fact, she had everything — home in the

house she'd never truly shoved from her thoughts in a town that offered the sweet simplicity of old memories, helpful neighbors, and of course, her good friends.

Yet even with a banquet of bounty, she couldn't deny a deep sense of inner vacancy. She wanted to think it was because Claire and Lexie had left, she wanted to think it was as simple as temporary aloneness. Or perhaps it sprang from the inevitable — that she stood on some precipice of the future with many doors open while instinctively knowing that even if she could enter them all-even that wouldn't be enough.

"And just what is it you want, Ms. Olivia Halsey?" she said aloud. And when the answer leaped so fast into her mind that she almost slopped her iced coffee, she took the glass to the kitchen and reminded herself that *that particular* want was no longer an option.

The sound of a lawn mower drew her attention, and she went to the back door, where she saw Trent in work boots, cutoffs, and a Cape Cod T-shirt. He was on the rider and making the first cut across the front yard. August grass mowing was never as frequent as in May and June because of the sparse rainfall. That in turn accounted for his infrequent mowing visits.

But to come today? Forty-eight hours after he rejected Claire? Either the guy had an excess of guts or a dearth of common sense.

Probably both, she concluded, opening the door and walking out to the yard. She waited until he came down the side of the yard and saw her.

He stopped the mower and shut it off. "Morning."

Olivia slipped her hands into the side pockets of her shorts. "I'm amazed you're here."

"Grass is getting shaggy even though it's more brown than green. August drought is tough. So how's it going?"

"A better question would be how is Claire."

"I already know how she is," he said flatly.

Olivia waited, expecting him to say more, to say anything. But he didn't.

Finally she said, "You hurt her badly."

Then he took off the sunglasses and looked at her directly. "What do you want from me?"

What did she want? His point of view? His excuses? And even given the possibility he'd done what he did because it was best for Claire, did she really expect him to explain it all to her? Probably not, but just the same . . . "How about a reason?"

"How about you mind your own business." And it wasn't a question.

Olivia planted her hands on her hips. Claire was fine; she and Jeff had never looked happier, but still she was appalled at what Trent had done. There was no way she was going to pretend she knew nothing of

370

what had happened. "How about she's my friend and I don't like to see my friends hurt."

"Fine. She won't be hurt by me again."

She debated, then decided why not. It was a way outside shot that he'd agree, but she figured if she couldn't get an answer one way, there might be another. "You did it deliberately, didn't you? You rejected her and told her you didn't want her because you really do care about her."

The sudden shift of his body and his refusal to look at her spoke even louder than a verbal denial. He did care and he had wanted more than an affair, but admitting it? Clearly he wasn't going to do that. "That's the craziest thing I ever heard," he snapped.

But Olivia knew, she was sure she knew. "It was the right thing, Trent, pushing her away even though we all wanted to kill you the other night."

His glower grew darker. "Kill me? What the hell are you talking about?"

"Trust me, you don't want to know. I'll leave you to your mowing." She then turned to go back in the house.

"Wait a minute."

She swung around, expecting something about Claire, but instead, he said, "We got the ringleader of the vandalism spree. Helene's daughter fingered him — it was Jessica's boyfriend."

Olivia sighed at the total subject change.

Let it go, she reminded herself. A guy like Trent doing confessions of feelings and regrets is probably a hopeless hope. Much easier to deal with teenage rebelliousness and small-town crime. "So what now?"

"They'll get some community service, plus the judge will order them to make restitution to you and to the others. Either with cash or work. The other news is that Ray Klayton — the kid in the patrol car that first day — actually prevented more destruction here at your house. He'd heard there was going to be some house breaks in this area. He came by and saw them here, confronted them, and told them to get out or they'd have to deal with him."

"And they did what he said?" Olivia asked. Four boys had been arrested and for all four to wimp out because of one kid amazed her.

"Klayton's tough, moody, and mouthy, but no one messes with him. He's got a loyalty streak for those who have treated him and his mother right. Guess you and your house made his list."

She was speechless. She hadn't seen Ray but that one time, and even then she hadn't been sure he remembered her. "I guess I should be grateful."

"Word is he had good memories of when his old lady worked for your parents. Said your dad gave her extra money a few times when things were really tough at home. According to Klayton, the vandals wanted to break windows and kick in a few walls. He axed that plan and they all split."

"I don't know what to say."

He shrugged. "Sometimes things aren't what they seem. Sometimes the bad stuff is really just a road to a better result." And with that, Trent started up the rider and once again began mowing.

Olivia digested his esoteric philosophy. He could have just said "when handed lemons make lemonade," but she found his more complex comment, well, interesting.

At three that afternoon Olivia was in the study paying some bills when she saw a delivery truck back into the drive. Two men in work khaki climbed out of the cab. When they opened the rear doors and began to haul out a wide, flat, rectangular box like a door would be delivered in, she frowned and rose to her feet.

She hurried from the study to the back door, where she called, "Excuse me, but I think you have the wrong house. I didn't order anything."

"You Olivia Halsey?" a short skinny guy with beefy arms asked.

"Yes."

"This" — He pulled a folded order slip from his shirt pocket — "457 Steeple Street?"

"Yes, but —"

"No *buts,* lady. We already been here once and no one was home —"

"That unable-to-deliver slip was from you?"

"Yep. We got orders to deliver and hang."

"Hang? Hang what?" She was beginning to feel like the straight man in a bad comedy routine.

The shorter man scowled. "Look, we got six more deliveries today. If you don't want this, say so now and we'll load it back in the truck."

"But I don't know what you're delivering."

"Was there a full moon last night?" the shorter one asked his partner, who just looked blank. Then to Olivia, as if she might be a dimwit, he said slowly, "It's a framed mirror. It's big and weighs more than a 400-horse engine. Delivery order says there's a prepared wall, so if you want it inside and hung, say so and lead the way."

Framed mirror, heavy, prepared wall. That could only mean the upstairs hall where her father had hung the huge antique mirror. She'd left the industrial-strength hanging hooks because she'd hoped to find a suitable replacement for the one the vandals had broken.

"Who arranged for the delivery?" she asked.

Both rolled their eyes, but the shorter one went back to his order sheet. "Name's Cafferty. Daniel Cafferty."

"But he never said anything to me. Why would he buy — ?"

"Lady, please. Take it up with him. We just deliver."

"Okay, okay." She'd sort it out later. She held the back door open for them and directed them through the house to the central staircase, bringing groans from them when they realized the prepared wall was upstairs.

Nevertheless, they carefully carried it up, unwrapped it, and after some overly colorful curses, they got it hung while she watched in awe. Not at their expertise in juggling and hanging without scarring the wall, but that this wasn't a new mirror. It was *her* mirror. The broken mirror. How was that possible?

"It's the same frame, but the same glass? No, that's not possible, but the mirrored glass looks old, and where would he have gotten vintage glass?" She muttered all of this as though saying it would glean answers. She stepped closer, touching the ornate frame, remembering her father's pride at his discovery in that old barn, his pleasure of ownership over the years, and how naked this wall had been since its breakage.

Now it was home once again, restored and wonderful. Home as she was.

"We need a signature, lady."

Daniel had done this for her.

"Hey, lady!"

She glanced at them, then took the grimy pen and scribbled her name. "What about a bill?"

"Already paid." He tore off the copy, handed

it to her, and the two of them hurried down the stairs muttering about weirdly wrapped women, and leaving Olivia staring with delight at the mirror her father had so loved.

Daniel was hot, sweaty, and tired. Moving Caitlyn from Greeley to Parkboro should have been a simple matter of a few boxes, clothes, and that semi-sized sound system he and Marsha had given her for Christmas last year. But instead of a few items, he'd ended up with his truck bed packed, stuffed, tied, and strapped with enough crap to fill a football field. Driving from Greeley felt like the Clampetts on the road to Beverly Hills.

All afternoon they'd hauled the stuff inside. Caitlyn had worked hard, but there was no question she was more interested in arranging than in carrying boxes. She'd taken one box full of clothes and a plastic shoebox full of cosmetics into her bedroom. He knew there were three or four more of those boxes, as he'd loaded them himself.

"Was there anything left in the drugstore?" he asked, peering at the array of cosmetics, hair doodads, and at least eight hairbrushes.

She looked horrified. "I buy at Neiman's."

"Marcus?"

"Really, Daddy. No one who cares about their skin and hair goes anywhere else."

"Maybe I should start looking for a second job."

"I only buy when they're on sale."

"Thank God." But he grinned at her and she smiled back, a moment, he realized, that was only the first of many he would adjust to with her living with him full-time.

Now he realized she hadn't returned after taking that last box. Arranging and rearranging, he imagined. But for all his minor complaints, he was glad she was here.

He was down to the last box — books — and he was most grateful when his neighbor, Jake, appeared, walked up the drive, and offered to help.

"Why didn't you give a whistle?" he asked as he and Daniel lifted the box and carried it inside.

"I kept telling myself I was seeing more than was really there." He swiped his forearm across his forehead. "Thanks for the hand — don't think I could've done that last one by myself. Want a beer?"

"Nah. The wife saw Caitlyn a little while ago and sent me over to see if she wants to go to the mall with us. Our niece, Kelly, is visiting and she doesn't know anyone, so we thought the two girls might hit it off. The mall is always a good icebreaker."

"Sounds okay. Caitlyn!"

She came around the corner, looking scrubbed and freshly showered. "Now I know where you disappeared to." But he grinned, thinking that was exactly where he was headed. "Caitlyn, this is Mr. Ballard. He lives next door." Daniel mentioned Kelly and the mall and was rewarded with new energy in her expression. "Need some money, I imagine."

"Fifty should do it," she said, grinning.

"Twenty you get." He took two tens from his wallet and handed them to her.

Jake headed for the door with Caitlyn following. Then he turned. "Hey, you wanna come with us? I figured we'd get pizza after the girls finish buying out the stores."

"Me go to a mall? Willingly?" He shuddered. "I'd rather drink a bag of vomit."

Caitlyn made a face. "Gross, Daddy."

Jake laughed. "I'll have to remember that one."

Moments later he was alone. He pulled a bottle of beer from the fridge, opened the top, and drank thirstily. It was near seven, and although he and Caitlyn had had some burgers and fries about three, he was hungry. He had a steak in the freezer — maybe he'd do it on the grill. But first he wanted a shower —

"Thank heaven you're here. I was afraid you were in Greeley."

He jerked around. "Olivia! What are you doing here?"

But before he could tell her how glad he was to see her, she'd launched herself across the kitchen and flung herself into his arms.

He grabbed her, trying to hold her back.

"Babe, I'm filthy and smelly and —"

"I don't care." She kissed him deeply, and all his resistance collapsed as he indulged her and himself. Finally, when they both came up for air, she began to talk as if she was on speed. "How can I ever thank you and why did you do such a wonderful thing and I love you and I don't want to lose you and you have to want to be together the way I do and —"

"Whoa, whoa. Slow down. I think I'm missing some pieces here." Then he grinned as she took one breath after another. "Can I assume some of this overjoy is about the mirror?"

And with that her eyes welled with tears. "I can't believe you did such a wonderful and thoughtful and, well, just plain glorious thing."

"To see you this happy makes it even more of a pleasure than it was."

"But how? You were going to the dump with it."

"I did go to the dump, but when I pulled it out and really looked at it — you know, you were upset and given the tension between us, neither one of us really examined the frame. I figured it was worth having an expert take a look — to me it seemed very repairable. So I brought it home, called a local frame shop, and they recommended a framer in Middletown. She specializes in vintage and restoration."

"But the mirror glass."

"That was a bit more complicated. Suzanne — that's the framer — made a lot of phone calls and finally found another old mirror through her sister-in-law, an interior designer in New Hampshire. She drove up and picked it up, and after some work with the frame, she made it fit."

"You are amazing."

He shrugged, grinning at her and loving that she was here and more than ever pleased that he was able to get the mirror she so treasured repaired for her. "I'm glad you're so happy with it. That place in the upstairs hall would not have looked quite right with anything else hanging there."

"Oh, Daniel," and then she was once more in his arms and kissing him and saying, "Have I told you I love you?"

"Tell me again."

"I do and I don't want to lose you. I really don't. The whole love-hate thing with the house — going back there and then finding out that was where I really wanted to be. And as wonderful as it is being there, I missed you. Maybe I took you for granted and then when I was going to lose you, I realized —" She stopped, gathering her emotions. Taking a deep breath, she said, "I know you're moving to Greeley, but I'm not going to let that be a deterrent. I want to keep seeing you. I'll drive up there or you

380

can come and see me . . . but, please, Daniel . . ."

"If I'd known a repaired mirror would do all this, I would have delivered it myself."

"It's not just the mirror — okay, I know it sounds as if I'm overwhelmed with emotion because of it and not thinking straight and saying things because I'm grateful. . . ."

"Yep. I could take it that way."

"Please don't." She took a deep breath, drew back, and leaned against the counter. "This is all my fault for what I did when you asked me to marry you and gave me the ring —"

"Which you returned."

"Not because I wanted to. You're moving to be close to your daughter, which is absolutely the right thing to do."

"I'm glad you see it that way." He folded his arms, watching with amusement and a deep reservoir of happiness for their future. Even as she talked, he knew it was all going to be okay.

"You made it quite clear that you were glad our relationship was over."

"That's not what I said." He looked pained that he'd given her that impression. "I was never glad it was over, but since we seemed to be getting farther apart, and there didn't seem to be much hope we'd ever get together, I began to think that maybe you were right. I needed to cut you loose and then, although I sure didn't like it, let you move on with your life." He finished his beer and tossed the bottle into the trash. "And I'm not moving. Caitlyn is here now, living with me."

"That's terrific! But what happened? What changed?"

He told her about Marsha's marriage and the arrangement the two of them had made that allowed Caitlyn to live with him and visit her mother. "So I scrapped the idea of moving. We just got all her things here today."

Olivia nodded, then asked softly, carefully, "What about us?"

"A commuting relationship?"

"Not very appealing."

"Then what?"

"You move back to Parkboro?"

And for far too long. Olivia was silent. This was not a choice she wanted to make. She wanted to live in the house in Bishop, but she also wanted to be with Daniel. On the other hand, how happy would she be with some long-distance relationship? Oh, she knew it could work for a while, but forever? No. And to leave the house — she shuddered at that idea. "There's no answer."

"A dilemma of the heart."

"Yes."

"I have a solution."

"You do?"

"And as soon as I take a shower —"

"Oh, no, you don't, Daniel Cafferty." She grabbed his arm before he could take three steps. "What's the solution?"

"Caitlyn and I will move to Bishop."

She stared at him as if he'd spoken bad Italian. "Are you serious? You'd do that for me?"

"Sweetheart, I love you and I want to marry you. Moving to Bishop is hardly a hardship."

"But your job is here and Caitlyn —"

"The job isn't a problem. I'd already spoken to my assistant coach about the football team when I thought I was moving to Greeley. And as far as my history classes, once Fisler knows, he'll find a replacement. I might have to stay this semester, but we can work that out. As far as Caitlyn — my guess is she'll be psyched. As you recall, her best friend lives in Bishop."

"Jessica."

"And her newest boyfriend. Ray Klayton. I've met him, and while he's a little rough at the edges, I liked him."

"I knew Ray from a long time ago." She told him of Ray's mother working for her parents and what she knew about the vandalism from Trent. "Apparently, Ray was the one who stopped those other boys from doing even more damage."

"Then it's all settled. Caitlyn will be happy,

you and I will be together —"

"And happily married."

"I hope so. But, Olivia, I don't think we should do it right away."

Now she scowled. "I don't believe you! Now I'm the one who wants to marry you and you want to wait?"

He hooked an arm around her neck and pulled her close. "Only until spring," he whispered against her hair. "I want you to be sure, and I don't want you to feel pressured."

She tipped her head back and looked at him, loving the warmth and the caring and the love she saw in his eyes. "I love you."

"Me too, you." He reached around and opened a drawer, taking out the package she'd left and he hadn't opened. "I think this is yours."

She opened it and handed him the ring.

He took it and slipped it on her finger, saying, "It really wasn't supposed to be an engagement ring. We can get a diamond."

She shook her head. "No, I like this one."

"I do, too." And he kissed her hand where he'd placed it.

Tears slipped from her eyes. "Oh, Daniel, I can't imagine a future without you."

"And you won't have to."

He drew her close, walking down the hall, and into his bedroom. And she was in his arms and they were kissing just as he kicked the door closed.